Susanna N

BUSHES AND BRIARS

SUSANNA M. NEWSTEAD

For Anne

PASTMASTERY PRESS

Cover art and design Charlie Farrow

Editing by Gill Whatmough

Published by PastMastery Press
Medlar House
Hanover Drive
Brackley Northants. NN13 6JS UK
sue@pastmastery.com

ISBN 978-1-916244429

BUSHES AND BRIARS

Through bushes and through briars I lately took my way;
All for to hear the small birds sing and the lambs to skip and play.
I overheard my own true love, her voice it was so clear;
Long time I have been waiting for the coming of my dear.
Sometimes I am uneasy and troubled in my mind,
Sometimes I think I'll go to my love and tell to him my mind.
And if I should go to my love, my love he will say nay,
If I show to him my boldness, he'll ne'er love me again."

English Folk song.

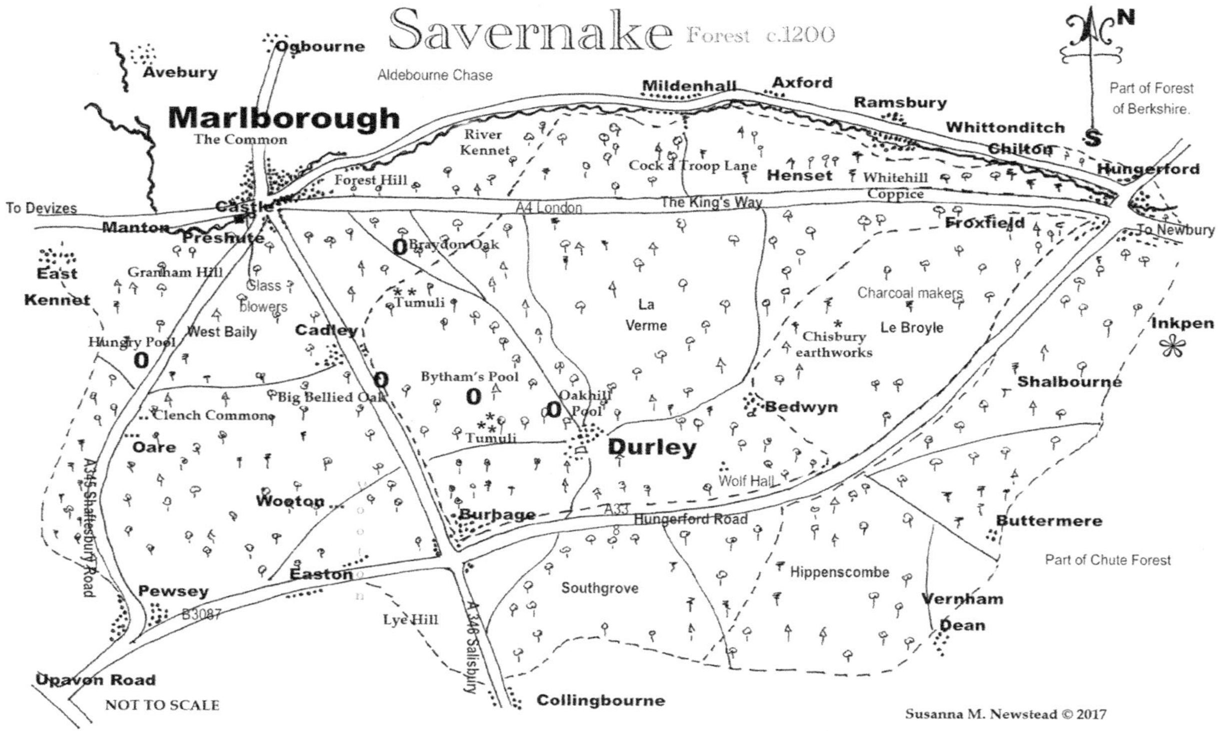
Savernake Forest c.1200
N
S
Part of Forest of Berkshire.
Avebury
Ogbourne
Aldebourne Chase
Marlborough
The Common
Mildenhall
Axford
Ramsbury
Whittonditch
Chilton
Hungerford
To Devizes
Castle
Manton
Preshute
East Kennet
Forest Hill
River Kennet
Cock a Troop Lane
Henset
Whitehill Coppice
A4 London
The King's Way
Froxfield
To Newbury
Braydon Oak
Grantham Hill
Glass blowers
Tumuli
West Baily
Cadley
Hungry Pool
La Verme
Charcoal makers
Le Broyle
Chisbury earthworks
Inkpen
Bytham's Pool
Big Bellied Oak
Oakhill Pool
Bedwyn
Shalbourne
Clench Common
Oare
Tumuli
Durley
Wolf Hall
Wooton
A345 Shaftesbury Road
Burbage
A33
Hungerford Road
Buttermere
Part of Chute Forest
Easton
Hippenscombe
Pewsey
B3087
Southgrove
Vernham Dean
Lye Hill
A 346 Salisbury
Upavon Road
NOT TO SCALE
Collingbourne
Susanna M. Newstead © 2017

Durley Village c. 1200

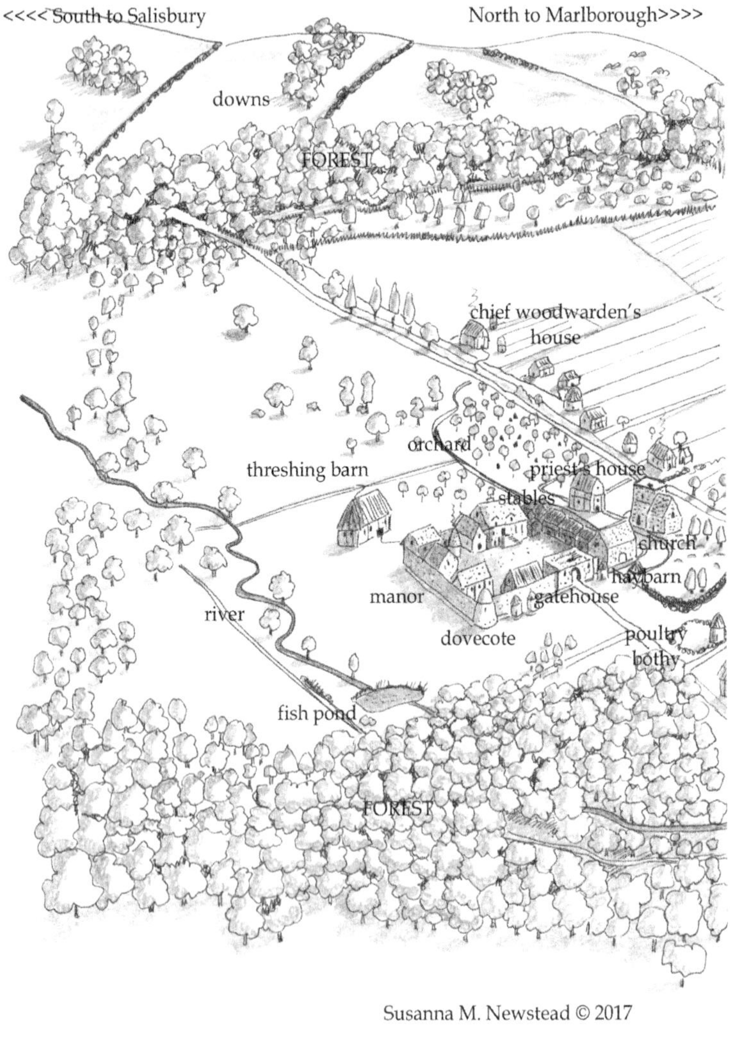

Durley Village c. 1200

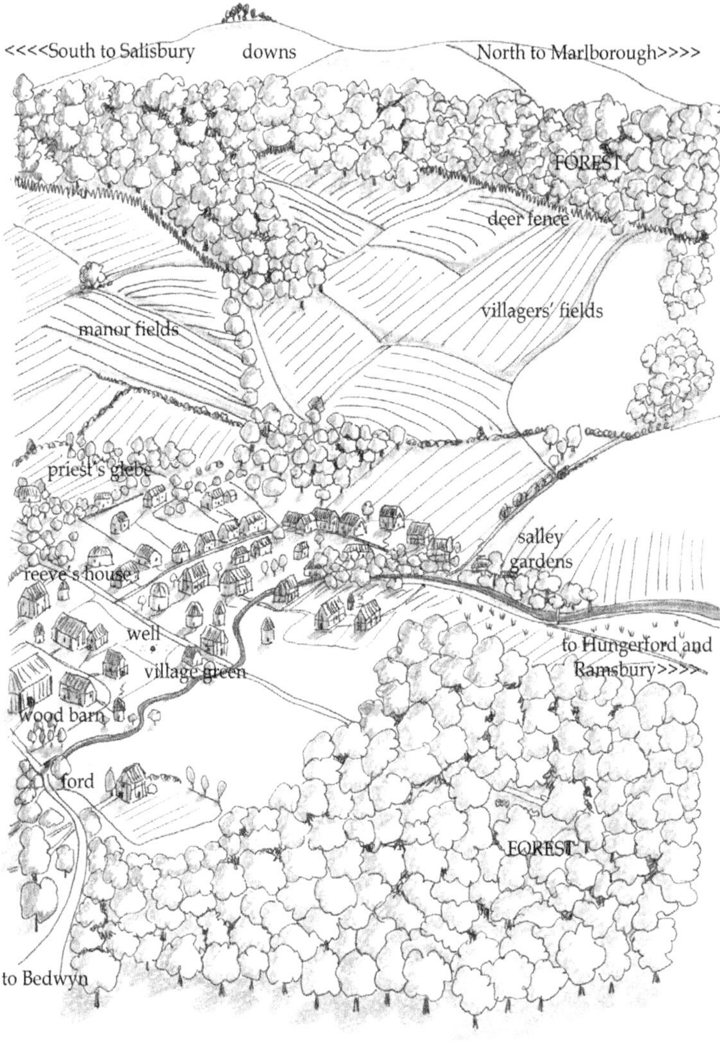

Susanna M. Newstead © 2017

Marlborough and Savernake Forest c.1200 (1)

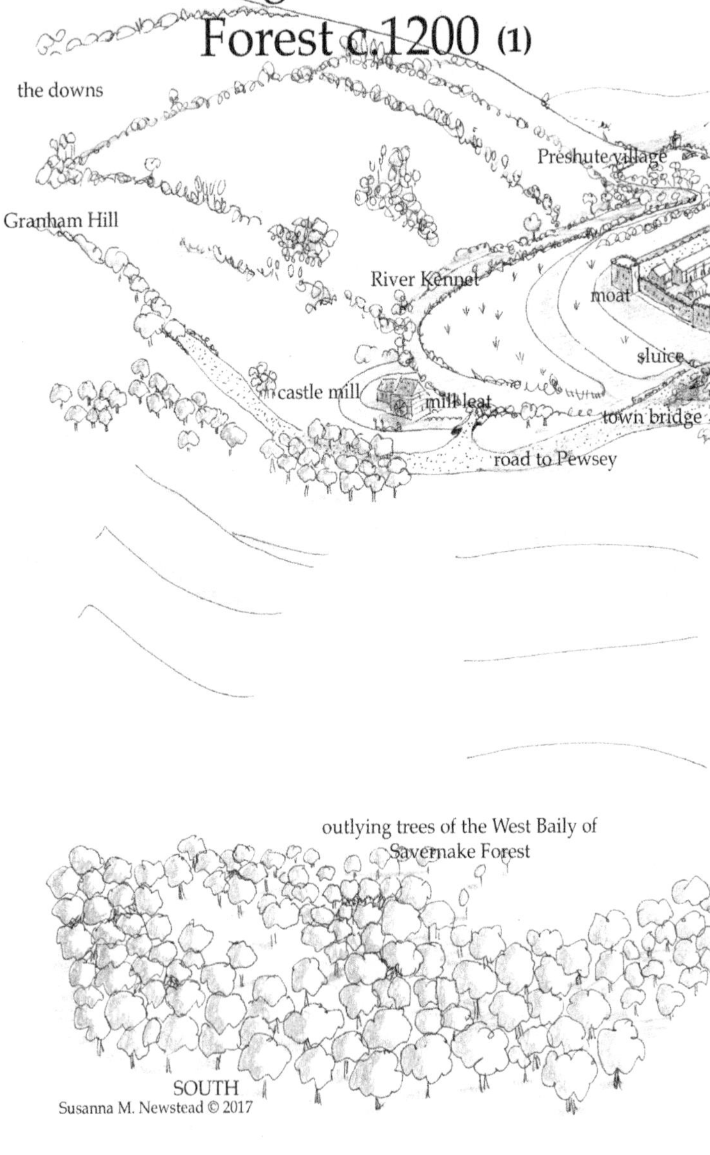

Marlborough Town and the forest c.1200 (2)

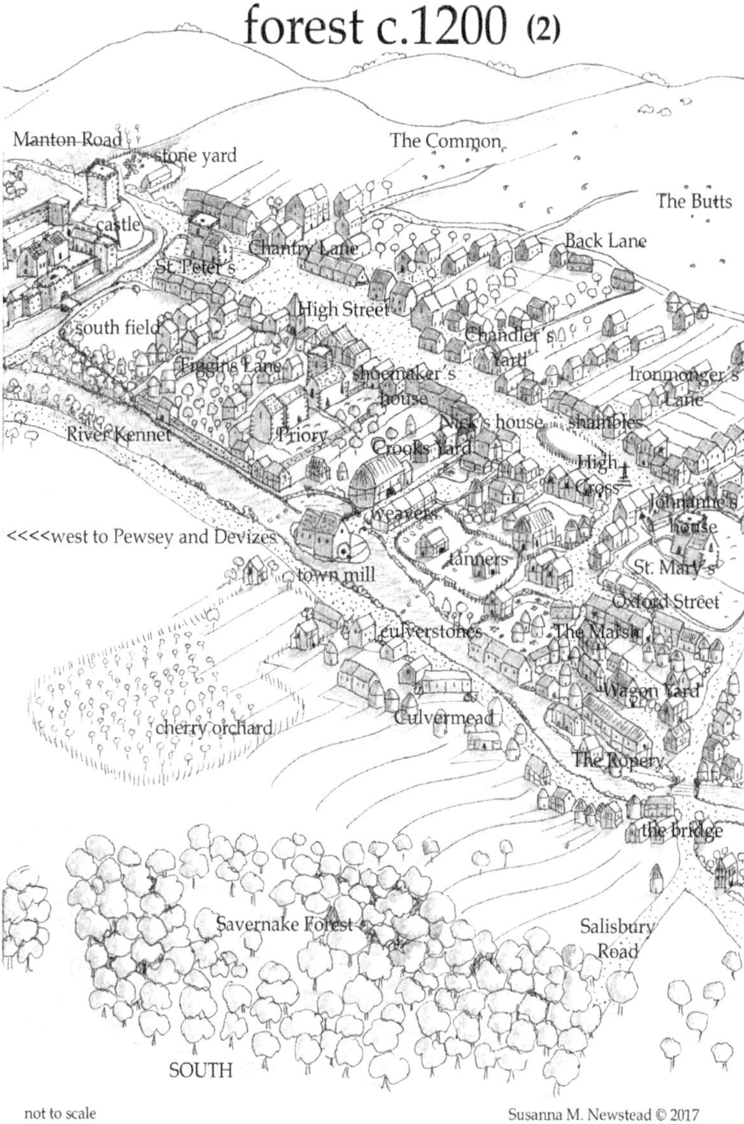

Marlborough and the forest c. 1200 (3)

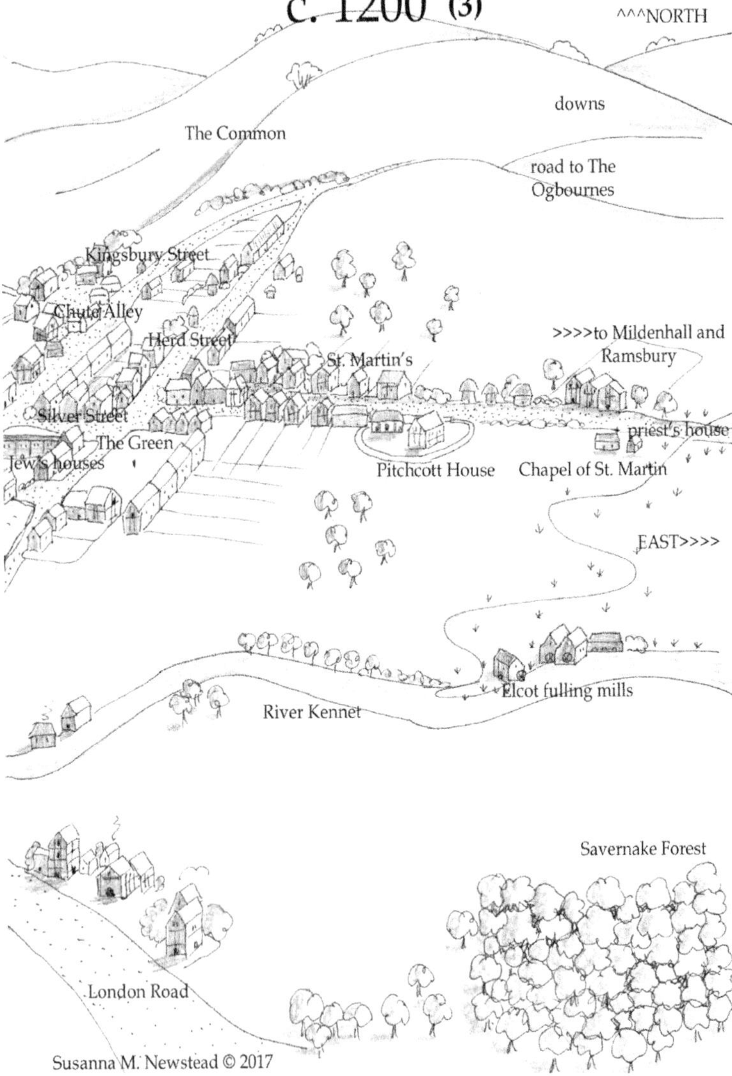

Chapter One

I remember the day quite distinctly.

It was high summer; the sun was a pale disc high in the sky behind a light screening of cloud.

The heat would begin to build that day and after this day in early June we would have warmth for weeks on end.

I stood and breathed in the scent of the rose bush my first wife Cecily, had planted at the courtyard's edge. I remember she'd found it in the forest and dug it up, transplanting it to the village. In just a few years it had grown tall for it was a vigorous specimen; cupped blush pink petals in two rows, with a cluster of bright yellow stamens to the centre. The bees were busy about it, coming and going to the hives in the orchard. The scent was mild but lovely.

It lay right up against the wall of the manor house along with a volunteer elder tree, their roots buried in a small patch of soil at the wall base. The elder was considered by some to be the witches' tree but I had no such worry and let the thing grow to accommodate the little sparrows who twittered about its branches all day and roosted there at night. The rose climbed the face of the manor hall, clinging tenaciously to the stonework into which one of my manor workers had driven nails. Around these, string had been wound and the rose's tendrils curled over it, though the brisk spring breezes and the profusion of blooms of this year, the year of our Lord 1207, had made it come adrift from the wall. It leaned out above us like a swaying green roof.

My steward Henry Pierson was up a ladder tying in the wayward stems.

"That one can go a bit higher I think, Henry," I said.

"It has so many blooms it's too heavy to go higher, sir," he replied, wobbling on his rung.

I leapt forward and grabbed the edge of the ladder.

"You're leaning too far out, Henry. Come down and we'll move the ladder."

"No... I can do it... just... there... now this one."

Henry took his hand from the rung of the ladder and leaned over to another branch.

"Ouch!" He sucked his finger. "Damn it... begging your pardon, m'lord."

I chuckled. "She's a feisty girl is our rose," I said. "Those thorns are lethal."

"I should've worn gloves," said Henry, smiling.

I leaned back to survey the work done so far.

"I think that's all the stems which have been blown off the wall. Now for the new growth," I said.

Henry leaned out a little further. I was about to put my booted foot once more onto the bottom of the ladder to steady it.

"Henry, let's move the l...."

With an 'oweee' Henry tumbled from the top and landed with a thump on the flagstones of the manor courtyard.

" Ow...ow... ow!" he cried, grabbing his ankle.

He'd been about twelve feet up and had fallen the whole distance.

I moved the ladder out of the way as Hal of Potterne, my senior man at arms, came running down the manor steps close by.

"Wha'sup?" he shouted.

"Henry has fallen from his ladder."

Hal was immediately down on his knees by the stricken man. I leaned over them both.

"Tsoo... looks like you mighta' sprained that ankle real bad," he said.

He took the booted foot in his hand and carefully probed for broken bones.

"I don't think it's broken nor anything."

Lydia, my wife, poked her head from the manor door, above us, having heard the cry.

"Bring him up here you two" she tutted. "Don't just stand there."

Before either of us could raise the young man to his one good foot, our arms under his armpits, there was a fleet scurrying of feet and the swishing of a kirtle and a young girl came running across the yard, her hair flying free behind her.

"Henry, you all right?"

"Aye... aye, Ancie... I'm fine."

"Well, you don't look fine to me, grimacin' and gurnin' like that," she said.

She pushed past me. "Excuse me, my lord."

Standing behind him and with two forearms under Henry's armpits this slight girl lifted my manor steward as if he had been a dry leaf. He stood shakily on his one good foot, his silken blond hair swaying over his face.

Hal took the other side. Henry lifted his arm over Annot's shoulder.

"Reckon we can get 'im up the steps, lass?" asked Hal.

"Reckon we can, sir," said Annot Wedgemoor, grinning.

Annot was the eldest daughter of one of my foresters. She was an attractive girl with light brown hair and hazel eyes, clear fair, freckled skin and a wide smile.

She would now be leaving sixteen behind, I thought.

My mind raced back to the day when I had found out that Annot had been set to work as a prostitute, by her uncaring and grasping father. She had seen no evil in it. Her father had asked her to do it; that was all, but once our reeve had pointed out that it was immoral, that the church frowned on it, and that her lord would not countenance this sort of behaviour, she had never again lain with any man of the village or forest.

I had fined and disciplined her father, we had kept quiet and no more had been said.

I followed them up the stairs. Heavens! Had this only been three years ago? Annot had gained in confidence and in looks and from the conversation I could hear between the girl and my steward, she had caught his eye and held it as surely as Henry had fixed those wayward rose stems to the manor wall.

"Sit there, don't put any weight on it," said Annot, depositing Henry on the nearest bench by the door. She deftly pulled off his boot.

Lydia caught my eye and her forehead wrinkled in a sardonic smile. I raised my eyebrow and folded my arms across my chest.

"Annot, go down to the kitchen for some cold water. Hal, fetch some linen from the store please. And some tumbler's cure all. We shall strap it up," said my wife. "Johannes is due to visit later today, he can have a look at it for you."

Johannes was my friend, Lydia's uncle, and the doctor of Marlborough, the small town three miles away.

"Thank you mistress," said Henry smiling up at her. "It's nothing, I'm sure." He sucked on his fingers.

"To be truthful... this hurts a deal more than the blessed ankle."

Poor Henry's hand and wrist were scratched and bleeding. On the way down he had sustained damage from the rose thorns.

"I told you we needed to move the ladder you stampcrab!" I laughed.

He smiled sheepishly, "Sorry sir."

This was the first day I truly realised that the relationship between my poultry girl and my manor steward had become a serious one. I had known that they had been seeing each other but I was unaware that their friendship had become a deal more than that. None of us had.

Henry was twenty six, Annot was seventeen in a few days. Some might have said that it was not a good match, there being nine years between them and one free, the other a tied villein, but I saw the light in their eyes that day and I was happy for them both.

*****

Three days later Henry hobbled on his stick into my office at the head of the stairs and by the screens passage of the manor.

I looked up. "How is it now?"

"Aw it was nothing, sir. I shall throw away the stick tomorrow."

"Good man!"

"Much worse were those damned rose thorns. I'm still diggin' 'em out."

"Aye tenacious little so and sos, they are," I said.

"Sir...might I ask you a question?"

I put down the piece of charcoal with which I'd been scribbling and dusted my fingers on a rag.

"Whatever you like."

Might I ask you, sir, if I could go and ask Ancie's..Annot's father for her hand in marriage?"

Just like that. Out it came.

I blinked.

"You are a free man Henry. You may marry whomever you wish."

"But sir, Ancie is one of your tied villeins. I need to ask you first in case..."

"I have no objection at all, Henry." I smiled, "You may marry your Ancie whenever you wish."

Henry's face broke into a huge grin.

"Thank you, sir."

"And we shall build you a new house out on the Green. Can't have you living in your small room in the yard when you're a married man now, can we?"

I came round my table and offered him my hand. "I can see that you love her dearly and she obviously thinks you're all right."

"She's a good girl, sir." He took my hand and we shook as if we'd made a bargain.

I tilted my head. "You know what she has...?"

"I know what she has been. Yes, sir. Although there are no records of it. She told me."

"Well, that's good. You heard it from the girl and not from someone else. And no, I managed to keep it quiet."

"She was young and her father is not a nice man, my lord. He beat her and..."

"Yes, I know. He hasn't beaten her this past few years, nor her younger sister. He hasn't touched Annot's mother either. I saw to that. I've had Walter Reeve keep an eye on the man. Hal too, wouldn't allow any nonsense. Nor the village elders."

"No, I know and I thank you for that, sir. All of you."

"We'll get her away from that house and at the other end of the village, shall we?"

"That would be a grand thing, sir" said Henry, grinning. "I shall go now and let her father know what my plans are....what our plans are."

"Let me know, Henry and I'll ask Father Crispin for a date for you to be married and get your intentions cried about the village and the banns said."

"You are so kind, sir."

"Your mother...what does she think?"

Henry chuckled. "You want me to tell you what she said, sir? She said 'oh good...this means that I shall have some grandchilder at last.' "

We both laughed.

He turned to leave and then drew back a little into the doorway.

"Sir, let me say...you are the finest lord it is ever possible to work for. It's not just me who says so..."

"Aw Henry. Off you go...you'll have me blubbering."

He smiled again, twisted on his stick and was gone down the manor steps.

I turned back to my tasks. I smiled to myself happily and set to work again, planning how I might prevent the flooding of the little river which ran through the village; flooding such as we'd had that last spring. I took up my charcoal to draw once more.

A new house had to be built. We'd keep it well away from the banks of the river.

Henry was back, without his stick just a few moments later.

His face was white and pinched. He had obviously been running despite a bad ankle; his sides heaved and he struggled for breath.

"Sir...please come...come now."

I noticed him shaking as he turned on his bad ankle and grimaced. Then he was off limping down the steps. I followed.

"Where to, Henry?"

"The Wedgemoor house."

"What's the matter?" I caught him up and saw him shake his head.

"Quick; before anyone sees."

"Sees what?"

"Annot's mother is out in their plot up the hill, with Darla." This was Annot's younger sister.

"Annot home Henry?" I asked.

"Yes sir, but.... Oh Jesu!" he cried out.

We rounded the corner of the manor wall and took the slight incline by the church. Just past the church wall we veered off towards the road and found the cottage of the Wedgemoor family. The door was open. I saw my young steward's stick lying on the grass.

Henry disappeared inside but did not fully enter the house place.

"Oh Jesu defend us," he said again, wrapping his arms around his body.

I could see why Jesu was being called upon so fervently.

There in the middle of the main room, by the large ash trestle where the family would take their meals, was a body.

And kneeling over it, a knife in her hand, was Annot Wedgemoor.

She looked up at me and pushed a stray strand of hair across her forehead smearing it with blood.

"My father....he..."

"Annot," said Henry gently.

"Oh Henry." She struggled to her feet and stood unsteadily. "Henry, my father, he's dead."

My eye met that of my young steward.

"Henry, close and bar the door," I said.

*****

Ah Paul, my scribe. Where have you been? I expected you on Friday.

What's that? Speak up boy...oh you can't...you have a sore throat. You've lost your voice?

Illness at the priory? Oh my...you've been ill then? Perhaps you shouldn't have come but stayed in the heat of the warming house at the priory and sweated it out.

Yes, it is a fine day today and so good for travelling from Marlborough to the forest. Are you sure you want to sit and write for me? You aren't going to sneeze all over the vellum are you?

Your sneezing has gone? Well, I'm glad about that. Just coughing...

Hmm...make sure you don't cough all over the writing then.

Today we are going to write about the summer of 1207 when there was a murder in Durley village, right under my nose; Durley the village of which I was lord. I've been rehearsing it out loud, before you came. So let's recap and you can now write it down for me.

Don't cough over me lad, put your hand over your mouth. I'm an old man of seventy three. I don't want to catch whatever it is you have. I'd like to live a few more years so I can write more stories about my days as warden of Savernake forest, underconstable at Marlborough castle and constable of the county of Wiltshire, and my time unearthing felons and bringing them to justice, amongst other things.

This is, as you know, just one of those tales. You have kindly written down the others, the previous ten, for me. I can't do it now, my hands are too gnarled and old and won't obey me. Oh! I've said that before have I?

Well, us old men, we tend to repeat ourselves you know. Let me know if I repeat myself too often...

Right... prime your pen... spring 1207...ready?

*****

Henry closed the door and walked towards Annot.

"No, Henry...step back. Don't come near. I want to look at the room, see what there is to be seen before anyone destroys what there is which might tell us something."

"Can Annot not tell you, sir?" he asked, his voice wavering.

"Take her over there, Henry." I pointed to the furthest wall by the door.

As they passed me I took the knife from Annot's hand.

The girl crushed herself into Henry's chest and started to shake and cry quietly.

"A moment only then we shall take Annot up to the hall."

The only light in the cottage was that coming in through the open window. I found an oil lamp,and lit it with a meagre flame from the covered fire. I started my examination by making sure that Annot's father, Bardol Wedgemoor, was indeed dead.

He lay on his front, his head turned to the side and had obviously staggered forwards when struck. One or perhaps two, knife wounds low in the back, had propelled him forward. He had grabbed at the bench as he fell, dragging it over, on top of him, I thought. I reached over and set it straight.

I peered at the wounds. Yes, two. Both to the lower back. There was a great deal of blood pooled on the floor. He had not died immediately but had lain unconscious, bleeding out his life force to the beaten earth before Annot and Henry had found him.

Beginning at the door and bending to the floor, I searched the whole area.

My eye raked over the table. Nothing here but mugs of fresh ale. Two ale mugs, one almost empty and some flowers in a small pot on the table top. A few petals had fallen from them.

I turned round and round and gazed across the rest of the room. Nothing here told me anything.

"Right Henry, let's have the young lady up at the hall. Wash her hands and forehead first in the water trough at the side. We can't have people staring at her and wondering what's going on just yet."

I opened the door once more and light flooded in.

There was no one about. Once we had exited, I closed the door behind me.

*****

Up at the hall, I sent Hal of Potterne, my chief man at arms, to guard the cottage and bade him let no one enter. If Bardol's wife and younger daughter returned, he was to send them straight here to the hall. I called for Peter Brenthall, my deputy wood warden's sixteen year old son and asked him to go to Marlborough to ask Doctor Johannes to come to look to the body for me. I would also send a man to Ramsbury to inform the coroner.

Dr. Johannes of Salerno was my good friend and the town doctor. He was a big man, tall, over six foot, near to 45 years of age. He had shoulder length brown hair, scrupulously clean and shining, with just a hint of grey at the temples, which was tied back in a queue and he was clean shaven, contrary to the current fashion, which dictated that men wore small beards, as I did myself. His eyes were an amber brown, clear and direct of gaze.

He had learned his doctoring in Salerno in Sicily, (where he had been en route from the Crusade with King Richard,) the best school of learning in the world for doctoring, he assured me, and though he had some odd ideas, as far as the rest of the profession believed, he lost fewer patients and cured more people than others could ever hope to. Cleanliness and orderliness was paramount to Johannes. He had been born in Oxford of a parchment maker and a seamstress but, upon his return from Italy, finding it hard to pursue doctoring in his hometown, had packed his bags and fetched up here in Marlborough. We were all glad he had. He had been a great help to me in my role as constable, responsible for all unusual deaths in the locality. This role had been bestowed upon me by the King a while ago and I have to say I could not have done the job half as well without Johannes' help.

We had quite a reputation now, Johannes and I, for the solving of local murders.

Lydia took hold of Annot, sat her at the hall table and gave her a small cup of burntwine. The girl coughed as she sipped it, never having tasted it before.

Henry sat down on the bench beside her and refused the wine. Quickly I told Lydia what we had found.

"Firstly, Henry. What did you see as you entered the cottage?"

Henry looked up quickly and then at Annot.

"Should Annot not..."

"I'm asking you, Henry. The truth please."

My steward shifted back on the bench.

"I finished talking to you, sir. I knew that Bardol would be in the cottage then, for I'd seen him come home from his work about the forest moments before I came to talk to you. As I walked back, up past the church, I saw Annot enter the cottage. She made no noise, sir. When I ducked under the lintel, I saw her kneeling by her father's body with the knife in her hand."

"This is the truth Henry?"

"Upon my father's soul, sir."

"Annot entered a little while before you stepped into the house?"

"A moment only."

Henry licked his lips. "I turned tail and ran up to you."

"Why did you not go to Annot?"

A feathery wisp of a smile wafted over Henry's lips. "I knew that it was important that you see what we'd found immediately...I didn't..... I did not think that Annot had killed him, sir. She wasn't hysterical and hadn't seen me coming into the house. You have often said that the most important thing to do when a body is found is not disturb anything. So I didn't."

"You did not believe that Annot had killed him and you didn't check to see if Bardol was alive?"

"No sir. I don't think she killed him." I noticed the change in tense. "She had not the time and no knife in her hand when she entered the house...."

Annot looked up. "It's his own knife. He was killed with his own knife." She caught her lower lip with her upper teeth. "It was missing from his scabbard." Lydia patted her arm.

"Thank you Annot," I said gently.

"And besides no man could bleed so much and not be dead, I thought," finished Henry. He had been bleeding some time, sir, hadn't he?"

I turned to the girl. "Annot, can you tell me what happened?"

She took a deep shuddering breath.

"He was in a bad mood this morning and went stomping off to work early. I went to my tasks and didn't see him until..."

"Why do you think he was in a bad mood, Annot?"

Annot's eyes flicked momentarily to Henry.

"I told him last night that Henry was going to ask you, my lord, if we could be married, that Henry would be coming to talk to him later today. He wasn't happy, for he said that I was needed at home to help work the plot and work on the manor fields. I told him, I'd be doing that anyway, to help out ma."

"He didn't want you to marry Henry? Become a free woman, step up in the world?"

"He didn't want me to marry anyone. He wanted me at home where he could use me as a slave like he's always done....like he uses ma and Darla. It's us that does all the work around the place, not him."

"Did you argue?"

"Last night. Yes, we did, but I didn't kill him."

"Then what happened?"

"I'd been to the poultry house and was out in the fields with ma most of the day. I was shutting up the hens and I saw Henry go into the manor to speak to you and then thought I'd come up here to be in the cott when Henry came out and walked up to us to speak to father."

"You were fairly sure that I would say yes, then?"

Annot gave me the ghost of a smile. "I was sure you would. You aren't the sort of master who is unkind, sir," she said.

I cleared my throat.

"Right...and so...?"

"When I came in, father was lying just as you saw him. The knife, his knife, was by his side. I dropped onto my knees and just stared. I picked up the knife, I don't know why, I just did."

"Perhaps because you recognised it, Ancie?" said Henry.

"Yes, I did."

"You knew he was dead....you didn't see Henry come in behind you?"

"No...everything was....mixed up and muddled in my head. I didn't like him... my father...but he was my father and the only one I have...had..."

She was dry eyed now.

"You, neither of you saw anyone about? Anyone coming from the house or about the place?"

They both shook their heads.

I sighed and looked up at the rafters. "Well, we shall wait to see what Doctor Johannes says about the body of your father, Annot. The coroner will come when he can and you will have to make a statement telling him that you found the body...."

My wife Lydia looked up at me with her large violet eyes. "My Lord Aumary, Henry cannot tell them that he saw Annot with the knife or the coroner will get the sheriff to arrest her for her father's murder."

"Yes, I know how it is, Lydia."

The first finder was the person who found and more times than not, reported the body to the authorities and they were often, sadly, the first person to be accused of the crime. Many times they were wrongly convicted of it too.

"Nor that they had argued, sir," added Henry.

I turned to Annot. I am a tall man, six foot and I was able to tower over many folk. This height came in handy when I wanted to use my authority and I towered over Annot Wedgemoor now.

"Annot Wedgemoor, do you swear upon your immortal soul that you did not harm your father? That you did not plunge a knife into his back?"

She stood and lifted her chin to look me in the eye.

"No sir. I didn't kill him."

I nodded. "Then it's my job to find out who did. The least we say about this to anyone for the moment, the better."

I picked up the murderous knife which I'd laid on the bench. "Henry, can you take this to Hal and ask him to....."

At that moment I heard small feet pattering on the stone steps of the manor stairs and Darla, Annot's ten year old sister came into view in the screens passage. I put down the knife once more.

Darla saw her sister in the hall but would not step forward until I beckoned her.

"Where is your mother, Darla?"

"Here, my lord," said a voice and the small figure of Winfled Wedgemoor came into view. She curtsied.

"Master Hal said we were to come up here, sir," she said with puzzlement in her voice. She noticed Annot standing with Henry and she smiled sweetly at her.

I stepped forward and caught her by the shoulder. "Step into the hall please, Winfled."

She looked behind her as if she thought someone was following and then came in to curtsey to Lydia.

"Winfled, can you tell me where you have been all day?"

"All day, sir?" she said in a surprised tone.

"From when you arose this morning to just now."

Her brow puckered. She fiddled with the hessian apron which was tied around her waist.

"Erm... after we broke our fast we went to work, at the reeve's instruction, in the top field, sir. Then Darla and I ate some dinner with Widow Deerman and went up to our own field. We came down about...."

"Yes, thank you."

I guided her to a seat. "Have you been within sight of someone all day, mistress?" The thought had crossed my mind that the poor woman's patience with her boorish husband had snapped and that some time today she had lashed out at him in a momentary fit.

"Aye, with the Widow Deerman, and Alice Reeve and others. Why, sir?"

Her eyes grew round and large as I told her that her husband of almost twenty years lay dead on the beaten earth floor of their cottage.

She reared up quickly, her fist going to her mouth. "No!"

"You cannot go to your home this night, Winfled. I will arrange that you stay with neighbours or at the priest's house."

Her pale oval face rose to look at me.

"Dead, sir?"

"Murdered, mistress."

Her jaw worked for a little while and then, to our surprise, she laughed. At first a small half concealed titter that barely escaped her lips. Then it became a fully fledged hysterical laugh.

Annot moved to her mother and embraced her, shushing her as best she could.

The laughter then turned to racking sobs and moans and Lydia moved Winfled carefully to a bench again, where she sat in a daze.

"Find someone to look after her, Henry... I don't know where Agnes Brenthall is...try the undercroft. Last I saw her she was there."

Henry nodded and turned to leave.

Winfled rose up from the bench, brushing her daughter aside.

"Well.." she said, shaking with fury. "Set the wolf to guard the lambs would you, sir?"

"What?"

"Look no further than Henry Pierson, for your murderer...oh yes...I have no doubt..."

"Mother!" cried Annot.

Winfled grew paler still. "Ask him where he was...ask him." And she fell down in a faint on the hall floor.

Chapter Two

I blinked once or twice in surprise and started forward but Henry and Lydia, aided by Annot, quickly lifted Winfled up onto the wide bench and laid her down. Lydia ran to the stillroom for some remedy which would bring her round.

"Henry... can you do as I've asked; go and find Agnes and then come back here please?"

"Yessir."

Little Darla began to cry. I gestured that she should come and sit on the bench by her elder sister.

"Annot ...why do you think your mother said such a thing about Henry? Do they not get on?"

"Yes sir...they are fine together."

"Have you any worries about Henry's innocence?"

"No sir...none at all. Henry wouldn't hurt anyone. He had no reason to hurt my father."

I thought back a few years. To 1204, when Henry had been a man of twenty three. He had played a part in a gruesome murder on my manor though he hadn't truly killed anyone. He had done penance for it. Did any of us really know what we were capable of in extreme circumstances?

The Widow Wedgemoor was beginning to come to her senses. She moaned as Lydia wafted a small vial of some foul smelling stuff under her nose. Then she coughed and opened her eyes.

Annot gave her a small beaker of ale and she sipped it with a nod of her head.

I hunkered down in front of her.

"With what do you accuse Henry Pierson, Winfled?" I asked sternly. "I will, as you demand, ask him, but I should like to know what you think first. Before he returns."

"Sir..."

"Be quiet, Annot."

Winfled Wedgemoor swung her legs from the bench and sat upright. I stood up again.

"I... it was a moment of... I ..."

"No. No excuses, tell me."

Her eyes strayed to her elder daughter and then back to me.

"I saw him, from the field, our field. Our strip lies directly at the back of our house, up the hill and I saw Henry go into the cottage at dinner time."

"You are sure it was Henry?"

"Who else has his bright silver hair, here in the village?"

I nodded.

At that moment Henry arrived with Agnes and together Annot, Darla and she got the unsteady woman out of the hall and across the courtyard. She would stay with Agnes Brenthall, my housekeeper, until her home was habitable again.

I went to the table and poured two cups of ale, one for Henry and one for myself.

"Why do you think she accused you of Bardol's murder, Henry?"

Henry took a sip of ale. "Probably because she saw me going into the house at dinner time."

Lydia snatched a breath.

"Oh? What were you doing there?" I asked innocently.

"Looking for Bardol...to warn him I was about to go to you and ask permission. He wasn't there though Mistress Forester the neighbour, said he was working with her husband Bird up at Burnt Wood today and wouldn't be back till later."

"Can she vouch for you?"

"Aye I've no doubt she will."

"Might she have heard anything you said?"

"I said nothing for there was no one to speak to, sir," said Henry, his beaker half way to his lips.

"Annot tells me Wedgemoor didn't want you to marry her."

"It's as Annot says. He didn't want anyone to marry her. He'd have her an old maid all her life," I saw him grimace at his choice of words, for Annot was no maid, "and a slave to him. He was cross that someone wanted to take her away from the home. Lose an able body then, wouldn't he? More work for him to do."

"You didn't argue with the man?"

"No sir. I didn't. I tried not to speak with him very often, if you must know. I found him...."

"Unpleasant is the word Walter Reeve uses," I said with a slight smile. *That* I knew was an understatement.

"Yes sir. He is...was. However he bred his girls to be so good, I do not know."

"Might have something to do with Winfled." I supplied, smiling.

"So, there was no body at dinner time."

"No sir. Like I say, I saw him go into the house just before I came up to see you this afternoon. The rest of the time I was working in my office."

"Who saw you, Henry?"

"In my office? Erm.... I don't rightly know. The door was open sir...it's warm today. Someone passing must have seen me with my head down over my books."

"Be sure I'll ask, Henry," I said in a level tone.

"Yes, sir. I've no doubt you will. You are a very fair man."

"Let's hope the doctor will confirm that the man died later in the day and about the time you say you saw him go into his cott."

"Indeed I do..." said Johannes coming in through the hall door.

I started in his direction, put down my cup and embraced him.

"I was half way here when I met Peter on Fitz. Seems I have a habit of meeting the lad on the road to the town."

I smiled. "You have been to look at our dead forester?"

"I have. Might I wash my hands?" Henry started up from his bench but Lydia waved him down.

She went to fetch the doctor a basin of hot water from the kitchen to wash off Bardol Wedgemoor's blood.

"So what do we think?" I asked him as I handed him a cup of wine.

"Dead only an hour or a little more... rigor not yet established and the body not cold. It's warm today of course."

"So Henry is vindicated."

Johannes looked over at Henry who had been turning his empty cup in his hand. "Is there any evidence that Henry is guilty?"

"Not really. Just the accusations of a shocked and disorientated wife."

Henry stood. "She saw me go into their house at dinner time, doctor, and so she thought...."

"Ah no, young man. Bardol Wedgemoor was alive and no doubt enjoying his last meal at that time."

"Somewhere at Burnt Wood," said Henry quietly.

"What are your findings, Johannes?" I asked as Lydia came across the room, put down the basin of hot water and embraced her uncle.

"Two strikes with a large bladed knife; no doubt the one which is lying on that bench there."

"Ah yes...Henry, run up to Hal at the door of the cott and ask him to drop it back on the floor by the body will you? Then he can come back to the hall."

"Yes sir," replied Henry. Moving to the knife and handling it with disgust he left.

I told Johannes the story so far.

As he washed his hands he told me what he thought about the death of my forester.

"As I say, strong blows to the back. The knife was driven in, twice in succession, around the kidney level. Almost to the hilt. The man died of bleeding both externally and his body filled with blood internally. He didn't die immediately...."

"For there was much blood which meant that his body was losing it still. I remember you telling me that if a man dies quickly the heart stops and blood ceases to flow."

"We don't know why... or how... but yes, it does," said Johannes. "You have no idea at all why the man should be killed?"

"None as yet," I answered, "though obviously I must ask around my folk and see if Bardol was at odds with anyone in Durley."

Henry snuffled coming back in at the hall door. "Who wasn't he at odds with?"

"Oh?" I said, turning around to face him. "You know someone with whom he might have had an argument?"

"Several, sir," said Henry. He itemised people on his fingers.

"Matthew Cook. They really disliked each other. His neighbour, Ackerman. He'd a foul tongue for him."

I looked at my wife. "And there was me thinking my village was nothing but peace and tranquility."

She shrugged.

"He'd argued with John Brenthall now and again. And Widow Giffard gave him a wide berth too."

"Ah yes. I remember some of these transgressions from the manor court, Henry."

He nodded "And that's not all."

Henry was the person responsible for organising the manor court and he had a better memory than I about the petty cases.

"Well, well," I said. "A list as long as one of Crispin's homilies."

I'd seen Father Crispin come in the door and set down his stole and little vial of holy water on a bench by the table.

We were old friends, boyhood companions until Crispin Darrell had gone off to Oxford University at the age of fourteen. He'd returned a while ago to be our priest after a long and fruitful career with the Bishop of Salisbury.

"Now, now, Sir Aumary Belvoir," he said laughingly. "You know full well that I hate long sermons as much as you do."

"Been to the dead man, Crispin?"

"Aye. His soul is as fit as I can make it."

"By all accounts he could have done with some help," I said.

"He was shriven at Easter," said Crispin, "unless he's been blacker than the devil's cotte since, he will be acceptable to God I think."

I nodded. "He's not been a popular man." I turned back to Henry.

"Can you write me a list of folk with whom he was known to have argued or been at loggerheads, Henry?"

"Yes sir. If you'll excuse me from some other duties. It'll take me two weeks."

Johannes guffawed. "Oh dear. Perhaps a list of those with whom he was friendly then, Aumary?"

I smiled.

*****

Naturally at the head of the list was my old village reeve, Walter. As reeve it was one of Walter's tasks to hand out punishments dictated by myself or Henry my steward, to errant villagers. Fines and spells in the lockup were very rare at Durley. Most people behaved most of the time. Now and again the young lads would have a set to, but a night in our little gaol usually mellowed them. Most of our punishments were fines. Rarely did we put someone in the stocks on the village green.

Bardol Wedgemoor had more than once been fined for striking his wife and children. Many felt, including him, that it was his right and indeed, in law it was. However I took a dim view of the striking of women and children for no good reason and fined him regularly until he stopped. He had, as I said, also prostituted poor Annot when she was younger and that too I had stopped and fined. Bardol had spent time in the lockup when drunk and beyond control. Our reeve was not a popular person with him.

Walter, now an old man, straightened his curved back and grasped his long staff with wizened and gnarled fingers.

"Aye sir. It's well known. He hated me, but then...he would. I've had to discipline him so often for this and that. I've pulled him off John Kellog so many..."

"He was idiot enough to tackle John?" John Kellog was the village butcher, almost as tall as I was and as broad as a Savernake oak.

"Oh aye."

"Why?"

"Drunk and disputing the fees for slaughtering his animals. He's argued with Hubert Alder about a fee too..."

He was our brawny blacksmith and farrier.

"And Matthew Cook?"

"Ah, that was about a patch of mushrooms."

"Mushrooms?" I scoffed.

"Matthew had found a patch of mushrooms in the forest and was gathering them: naturally he's a cook. Wedgemoor disputed ownership. Told him to go away from there."

"They belong to me....really."

"Yes, my lord they do, and they were destined for your table."

"Ah. I see. Why did Ackerman fall foul of him?"

"I think that one was noise, sir."

"Noise, Walter?"

"As you'll know they are close neighbours. Wedgemoor again, was drunk and singing at the top of his voice and yelling and blaspheming at night. Cynn was trying to sleep. One thing led to another and blows were traded."

"Gods, the man was an abomination. I had no idea."

"We try to keep... erm..." Walter scratched his chin making a rasping sound, "petty squabbles from you, my lord, so you might go about your lawful business... you're a busy man. Master Henry and I dealt with most of it."

"Yes, well....I thank you for that but I should really have known how troublesome the man was becoming."

"Yes, sir." Walter bowed as best his old back would allow. "There's many glad he's gone."

"One made absolutely sure he did go, Walt," I said.

Widow Giffard, I was told, had barred him from her home. She brewed ale here in the village and when she had made a new batch, she would hang a green branch from her eaves to signal to the villagers that they could come and buy.

Wedgemoor had more than once been drunk upon arrival at her house and the widow refused to sell him any of her ale. He had then gone about the village sniping about the woman and after a while a couple of her 'friends' had apparently taken the man aside and taught him a lesson. I would never find out who they were. And to be honest, I wasn't worried. It was a far cry from beating someone to sticking a knife in them twice.

Ah well. He was gone and could cause no more trouble. Even so, I needed to find out who was responsible for his death, for my role as constable warranted that I look into it, no matter how I felt about the man. The fact he was unfree meant that I had no great need to investigate, but he was one of my villagers and besides, I loved a puzzle.

I sought out John Brenthall, my chief wood warden, and found him chopping logs at the back of his cottage.

"Good day John. I trust you have no objection to sharing your home with the...well, I suppose we must call her Widow Wedgemoor now...this evening?"

"None at all sir. Agnes and Annot have just brought Darla and her mother into the house place. We have a spare space, as you know. They'll be comfortable there."

"It will only be until the coroner has seen the body."

He put down his axe.

"Any idea what happened, sir?"

I leaned against the house wall. "Well, you know he wasn't a pleasant man and was welcomed by folk in the village about as much as a nest of wasps in a roof. Someone has snapped I expect."

John chuckled. "Aye. He was as angry as a wasps' nest most of the time. I can't count the times I've had to ask Master Henry to punish him for poor time keeping or being disrespectful, drunk at work or simply not doing his job properly. I wasn't popular with him, I have to say."

"Neither was Walter."

"Ah no...it's the same story there. Peter told me he used to walk across the orchard to get to the road, rather than go the long way round. He pushed a path through the hedge we'd laid, Peter and I. We asked him not to, but he took no notice."

"I wondered how that had happened," I said, picturing the gap in the orchard hedge, which we had laid only a couple of years ago.

"Anything in particular lately, John?"

John wiped his hand across his perspiring face. "Lately? No not really....wait yes....the last time. A couple of weeks ago, he should have been at Birch Copse with the other lads. I rode by just to see how they were doing and he wasn't there."

"Hadn't been there or gone missing?"

"Missing."

"Who were the lads?"

"Hartshorn's gang. Wilfrid, Bird, Ackerman...."

"Ah. Did they say anything about him going off or being missing?"

"Nah. Just swore at him."

"Hmmm," I chuckled.

"Wilfrid said it wasn't the first time he'd gone missing that week."

"This was the last week but one, in May?"

"It was, sir."

"You question him?"

"I did." John folded his arms. "He said he'd been taken ill and had to return home here. But Winfled said he hadn't been there all afternoon. At the next manor court he'd no doubt be fined with your permission and he'd be warned that next time it would be a flogging."

I pushed off from the house wall.

"So he was still in the forest or one of the villages round about?"

"Looks like it."

"Do we know where he'd been?"

John looked around the corner of the house and stepped a pace closer to me.

"I wondered if he'd got another woman out somewhere, you know in one of the villages or isolated groups of cotts," he whispered.

"It's a possibility. Can you make inquiries, John...discreetly please? I don't want Annot or Winfled any more upset than they have to be."

"Yessir, I can ask about...carefully."

"Though why a woman should be interested in Wedgemoor..."

John chuckled low in the throat."Doesn't make sense does it, sir?"

"No, it most certainly doesn't. What else might he have been up to?"

John shrugged.

"I have no idea, sir."

*****

I was walking away from John's cottage when into my mind came the picture of the table at the Wedgemoor house. I turned about and scratched on the door at the front of John's cottage. There were two doors to this house and this one faced south.

Agnes came to the door adjusting her headcloth.

"Oh sir...come in. We're just settling the girls here now."

"I just want a quick word with Winfled, Agnes."

"Aye sir. She's in the front room. Go through."

Winfled was stooping to play with Peter's wolfhound Maxime as I poked my head around the doorway.

I smiled. Although the family had lost its major support, truly they would fare well. As Annot had said, most of the hard work was done by the girls anyway. Bardol was no loss to them and it would be easy to transfer the cottage and ground to her as Bardol's heir. I saw Winfled smiling as she played with Maxime at a game of lifting paws and pretend biting.

Maxime saw me first and bounded over to me. I gentled his coarse pricked up ears.

"Winfled...just a word."

She curtsied again and stood with her hands clasped before her, her eyes downcast.

"When I went into your house today, I noticed two ale cups. One was drained, the other half full. Were they yours?"

Her forehead wrinkled. "No sir. I washed up all the cups before we left the house this morning. We had no ale to be drunk. I was going to fetch it after... when.... We didn't return to the house all day. We took a flask with us up the hill."

"Yes. I see. So neither you nor Annot had filled those cups and drunk?"

"No, sir."

So this meant Wedgemoor had had company. Company he was happy to drink with.

"Thank you." I smiled "I'm glad you are feeling better."

She shrugged. "It was a shock...him being dead and murdered but....but truly we shan't miss him, sir."

"No, there's many in the village who will say the same thing, Winfled."

"I know it sounds...well...awful, him being my husband and all but I shan't grieve too hard for him, sir."

I smiled again. "I do understand, though..." I lowered my voice. "I wouldn't make that too widely known, mistress."

Her eyes widened and her fingers went to her lips. "Oh no, sir. I see what you mean!"

I left her staring into space, thinking, no doubt, about her new found freedom. Never once did she question me about who I thought might have killed him. Too many suspects to wonder about perhaps?

So Bardol had shared a jug of ale with someone before he'd been killed and the cups had been left, perhaps by him and his murderer. It was obviously someone he knew. The jug or flask was nowhere to be seen.

The coroner came and went, the next morning. Johannes gave him his observations and a verdict of murder was brought in.

I told Sir Hugo Ramsbury that I would investigate the killing.

"As is your right, Sir Aumary," said the man. "Though if it were me, I wouldn't bother to waste my time on such an unpleasant churl."

"Murder is murder, no matter who the victim is, Sir Hugo," I answered in a level tone.

He scoffed. "I suppose you must do your job even though it is a villein."

"My villein, Hugo."

I'd listened as Annot, the first finder, had explained to the coroner how she had found her father and told him a little about his character, without telling him that she and Bardol Wedgemoor had been at odds. She did say that half the village had been his enemy though.

"And so any one of at least a dozen people might have killed him?" he'd asked.

"Yes, sir, I suppose so. He was very unpopular in the village and the forest."

"You know of no particular reason why he might have been killed?"

Annot looked over at Henry who had been asked to be one of the jury.

"No sir. Nothing in particular."

I stood at the back of the crowd, watching faces and noting who was not paying attention and who was perhaps paying too much attention. The body was moved to the table and the wounds revealed. There was a general shaking of heads as the coroner pointed out the two stab wounds.

Johannes said that to push the knife in as hard as it had gone into Wedgemoor's body would have taken some strength. He demonstrated with his probe how far the knife had penetrated. The assembled crowd sighed as Johannes brought it out.

"You grasp your victim around the body and draw him onto your knife, pushing at the same time.

"So the murderer was a man?" asked Hugo.

"Possibly," said Johannes, "or a very strong woman."

Again the crowd hissed. They all looked around at one another. 'What a terrible thought,' they said, and 'No, it cannot have been his wife for she is a small weak woman and besides she had been half a mile away with witnesses when the deed was being done.'

"Did anyone see a stranger in the village at that time?"

No strangers in the village. Just village folk returning home from their work. And people passing through the village on the main road to Ramsbury some distance away.

"Ah...did anyone recognise those people?"

Villagers conferred. No, they didn't remember anyone in particular. Durley wasn't really on the beaten track but you could pass through on the way to the small town of Ramsbury, through the forest. People did and no one took much notice.

The little house emptied of its jury, the yard around emptied of villagers who had come to hear the verdict.

Henry exited and nodded to me. "We shall now have to wait a decent amount of time, sir, before Annot and I can be married."

"I'm afraid so, yes. There's no fixed time for it in canon law, you know, but let's get the burying done and the mourning period over with and then we'll think on it, Henry," I said, ducking my head under the lintel of the small door. Candles which had been lit for the coroner to make his examination, were being snuffed out. There was an unpleasant smell of extinguished tallow wax.

Annot sat down and exhaled loudly.

"Shall the body of my father be taken to the mortuary now, sir?" she asked.

She looked up at Johannes who had stayed behind.

"Thank you sir, for your help," she added.

"It was nothing but that service I would normally perform for the constable, girl," he said. "It helps the coroner and the constable to know how a man died, when and if there is anything odd about the body."

Annot looked down at her shoes. "Yes, I suppose it does."

Henry came back in the door with a plank of wood and a blanket. "Bird and Hartshorn will help me carry the body to the mortuary, sir," he said.

Our mortuary was a small round building built onto the back wall of the manor courtyard. Here lay the parish coffin and Bardol Wedgemoor would be laid in it within the hour.

Annot and Winfled stood and crossed themselves as the body was heaved on to the plank and covered by the blanket. Crispin the priest, standing outside, accompanied it down past the church.

Winfled tutted as she went to draw some water from her barrel outside the door to scrub the table clean. Annot rearranged the items on the table.

I idly watched her.

"The two cups which lay on the table when you came in and found your father Annot, are they still here?"

"Aye my lord, and cleaned up."

"Ah.You found no flask or jug here, rolled anywhere?"

She looked up puzzled. "No sir."

"Hmmm."

"But I'll tell you this..." she said looking round... "the little flowers...the ones my father brought home yesterday and put on the table in a small pot...they're gone, sir. Oh the pot's here but the flowers are gone."

"Gone? Where?"

"They aren't here. In the house. Maybe when someone moved my father's body to the table they....."

"You weren't here then?"

"No, I was at Master Brenthall's still. Maybe they got moved then."

We searched but couldn't even find the flowers on the midden.

"Your father brought them home? Not like him is it, Annot?"

"No sir...not really. He said he liked them and they smelled pretty. Been bringing them home for a few days."

"Why on earth did he....?"

"He hadn't done it before, sir, before this year."

"I can't really see your father as the flower picking type, Annot," I smiled.

"No sir, he isn't...wasn't. Mam and I used to pick a few if we had time but never my Da."

"So what made him pick these, I wonder?"

Annot shrugged. Her mother came in and started to boil the water on the fire.

"What kind of flowers were they, Annot?"

"Kind sir...? Oh I see...why they were roses sir. Yes, roses."

*****

Satisfied with the state of the table, eventually the women then went down to the mortuary to begin the laying out of father and husband.

I stayed to look round again. I could find nothing which was helpful and so followed the women down the slight incline and back to the manor.

Waiting for me was a letter.

I broke the wax and sitting at my office table I read the contents.

'To the Lord Aumary Belvoir, Master of Durley, Greetings in God.

I am today, my beloved son-in-law, writing to tell you of the death of my husband, Toruld Congyre.

For much of this past day he has lain in a stupor from which he rarely truly woke.

I called for the doctor, your friend Master Johannes of Salerno, but he was away from home and my missive would have been too late to find him, for Toruld died in the early hours of this morning.

I grieve to bring you this news. Let us see you as soon as you are able.

Think of myself in love and farewell.

Given this day June 6th at Bedwyn. Evisa Congyre.'

A lump came to the back of my throat. In truth I had known it was coming for my father-in-law, father to my first wife Cecily, had been unwell much of the year and in much pain. He had failed and rallied for months. It was just the suddenness of his actual death which shocked.

I scribbled a note to Evisa and sent it quickly back to Bedwyn, by one of my grooms. I would visit later today. Her priest would read it to her.

Toruld Congyre had at last gone to meet his daughter, my first wife Cecily and his grandson Geoffrey.

I bounded up the solar stairs and sought out my second wife Lydia and told her of the news.

She sat down heavily on a chair and put her hand to her mouth.

"Oh poor woman," she said. "She has been with Toruld since they were little more than children, Aumary. That's forty years. It's a long time. She'll be distraught."

"Her letter was matter of fact. I know she will have had the manor steward write it, or father Godfrey for she can't read or write but still.... I hope she will manage all right."

"Shall I come with you?"

I reached for her shoulder. "I'll send you a message from there when I know when the interment will be. You can bring Hawise up then. She ought to know. Will you tell her?"

"Yes, I can do that."

Hawise had been particularly fond of her grandfather.

"And Simon too must come to Bedwyn." Simon was my son and heir.

"I will arrange it when I know when you want us," said Lydia. "You must go now and be with Evisa."

"Thank you Lydia."

She smiled, rising. "I'll fill you a pack."

*****

A few hours later I was off to Bedwyn, a short ride through the forest to the manor which lay to the north of the main road and like Durley, was buried in the forest.

Bedwyn was a village a little larger than Durley but still belonging to the crown. It was rumoured that it had once belonged to that great Saxon king Alfred, along with other villages nearby. There had been a mint here at Bedwyn earlier and this had been transferred to the castle at Marlborough. In 1201, there had been a disastrous fire in the village and after this the place never really thrived, probably because of the proximity of Hungerford and Marlborough.

The abbey at Abingdon had been given the place during the reign of a subsequent king but King Athelred had recovered the village and manor from the abbey and now they both lay within my forest. However, in recent history the place was not part of the forest holdings and was autonomous. Toruld Congyre had managed and farmed here for over twenty years. He was without a male heir and so I knew that the village and its environs would pass to me, for he had told me as such and it was written not only in his will but in other charters kept at Durley.

I clattered into the manor yard to be met by one of the grooms.

"Ho! Alfred… where's your mistress?"

"Up in the solar sir, I think," he said."

I took the steps two at a time and scratched at the solar door. A lady's maid opened it and curtsied low.

"Hello Annie, I trust you are well," I said as I entered and bowed to my lady mother-in-law and the grandmother of my daughter.

Evisa Congyre rose shakily. "Aumary! I did not think for you to come so quickly...I..."

"Do not put yourself out on my account, Evisa." I said, embracing her and pecking her on the cheek.

"We are not ready to receive you...it's..."

"No, no, I need nothing special. I can lay my head on the hall floor if need be."

I looked round to the main bed. "Where is Toruld?"

"In the church. He wanted to be there. We shall lie him under the nave as soon as we are able."

I nodded.

I had loved my erstwhile father-in-law and I wanted to go to see him one last time.

"Might I go there now, see him and pray for him?"

"Of course. You may do as you wish. I'll have a bed made up for you in the upper chamber."

"Thank you. My pack is with my horse in the stable."

"I'll have it brought up."

*****

I walked across the road and entered the little church. It was much like my own at Durley. A rectangular nave block with two small side aisles and a chancel, but this church had lain on this spot since the Saxons had farmed the land. Mine had been built by a Norman, my great grandfather.

Toruld Congyre was lying on a black pall before the altar. Two black candles burned slowly there and the light reflected from the two containing silver candlesticks. It was quite dark.

I bowed my head to the altar, reached for some holy water from the nearest stoup and crossed myself.

Then I gently tiptoed to the bier.

I drew back the cloth. The lined face of my father-in-law came into view. He had always been brown with wind and weather, this man, but now he seemed too pale apart from patches of redness and blotchiness about the forehead and cheeks. The light picked up his grizzled beard and moustache; his aquiline nose; it reflected from the hands where lay two rings; one of silver and ruby and the other plain gold.

I tilted my head to look carefully at him. There was a whiteness around his eyes and a thinness to his face I'd not remembered before. He was sixty.

Here was one of the last links to my old life. I swallowed down sadness.

I bent my head and prayed for his soul. My mind however would not stay on my prayers for into my head kept coming the picture of my first wife Cecily on our wedding day, she seventeen and me nineteen. It had been fourteen years ago but it was as sharp as the polish on the candlesticks before me. It had been 1193. By 1203 my lovely wife was dead by a murderer's hand and buried in the churchyard at Durley.

I thought too of my son Geoffrey, five years old - dead by that same murderer's hand; also in that year 1203. Before I knew it, I was weeping into my beard, for Cecily, for Geoffrey my son and for Toruld Congyre.

I felt a hand on my shoulder. I turned to find old Father Godfrey, the priest here, smiling at me.

"Peace, my son," he said, and we walked back together out into the summer air. I wiped my eyes and nose on a small piece of cambric I kept in my purse. Father Godfrey had been the man who had married Cecily and me all those years ago.

"How did he die?" I asked the priest. I knew he would know.

"He took to his bed on Friday saying he didn't feel well again. And he slept. He woke a little in the night and I was summoned to give extreme unction. He was, I think, in a lot of pain and had been for some time."

"Aye."

"And then he slept again. We did not think it would be so quick. The Lady Evisa would have sent for you but by the time we had pen to parchment....he'd gone."

I nodded. "Peaceful then?"

"Yes, it was a good passing."

"Were you there then...at his last breath?"

"No. I'd gone downstairs to write to you. I had to re-write my missive."

"The Lady Evisa...?"

"Was missing for a moment. She had to see to the visitor who arrived. She went to see him off. When she returned the Lord Toruld..."

"Visitor?"

"The Lord Toruld's brother had come. From Chilton. To see him in his illness. The Lady had me write to him the day that he last took ill. He farms there. They have been estranged these years but the Lady Evisa had been asked by Lord Toruld to..."

"I wondered why I'd never met him." I turned round to face the priest. "What's he like, this brother?"

Godfrey chuckled. "As like as two peas in a pod they were, though Sherwyn is the younger by ten years."

"What was it that made them fall out? Toruld was such an even tempered man; I cannot imagine him falling out with anyone."

"Ah for that, my lord, you'll have to ask the Lady Evisa for I don't know."

"Thank you father, I will. And so his brother came to see him? Were they reconciled?"

"Sherwyn told me they were. All was forgiven."

"You didn't hear this forgiveness, Godfrey?"

"Bless you no, sir. I was here praying."

"And the lady?"

"She was there somewhere but I don't think she was in the room. It was private you see."

" Sherwyn, was alone with Toruld, for how long?"

Part of my brain was saying to me, 'Oh for goodness sake Aumary, do not see ill where there is none.'

The other half was, shall we say, interested.

What Paul...yes...you are quite right...some might think that another word for nosy. You know how nosy I am, well I certainly was in those days. I had to root out ill wherever I thought it lay.

"For a short while sir. The time it takes to say twenty Paternosters."

"And then?"

"He went home, my lord. As the crow flies it's not so far, just six miles and it was early...very early, getting light."

"Yes, I know where Chilton lies."

I moved back into the church and Godfrey followed. Once more I gazed on the face of my father-in-law.

Then I drew the black cloth over him again.

*****

That night I slept badly. The story which Evisa had told me kept going round in my brain.

The story of why the two brothers Toruld and Sherwyn fell out.

It went back to the days when John, our present King, had been regent for the absent Richard who had gone on crusade.

In this area of Wiltshire there was great respect for and support of Count John, as he was known then. Many landowners and officers of the crown were secretly for John, as I was myself. My father however had been a King's man. That King was Richard and so, as had happened in Durley, families were split over which man they followed, John or Richard. When Richard was released from prison, John's star fell from the sky and what support there had been, dwindled. Then Richard died and John became King.

Those who had followed John were rewarded. Those who were out and out Richard's men, didn't prosper quite so well, in the main, with some glaring exceptions.

Toruld had been for John, Sherwyn for Richard.

And a war had waged between them. For almost ten years they hadn't spoken a word to each other.

Yesterday, before Toruld had died, Sherwyn and he had been reconciled.

All those years and nothing had been said. Suddenly Evisa had been asked by her ailing husband that if he should begin to seriously fail in health, his brother was to be contacted and they should meet. Evisa did as she was asked.

She left them, she said, to sort out their differences. Sherwyn felt his brother a traitor; Toruld felt his brother a man with no sense, for even though Sherwyn must declare his allegiance to John as monarch by swearing an oath which we all had to do last year, he had in his heart of hearts refused to countenance John as King. At the beginning he had backed Arthur Prince of Brittany - John's nephew and rival for the crown. When Arthur died, apparently he favoured another, though Toruld wasn't sure who this could have been.

John had been King eight years. It hadn't been an easy eight years but it had been fairly stable, this land of ours. John was King and would stay King and Sherwyn was unhappy about that.

No Paul, we had not yet descended into the mayhem which was to blight the latter years of John's reign.

A land owner of Saxon descent, Toruld's brother could not inherit his sibling's estate for I was named his heir. Why did I worry? Something niggled me. It niggled me all night.

Next day, I sent to Lydia and asked her to bring Hawise and Simon to Bedwyn.

They came in late that afternoon and were ensconced at the further end of the solar with their grandmother and Felice their nurse.

Lydia and I slept together in the little room at the other end of the hall.

Johannes, and Hal who had accompanied them, slept in the hall.

I tossed and turned.

Eventually I left Lydia sleeping and padded out in my soft shoes to the hall.

Hal opened one eye.

"Can't sleep, lad?" he asked.

I shook my head.

"Something isn't right here, Hal. I cannot for the life of me work out...."

"Are your thumbs prickin'?"

"Aye, they are."

"Ah well then. Must go with the prickin' of yer thumbs mustn't you?" whispered my man at arms.

Johannes reared up on his elbow, on his pallet.

"Will you two be quiet. Some of us..."

"Johannes... will you come out to the church with me...just this once...?"

"What?"

Hal was getting up and pulling on his shirt.

"Before we bury him tomorrow. Please just come and look at him and tell me I am being foolish."

"He was an old man, Aumary...old and failing..."

"He wasn't that old and besides, he'd failed before as you know and rallied."

"Let him go, Aumary," said Johannes, lying down again.

"Please, Johannes. I won't rest until..."

We tiptoed out of the building, like three naughty scholars and entered the church.

New candles had been lit that evening and were burned to half their height. The sanctuary light winked red at us.

It was in the hours just before a fine June dawn.

I fiddled in my purse and brought out a candle which I lit from the black candles on the altar. Hal lit one from my own, Johannes took hold of one of the candlesticks.

I peeled back the black pall.

Carefully Johannes looked at the body of my father-in-law.

"I can't see anything untoward. There are no wounds. We should have known about those when he was laid out."

I looked up at him, his handsome face picked out by the light of the candle he held.

"Remember Quimper?"

"Quimper... yes I remember him."

Quimper had been my brother's, my half brother's tutor, dead now these few years and he too was buried in the churchyard at Durley. He had been murdered in his own bed.

Johannes searched my face, then his eyebrow raised.

He lifted the eyelids of Toruld Congyre. He peered closely at the man's face. He lifted the hands. He fished in his purse and took out a small blunt looking knife.

He ran this under Toruld's fingernails. He looked around and found a small dish by the altar. "God forgive me," he said under his breath.

He placed the result on the dish and took the candle to it carefully.

Hal bent over and lent his light to the job.

"Skin, blood and...yes, hair."

"His own...?" I asked.

"Perhaps."

" 'E isn't scratched about the beard and face," offered Hal.

"No, he isn't."

Johannes stood up. "Yes, I remember Quimper. I remember how he died."

"He was smothered with a cushion wasn't he?" I said.

"Was 'e?" said Hal, "Oo did that then?"

Both Johannes and I looked at him. Our lips had to be sealed for we were both bound by oaths not to tell.

"Ah yes..well..." said my man at arms. "I 'spose I can guess. If yer won't tell me."

"Was Toruld...?"

"What is the meaning of this, my lord?" said a voice.

Father Godfrey, tousled and sleepy, stood raising a flare just above his head. I was worried that he was going to set fire to his hair.

"Father...it's not what it seems..."

"Oh, sir, and what does it seem?"

Johannes turned to face him.

"Put up your cudgel, sir priest. You have no need of it."

Hal made his way down the nave "It's only us, Godfrey," he said.

"I know that, Hal of Potterne, but what are you doing?"

"Examining the body of my father-in-law," I said.

Godfrey exploded. "What!"

He stuttered and stammered and we could get no sensible word from him, until Johannes raised his voice.

"Godfrey, we can have no burying tomorrow. We shall be calling the coroner instead. If I am not much mistaken, Toruld Congyre was suffocated."

"Godfrey..." I said, "Toruld was murdered."

Chapter Three

The coroner, Sir Hugo Ramsbury, looked at me severely.

"Sir Aumary, murder seems to be following you around these days."

I did not answer him.

Johannes of Salerno cleared his throat.

"I have examined the body, sir, and it appears that Toruld Congyre was suffocated. There is petechia of the eyeball, breaking of the small blood lines in the eye, squashing of the teeth against the gum and the patchy redness which is associated with...."

"Yes, yes, yes." Hugo looked up " Could this not just mean that he was old and...?"

"The man was not red of face in life Hugo. Remember, I knew him well. Tanned with wind and sun but never red nor blotchy."

"It happens when someone is starved of their breath," said Johannes, "When a man dies the blood falls to the lowest point. In this case there's a rupture of..."

"Oh spare me doctor. I believe you."

"And I fished this from his nostril..."

He brought out a small piece of parchment folded over and carefully unwrapped it. There was a tiny feather, a feather the sort with which one might stuff a pillow.

"The Lady Evisa's maid says that the pillow in Master Congyre's bed was indeed stuffed with such feathers."

"Could he not simply have breathed it in?"

I folded my arms across my chest. "Sir Hugo. If he had done that, he would sneeze and expel it. He had no time to do so for..."

"Yes, yes. I see."

"Then there's this..." went on Johannes and opened up his small vial. He tipped the contents onto the parchment beside the feathers.

"The person who attacked him felt the scratch of Master Congyre's nails. He did fight back but weakly."

Hugo of Ramsbury leaned over the evidence. "Hmmm. Hair from a head?"

"It isn't long. It's quite coarse; I'd say that it's a beard, sir."

"Hmmm," he said again.

"And then, there's the mystery of the missing will," I said.

The coroner straightened up. "Will?"

"I know, because I was present when it was made, Sir Hugo, that my father-in-law made a will. It lists bequests of a personal nature and leaves the estate to me as his only surviving male relative. It's gone."

"Only relative, but the servants tell me that Congyre has a brother? Might the estate not go to him...?" he stopped, for he saw my face.

"They were estranged until yesterday and Bedwyn is encompassed within the forest. My forest, sir. Only the King can take it away from me and bestow it elsewhere. And it's unlikely he would do that, before you ask."

"Hmm." He scratched his cheek.

"Where was the will?"

"The Lady Evisa says it was on the side table. They had looked it out from its place in the chest there in the solar, before Toruld breathed his last. The fact it is missing does not alter the eventual ownership of the village. I have other documents at Durley which will substantiate my claim, but it matters to the occupants of the village. Without that will we cannot enact the wishes of its lord."

"Hmmm, I see."

He screwed up his face. "We think then that Congyre was murdered by his newly pardoned brother?"

"It seems likely, Hugo, for he is the only person who visited him in his last days. However we must not jump to conclusions. I will go to Chilton and question the man. We must have proof of his guilt."

"And if we cannot obtain it?"

I shrugged. "Then, I cannot move against him."

*****

Go to Chilton I did, later that day.

It was, as Godfrey had said, only six miles away.

The house in which Toruld's brother lived was a large single storey farmhouse with a thatched roof and several outbuildings.

I looked around as I entered the yard. There were fields about the buildings where dairy cows grazed happily on lush grass watered by the River Kennet. It seemed a well run and prosperous place.

A young man came out of the house.

"What can I do for you, sir?" he said in a wary tone but with a smile.

I introduced myself, in my role as Constable and then my relationship to Toruld Congyre.

With the latter the man's face lost its smile. "I'll fetch my master."

I was not invited into the house. The master was fetched out to me.

He bowed.

"You are Sherwyn Congyre?"

"I am, my lord." I looked into eyes that were like my father-in-law's, deep and brown. The high forehead too was there; the upright stance. Toruld's beard had been dark grey and close cropped. This man wore a brown beard, with little grey in it but not closely snipped like my own. This beard covered his throat.

"You know that Toruld your brother is dead."

"Aye, he died when I had finished speaking to him. As I was taking drink in the hall before I left for home. It was dark and I wanted to be home soonest."

"We have had to postpone his funeral, Sherwyn. We should have buried him today but we have discovered that poor Toruld was murdered and so we have had to wait until the coroner had convened his jury and made a pronouncement."

"Murdered...no!"

"He was smothered with a pillow."

"No, it cannot be. He was weak and near to death. He died when ...."

"He was murdered," I said again.

Sherwyn Congyre paled. "And you think because he and I were not the best of friends, that I killed him?"

"I think you had ample opportunity to do so, when Evisa left you alone with him."

"Why? Why would I do it? I don't gain anything by Toruld's death," he shouted, lifting his hands in a gesture of disbelief.

"People can kill for very little, Master Congyre."

"Aye..I know it." His chin jutted "But I repeat, what have I to gain? Why would I kill my brother? A brother I have not spoken to for eight years and who in one of his last acts, gave me his forgiveness and I him."

I shrugged. "Did you remove the will from the table by his bed?"

"Why should I do that? I don't believe I'm mentioned in it."

I turned to my horse and gentled Bayard's nose.

"Perhaps you thought that you might inherit..."

"No! I know I cannot. You are the beneficiary. That I know, my lord."

"How do you know this?"

"Toruld told me. In the last words we had. He told me that his daughter's husband would inherit."

"And you did not think this unfair?"

"Why should I? I know that Bedwyn lies within the forest, that you are warden and that all lands within it are to be held from you. I know that the estate is to come to you."

I nodded. "Very well. What did you speak about, when you and Toruld conversed that last time?"

"About a private matter, my lord," said Sherwyn, folding his arms.

"About your distaste of our monarch, John?"

"A man's feelings about his monarch are his own, sir. I swore my oath last year. I'm not about to break it."

"My lady mother-in-law Evisa has told me about the reason for your quarrel."

"It's over with now," snapped Sherwyn. "The King is the King and there's an end. Until the next one."

"And your brother lies dead in his coffin."

"He supported John, I was for Richard..."

"And for Arthur Duke of Brittany?"

"It's no secret. Now."

"No. Best it remains...quiet though, Congyre," I said.

I walked around to his back.

"My father-in-law wounded his attacker. Did you know that, Congyre? He scratched him, quite nastily."

"No!." Sherwyn's hand flinched and almost rose up to his neck but he stilled it in time.

He turned to look at me. "I repeat, what have I to gain by attacking my brother?"

I reached out for Bayard. "We shall let you know when we will bury him. I assume you'd like to be there, Sherwyn?"

He bowed again. "I would, my lord."

"And if you come across the will, might you return it to us? It doesn't change the ownership of Bedwyn but it does deal with small bequests to the church and such like. Toruld wanted to leave some monies to his staff. He's also made provision for his wife. That will would be useful to us."

Sherwyn breathed in angrily.

I mounted Bayard. "I will see you in a day or so, sir," and I rode away.

*****

When I reached Bedwyn, there was a commotion in the hall.

Hal was standing listening to Evisa berating one of the maids.

"You stupid girl. Why did you move it?"

"I thought, ma'am, that..."

"Oh never mind...go away!"

Evisa turned on her heel and sat down at the table slowly with a grimace as if her knees pained her. I noticed she held a piece of parchment in her hand.

Hal looked over his shoulder at me. "Domestic matters, sir."

"Ah..."

Evisa looked up. "Oh Aumary, I'm glad you have returned."

She waved the parchment in the air. "It's been found. The will. The stupid girl...it had fallen down behind the table. The girl says she didn't touch it but... how else can it have got there?"

I eased off my riding gloves and chuckled. "Easily done, mother-in-law."

I sat down. Hal poured me a mug of ale.

"And I have just more or less accused Sherwyn Congyre of purloining it... ah well..."

I took a drink of the ale.

"Can I see?"

Evisa handed me the will.

I read...

'On June 16th 1206, I Toruld John Congyre, sound in mind and memory make my will in this way....'

I frowned.

I sat up straight.

"Evisa," I said, "This was found where?"

My mother-in-law was arranging her dress about her shoulders.

"Why, at the back of the small night table, fallen from the surface."

I turned it over. I put it up to the light. I swivelled round to the table and laid it flat and read it again. I checked the seal.

At last I let it roll up.

"I sighed. "No Evisa..." I said. "This isn't the will."

"But Aumary...."

"Oh yes...it's a will but it isn't the will that I watched Toruld make last year."

Evisa's face paled.

"This is a forgery."

*****

My lady mother-in-law shifted to the front of her seat. "A forgery but... why would anyone want to forge Toruld's will?"

"The terms are changed. There are still the bequests to the church and to staff here at Bedwyn. Your 'bride piece' naturally is reserved for you as a widow, as is your right, but a part of the estate, land towards Ramsbury goes to..."

"Not 'is brother?" asked Hal.

"No, Hal, a man called..." I unrolled the parchment again and read "Sir Jacques Garner."

Evisa started, "No. It can't be."

"No Evisa, you're right, it can't be."

"The manor is yours, Aumary. All of it. Toruld always said so."

I patted the back of her age spotted hand. "Don't worry, Evisa. This can be sorted out."

I looked carefully at her. "Do you know this man at all?"

"Yes, I do. He holds lands towards Ramsbury at a place called Whittonditch. Just outside the forest."

"Why would Toruld leave him part of the manor? What is he to Toruld?"

She frowned. "I don't know. They knew each other, that's all I can say. He's a neighbour."

"Had the man seen Toruld recently?" I asked.

"Not in the past few months. As you know Toruld had been ill for some time. He didn't see anyone. You, Lydia, Hawise and Simon were the only people who visited regularly."

Her eyes filled with tears.

"Don't fret, Evisa, the man cannot get his hands on the place. The King will confirm that Bedwyn lies in my land. The documents I have at home will negate this will."

"Can we bury my poor husband now, Aumary?" she asked tearfully. "Why have we had to wait?"

"Ah...we...." I had not yet told her that Toruld had been murdered.

I saw Hal coming round the table to stand by her side. He smiled sweetly at her as he slid onto a bench pulled up to the table.

"We 'ad a little problem with that, Mistress Congyre," he said gently.

"Evisa... I don't know how to tell you this..." I began, "but Toruld did not pass to his rest in God's good time. Someone helped him on."

Her face paled and her pupils contracted. I grabbed for her hand. "He was ill, yes, and would have died, we know this. What we don't know is how long he would have lingered. Someone helped him out of this life. I need to find out who? He was smothered, Evisa."

"No, no."

"I'll find out who did it, Evisa. I'll begin with this man Garner."

"How could 'e 'ave killed him sir, if he were nowhere near?" asked Hal.

"We don't know that Hal." I said, looking concernedly at my mother-in-law who was shrinking into her seat. "He may have had inside help."

"Someone at the manor 'oo..."

"No, Aumary...no one here," said Evisa suddenly, "No servant at Bedwyn. Not one would....kill Toruld."

"We need to find out why this man Garner is mentioned in this document and why suddenly it says he is entitled to part of the place."

"Seven miles by my reckoning" said Hal. "From Whittonditch to Bedwyn."

I nodded. "We shall pay him a visit and we shall find out if there's a connection between this man and Toruld's brother."

Evisa sniffled. "Why, Aumary?"

"If no one has seen Toruld but his brother and this man Garner benefits from this will which we know has been substituted, then it's not unlikely that the one is in league with the other."

Evisa shook her head. "I cannot believe it."

"The coroner has seen Toruld, Evisa...."

"I wondered who that man was and what was happening in the church."

"It pains me that we had to keep it from you but we wanted to be certain."

"Yes, yes I see that now."

"We can bury him soonest."

Lydia had come in with Hawise and Simon and stood at the hall door. I nodded to her. Hawise flew to her grandmother and buried her head in her shoulder.

"We shall do it tomorrow."

*****

We buried my father-in-law the next morning, in the nave of the church, settling him beneath a stone before the altar, as was his wish.

Sherwyn Congyre came and stood at the back and when all was over disappeared quietly. He brought no will with him. Village folk, heads bowed, conversation stilled, filed out into the summer day and went about their work. Some wept.

I left Evisa standing staring at the ground by the altar and ushered my family out of the church saying, "Let her be alone there for a while."

A pair of doves wheeled around the space before the church building and came to rest on the roof of the manor house. Simon looked up and pointed. "Bird" he said clearly. I would always remember this day as the first time Simon spoke an intelligible word, bar dada and mama.

I picked him up and settled him on my arm and he pointed again. "Bird."

"Yes, birds. They are doves, Simon," I said, looking back into the church and watching my mother-in-law muttering low, her chin on her chest.

"Evisa...come...come and hear your grandson speak his first word."

She looked up then. "Aye. I remember Geoffrey's first word too," she said walking slowly down the nave towards us. "He said 'What's that?' over and over."

The moment of sadness was broken.

"Aye, he was an inquisitive child," I said.

"Bird!" squealed Simon again and we all chuckled.

We stood in front of the church building and watched the sun speckling the old manor of Bedwyn. A little breeze had blown up and the birch trees behind the house were shivering with a silken rustle.

"Would you like to come and stay with us for a while, Evisa?" asked Lydia, linking her arm into that of my mother-in-law. Lydia smiled at me over Evisa's head and I realised just how small and shrunken the old woman had become.

"Yes, my dear, I think I would like that."

Hawise came forward and slipped her hand into that of her Grandma's. "Don't be sad Gramma," she said. "Grandfather Toruld is with the angels now. I know he'll be having a lovely time."

Evisa looked down at her only granddaughter.

"If I know Toruld, Hawise, he'll be organising them all into a choir."

"Yes, he always did love singing," replied Hawise. "He was very good at it."

"We shall miss him at Christmas when we sing our Yule songs," I said, a wave of nostalgia washing over me. "It truly won't be the same without him."

Evisa put her hand on my sleeve. "He was in much pain latterly, Aumary," she said. "He did no singing almost all year. That is how I knew he was failing and slipping away slowly to God."

I nodded. "It must have been very hard for you to watch."

Evisa sighed. "It was excruciating. Every day a little less of the man I had known was there. He was always such a forceful man, a man larger than life, a huge personality. Slowly it went. He became a weak, sobbing, sighing wreck."

Her eyes filled with tears. "It was more than I could bear."

Lydia drew her tighter to her side. "We shall remember him as he was last Christmas then, singing his heart out, laughing at the mummers, playing games with Hawise and Hal...."

Hal chuckled. "Cheatin' yer mean!"

"Aye cheating, Hal," smiled my mother-in-law. "He was such a fun man. All our life together he has made me laugh. From the very first when we were scarce more than children. We have laughed all our lives. He laughed less though, after losing Cecily and Geoffrey. That was a severe blow to him."

"To us all, mother," I said.

*****

We returned to Durley that day and after I'd settled everyone in the house again, Hal and I set to ride the eight miles to Whittonditch and back to Durley before the afternoon became evening. The light was clear and we could ride there and back before nightfall, for fine June evenings were long and the weather was good.

We crossed the London Road and made our way to Chilton and thence to the town of Ramsbury. A little while along this road the track became wooded on both sides and the trees shaded us from the sun. I shivered.

"What is it about this road which always makes me shiver, Hal?" I said abstractedly, "every time I travel this piece of road."

"Perhaps there's hoppergubbelins," chuckled my man at arms.

"Ah yes... the prior of Avebury's Hobgoblins. Perhaps."

In 1205 I had investigated a murder at Avebury manor and the local churchman had sworn that the place was infested with this type of evil creature. We laughed about it often.

A couple of yards further on Bayard pricked up his ears and stopped dead.

"What's the matter, old friend?" I asked.

Hal held up his hand..."Listen."

We sat in silence for a moment.

In the distance, somewhere in the trees to our left, men were shouting; there was a yelling and scrambling, the neighing of horses.

Bayard pawed the ground. "Steady lad," I said to him.

Hal cocked his head on one side. "A party of men travelling fast through the brush. Some mounted, others on foot."

"I hear it Hal."

Suddenly from the scrub at the side of the track, two men burst from the cover of the waist high ferns and bracken.

Both were breathing hard and were covered in sweat. They stopped dead when they saw us.

"What's going on?" I yelled.

At that, the men, realising I suppose, that we were not about to attack them nor impede them in any way, skirted our horses and plunged into the brush at the other side of the track.

An arrow came out of the further trees and caught the first man square in the back as he fled. He squealed and fell headlong into the brambles at the base of an ash tree. He screamed and writhed for quite a while then lay still. His fellow, following too quickly on his heels, tripped over him and rolled away.

Into our view came a man on a grey horse, followed by two others on brown rounceys. One man was reloading his bow.

"Stop!" I yelled. "I am the Constable of this county and I order you to stop."

Hal had scraped his sword from his scabbard and sidled his horse, his favourite mount Grafton, up to Bayard's flank.

The three men pulled up their mounts and scuffed up the chalk of the track.

Six more men now followed on foot. All of them were armed with bows. The man on the grey held out his hand to them. They stood still.

"Ah, Sir Aumary Belvoir," he said at last. "I'm glad we have met you."

*****

I nodded to Hal who left his horse and strode into the underbrush. The fallen man backed away hastily, blubbering and begging.

I saw Hal's head shake. The other was dead.

"Stand up man!" said Hal, "Yer quite safe now. This is the Constable of the county. 'E'll see you right."

The pursued man continued to blubber and shake. Hal lifted him by the neck of his tunic.

I turned to the man on the grey horse.

"You have the advantage of me sir. I do not know..."

"Garner, Jacques Garner, my lord Belvoir. Lord of Whittonditch." The man bowed from the waist.

He nodded to the blubbering wreck and the dead man "And these two are my tiresome churls, men of Knighton."

He chuckled. "We have tracked the beasts almost from there to..."

"These are men, sir, not beasts."

The smile left the Lord of Whittonditch's face. "I call them beasts when they steal what is rightfully mine."

"What have they stolen?"

"Food, my lord. Food destined for my table."

I turned to the man now in the grasp of Hal of Potterne. "Tell me, is it as your lord says? Did you take food which was not rightfully your own?"

The man blubbered still and no coherent word escaped his lips.

"Pah! Useless pizzle. Foreman, bring him down!"

"STAY YOUR HAND, at peril of the law." I shouted. "No further violence will be attempted."

Hal stepped bravely in front of the villein.

Garner tutted. "He is my property, Belvoir. I may do with him as I wish."

"Not on my land you won't."

Garner took a deep breath. He looked to Heaven. "Are we in the forest now, Foreman?"

The man called Foreman, seated on one of the rounceys, tugged his forelock. "Begging yer pardon, sir, I'm not quite sure. We may just be on our own land. But that side of the road is forest I think."

"You crossed the river a while back. The Kennet is the boundary here."

Garner threw his leg over the ears of his grey and jumped from the saddle. Foreman, followed suit.

"Ah! But now I think you'll find this piece of land belongs to me, Belvoir."

He stood in front of me, his feet wide planted, the fingers of his left hand clasped around his sword pommel.

"Correction, sir. This is the King's land. It belongs to neither of us."

Garner narrowed his eyes and there was a little silence. "It's no accident we meet here is it?"

"We were on our way to speak with you, sir," I said. "At Whittonditch. Your manor."

"Well, you have found me here. With my men. On my land."

"Why do you persist? You know that were we to try this before the King, Savernake would win."

"You are sure of this then, Belvoir?" scoffed Garner. He leaned forward. "How do you know that I don't have the ear of our King?"

"I don't, sir." I looked down at him from Bayard's back. "But I know that I do."

Garner blinked at that.

From the corner of my eye, I saw Hal smirking.

"The Lord Belvoir is a bosom brother of John our King, 'e is," he said. "I wouldn't give a fairy's fart for yer ear. No matter 'ow big it is." He smiled sweetly. "My lord," he added, crossing his arms over his chest.

Garner was angry but he contained it. "John is bedfellows only with those with, shall we say, deep money chests, Belvoir." He made a gesture as one feeling a deal of coin between his fingers. "How deep are yours?"

"My coffers are my own business. This forest is my business. This parcel of land is forest land. Go home, Sir Jacques."

The man laughed and his laughter rang out through the forest. Several pigeons and a startled woodpecker made out over the treetops. "You arrogant puppy."

I saw Hal bridle at that.

Sir Jacques Garner was a decade older than myself. He wore his hair cropped very short and it was already greying. He was of middle stature, not as tall as I was and thin as a lathe. I looked him over. I could see no muscle on him. So he was not particularly a fighting man. Not any more. No, I thought, he'd leave that to his bullies.

"Arrogant I may be but my arrogance will not alter the truth. This land belongs to Bedwyn Manor. Bedwyn Manor belonged to the Congyre's. With the demise of my father-in-law, it belongs to me. I am the warden of this forest and the law in it. In fact, I am the law in this part of the country and have a sealed document, incidentally now in my scrip, should you wish to see it, proving that I can and I will, see the law upheld."

Garner was riled now.

"That man..." he jabbed his finger at his villein, "is my property and the law says he must be handed back to me for punishment."

"I have no doubt of it. However, since I am the law here and I can see no evidence that the man has stolen from you, I am within my rights to detain him and question him about the matter. He stands on my forest floor. I extend sanctuary to him for the time being. If you can prove that the man has committed a crime and the man you murdered, or caused to be murdered..."

The man, I suspected, whose bow had delivered the arrow which killed him, grimaced and looked away.

"Then I will return him to you for, as you say, punishment."

"He's a churl, man. A filthy Saxon. Let's have done with him here." He chuckled, "save us the trouble of chaining him up."

The man called Foreman spoke with due deference, to me. "Sir Aumary, my lord Belvoir, it was no murder, sir. My lord Garner is within his rights to seek and detain, nay even kill a runaway villein from his lands."

"If it can be proven that he is indeed a tied man and has broken his word to his lord, yes certainly. The Lord of Whittonditch is within his rights to seek out the man and fetch him back. He can use force to do so. However, I take a dim view of a man who hunts another living being as if he were a hart, Foreman, and kills out of hand."

"We...."

"There are nine of you. Three of you are mounted. It would be no small thing for you to capture these two men unharmed and return them to your lands and try them in your manor court. It's murder, Foreman. However you look at it."

I saw the man chewing the inside of his cheeks. He risked a sidelong glance at his lord.

"Come, Sir Aumary..." said Garner, suddenly friendly. "Can we not come to some..."

"Go home, Sir Jacques. Take your men. I will, as I say, detain this man and have words with him..."

Garner licked his lips at that. He began to look worried. 'Hmmm,' I thought, 'I wonder why that is something the man really doesn't want me to do.? To speak to his villein?'

"And if I feel that you are correct and that he has committed a crime against you, he shall be punished."

Garner began to speak but I rode over him. "And as to this piece of land you so fervently desire; a patch of scrub, forest and a small meadow or two..what is there in it which is so important, so overwhelmingly desirous, that you must flout the law to get your hands on it?"

Garner shrugged. "Nothing...it's the....the principle of the thing."

Now it was my turn to laugh.

"I cannot see you forging a will, nay perhaps even doing away with Toruld Congyre...."

"Congyre had been ill, he died of..."

"Ah no, sir. There I have the advantage. My father-in-law was murdered. And I will see the man who did it dangle from a rope."

Garner blanched. "It was not I who dealt him his death blow. I hadn't seen the man for several months....I"

"Why would Toruld want you, of all people, to have this piddling piece of forest, sir? Tell me that."

"Our friendship..."

"It was not for friendship, Garner, of that I'm sure."

The man turned his back to me and returned to his horse.

"There is no reasoning with you," he spat. "Our lawyers must thrash this out."

"As you wish." I nodded. "But rest assured, I'll get to the nub of this deception.

If you wish to waste your money and time on attempting to acquire what amounts to a few square miles of venison and vert, that's your problem. It's a futile quest sir. You might as well try to empty the River Kennet with a bucket for all the good it will do you."

Jacques Garner mounted his horse and turned its head. "The land was willed to me. It was land which was once owned by the monks at Abingdon, as was Bedwyn. My family had it then. We shall have it again."

"Two hundred years ago...? Don't be a fool, man."

"We shall see who is the fool, Sir Aumary," he said as he rode away.

*****

Was I rattled, Paul? No; not rattled. Just irritated. And intrigued.

Hal let out a huge sigh as Garner's men turned their horses and heels and disappeared into the brush. He shoved his sword back into its scabbard.

"God's Cods, I thought for one moment we were done for, m'lord."

I wiped my hands over my face. "I think if we had been what he might call, 'lesser folk' Hal, then we would have been dispensed with like that poor man over there. As it was, my warrant and position as warden saved us. It's one thing to put an arrow into the back of a villein, quite another to murder the lord of Durley and Constable of the county."

"Aye..." Hal looked back at the body of the murdered villein.

"What's your name, man?" I asked the living one.

He was still shaking but gave it quite confidently "Oswald, my lord. Oswald of Knighton."

"Well, Oswald...you had better come back to Durley with us. No, no don't look so stricken. You do one of two things, you run away now and risk being found by your lord, or you come with us and help us get to the bottom of this unfortunate incident. I want your word you'll speak the truth about this happening when we get to my village."

"You... mean... that I am free to...to run off if I want, sir?"

"If you want to go... I shan't stop you but if I find you in my forest as an outlaw, a masterless man; that's if your master doesn't find you first; then I must arrest you and the law will take its course."

The man grabbed my leg and I saw Hal flinch.

"Oh sir, sir, thank you. Thank you for saving my life. I..."

"Aye I do think we did," said Hal, mounting his horse once more. "You would've been like yer friend there, a few 'eartbeats after we found you I reckon."

"Poor Dulf.... Hrodulf sir," snivelled the man. "He were only...." and he dissolved into tears, shielding his eyes with the palm of his hand.

I looked at Hal and grimaced.

"Are you coming?" I asked eventually.

"Aye, sir. I'll come," he replied tearfully.

"We'll send a party out to recover your friend."

"Brother, sir."

"Oh...I see...well then, your brother. I'm sorry for your loss."

The man sniffed into his sleeve. "I'm older by two years."

"Why did your lord want you two dead, for I think he did?"

"I'll tell all I know, sir. When we are..." he looked round the forest trees, "safe, sir."

I nodded. "Lead on then, Hal."

*****

We traipsed back the way we had come not a short while before. Towards the turning to Durley village, it seemed to me that the whole atmosphere lightened and the birds began to sing again. I heard the chaffinch with his 'pink, pink' and the gravelly rattle of the whitethroat. The lane was bordered by waving frills of cow parsley which made the edges as white as frost. I smelled the pungent aroma of the ramsons or wild garlic and the sharp smell of the yellow archangel, now dying down.

We rode slowly so the man Oswald could follow, though we spoke not a word to him. Had he chosen to dip into the brush and disappear, I would not have followed him.

But no, he was there behind us, as we clopped into the village, over the green, through the arch to the courtyard and up to the stables.

I led Bayard into his stall and Cedric took him from me.

"You weren't gone long, sir," he said, his brow creased in puzzlement.

"No Cedric. We had reason to turn back. We had company."

"Oh!"

"And it looks like we have company here too?"

Hal ducked under Grafton's tossing head. "We know that 'orse don't we, sir?"

"We do indeed Hal.If I am not much mistaken we have a visitor from Crofton."

Hal chuckled. "It's ol' Pebbles i'n't it?"

"It is," I said as I fondled the muzzle of our visitor's old horse.

"Come, let's go up to the hall. He'll be up there with Lydia and if I'm not much mistaken, his son too."

"Aye, there's 'is 'orse...what's its name now?"

I laughed. "He always chooses the strangest names for his horses. That one's called Rock!"

*****

I sent the man from Knighton off to find Henry my steward, with instructions to feed and house him. I'd speak to him after I'd greeted my visitor. A party was to go out to recover his brother's body.

I took the manor steps two at a time.

"Where are you, you old toad?" I shouted. I heard Hawise giggling as I burst in through the hall door.

"Aumary!" remonstrated my wife. "Really!"

"No, no, Lydia... I've always been an old toad to Aumary."

I clasped my old friend round the body and embraced him tightly. "Welcome Percy...it's been too long."

I turned about. "No, this can't be..."

"Aumary, don't embarrass the poor boy," said Lydia, chuckling.

"Aye..he's shot up, hasn't he?" said his father. "Jocelyn, don't slouch, stand up now."

"How old are you now Jos?" I asked my friend's son.

"Twelve, sir." He smiled shyly. "Nearly thirteen."

"Twelve! And I remember the day you were born."

"I said don't…Aumary," said Lydia chiding me gently. "It's unkind to go on so."

"It was just after our son was born, wasn't it...when we saw you last?"

"Yes. We came to make sure the rumours were true."

"Oh yes?"

"That you had a son at last. That you weren't only capable of getting girls."

"Oh Percy!" giggled Lydia. "You don't get any better for keeping."

"Aye...he's over two now. Sturdy as a Savernake oak," I said laughingly.

"I'll fetch him..." said Lydia, making for the solar steps.

I marched to the table and began to pour out the wine left there in a covered jug.

Hal helped himself to ale.

Percival, Lord of Pewsey and Crofton (for which he paid seisin to me as his overlord), turned on his heels and slapped Hal on the back. "You still alive 'ol Hal? Thought you'd be moulderin' years ago?"

"I'll live till I die, thanks," said Hal grinning. "Good to see you too, Sir Percival."

I sat down beside my daughter who was strangely quiet through all this banter.

"Hawise, have you said hello?"

"Yes father. Before you came in."

She sat demurely, her hands folded in her lap; her copper curls held back with a green ribbon. Her sweet oval freckled face was shining and pink. She always looked good in Lincoln green.

"So what brings you to Durley? Save just to see us of course."

"And why shouldn't it just be to see you all?" asked my old boyhood friend Percival, cheekily.

"You staying?"

"That depends on you and your good lady wife."

"Of course you'll stay," I said. "How's Frida?"

"Got her hands full with our latest addition," said Percy, "Alfred. He's four months now."

"Ah yes. I remember. Bit of a tough time entering the world, hadn't he?"

"Poor Frida, but she's recovered now."

"Our poor women. What we put them through for the getting of our heirs, eh?"

Percy chuckled into his wine. "All worth it when you've a lad as good as I've got."

"And a daughter as good as we have," I said drawing Hawise close to me.

Percy scratched his head. "It's erm...about that...I've come actually Aumary."

"Oh?"

"Well, that and to see you all of course...like you say far too long...too long ago we came last."

"Good daughters and sons?" I said puzzled.

"Well, yes. You see, well....Jos is twelve soon to be thirteen and Hawise is what, eight now?"

"Yes..."

"I was wondering, well..."

"Oh father!" said Jocelyn in exasperation.

I felt Hawise sit up straight under my arm.

"Our children have to be married at some time...and well, I was wondering...."

I heard Lydia coming up behind me, take in a small startled breath.

"I was thinking what a good thing it would be if my Jos could marry your Hawise."

Chapter Four

My hand convulsed on Hawise's shoulder. She looked quickly up at me and then down at her feet. I swear she'd known what had been coming.

There was a shocked silence.

"Hawise is only eight, Percy," I said after a moment.

"Well, yes. But I remember you and Cecily, God bless her, were betrothed at what, four or five? Obviously you waited until you were nineteen and seventeen to marry."

My mind was searching for obstacles, excuses. My daughter, my angel, my chick. Betrothed? I was I suppose, tender about it. All fathers of girls must feel so.

"I have always said, have I not Lydia, that Hawise will choose her own bridegroom, when the time comes."

Hawise raised her head. "Have you dada?" she said.

"Your father wants you to be happy with the person you marry, Hawise," said Lydia. "We both do."

"Like you are with father and he with you?"

"Yes, indeed," said both Lydia and myself simultaneously. We smiled at each other.

"And why might Hawise not be happy with my Jocelyn?" asked Percy in hurt tones.

I stood up and paced a little way towards him. "She might. Indeed she might. If she chooses Jos, well then, that's good. But I'll not force her."

"So you don't think it's a good idea?"

"I think it's a good idea to let them get to know each other," I said truthfully. "Naturally as children do. Not tie them into marriage at their tender ages."

"Ah well, it was only an idea," said Percy, looking crestfallen.

I turned to Jocelyn. "What do you think about it, young man?"

Jos shrugged. "I will do as father sees fit. If he wants me to marry Hawise and I can, then I will."

I looked over my shoulder at my daughter, still calm and quiet on her bench.

"Hawise? What do you think?"

She smiled sweetly at Jos. "I like Jos. He's nice. But..."

"But?"

"I don't want to marry anyone."

"Not now, no. But in years to come you'll find a nice man who will care for you and..."

"No, I won't."

"Why not?"

"Because no one will be as nice as you, nor as handsome, nor as clever, nor as..."

"Stop daughter! Stop!"

Everyone was chuckling.

"You cannot marry me."

"All girls want to marry their fathers," laughed Lydia, hoisting a wriggling Simon up onto her other hip.

"We'll say no more about it then, for the nonce," said Percy. "Maybe another time eh?"

He sidled up to Lydia. "And this is the doughty Simon Belvoir, eh?"

He took our son from Lydia. "My...he's a big lad."

"He'll be tall like his sire," said Lydia proudly.

"I have no doubt."

"I'm tall too," said Hawise standing for the first time. "For a girl" she said and we all laughed some more.

No further discussion was had about the marriage of Percy's son to my daughter.

*****

We sat late into the evening, chatting and reminiscing over our wine cups. As usual Percival kept us all laughing well into the hours of darkness.

"Dada?" said Hawise suddenly "I'm sorry to interrupt, might we have some birch bark please?"

I looked up at my daughter sitting primly at the table next to Jos.

"Paper? What for?"

"Jos wants to do some drawing."

"Drawing?"

"I'd like to show Hawise sir, what our garden looks like at Crofton."

"Ho, ho! You have a garden?"

"Yes, sir. Father has made it for mother."

"These ladies like their flowers don't they?" I chuckled. "Hal will get you some graphite and some parchment from my office."

For a long while into the evening the children sat, heads together scribbling and laughing happily over their drawing until Lydia left us and took Simon and Hawise to bed.

Young Joscelyn curled up on a bench at his father's side and snoozed away until, yawning he too bade us good night and made for the guest room on the southern wall of the manor.

"You're right, he's a good lad, Percy," I said, "have you placed him anywhere yet?"

"You mean to squire for someone? No, he missed out on a page's training. I meant to send him to old Fulke de Cantiloupe in Calne but it never happened. He's useful to me on the estate, even though he's young."

"I didn't go anywhere to earn my knighthood; I stayed here at Durley and learned at my father's knee. There's no harm in it."

"Yes, but you had a definite role - warden of the forest - to grow into."

"Jos will be Lord of Pewsey after you won't he?"

"Aye he will, and my younger son will take Crofton, with your permission of course."

"There's nothing wrong with that."

"No, I suppose not. And his mother will be happy to keep him at home."

"Well then?"

"I was wondering...if you might take him?"

"Me?"

"Have you no need of a squire then? And you are close enough for Jos to be able to come home now and again... to appease his mother."

I chuckled. "I don't really have a need. John Brenthall's son Peter acts as my squire when it's needful and old Hal of course is always on hand."

"You're not really a fighting man are you, Aumary?"

"I can fight when called. I keep my skills honed. Who knows when I might need to defend myself in my job? Jobs." I laughed out loud... "I've needed to recently, but no. I'm not really the sort who runs off to the King every other day itching to come at the enemy. I've too much to do and my enemies are of a different kind. The King would have me here in Savernake."

"Ah yes, secret malefactors ripe for the unmasking. I've heard you are quite good at this role of yours, unearthing murder and foul deeds."

"The King prefers me in this role, though no doubt should he be seriously engaged in war, then I should have to go out with my battle gear and my mesnie." I laughed out loud. "He still makes me pay scutage."

"Until that time you ride about Savernake pursuing villains."

"I must admit, I find it....diverting. If someone a few years ago had told me I was going to be running around the county chasing felons, I would have said they were raving. There is a certain...satisfaction in bringing evil deeds into the light and unmasking the perpetrators, I have to say."

I stretched my stiff shoulders and yawned. "Not every time though. Sometimes, I have sympathy for the murderer, but that doesn't mean I don't act."

"Aye murder is murder."

"Take my latest task. Right here in Durley. One of my tied men, murdered in his own home, with his own knife, almost in front of his daughter and I have as yet, no idea how the murderer got into the village without being seen nor why he singled out Bardol Wedgemoor."

"Strange," said Percy, tossing back his wine.

"The man was a pain in the backside to many of his neighbours but I can't see them sticking a knife into him for all that. One of the most unpleasant men it's been my displeasure to know," I said. "I almost take my hat off to the person who rid us of him!"

"You'll probably find it was his wife...nearly always is...men like that. Or this daughter you speak about."

"No, not them. They were half a mile away."

Percy caught my yawn and started one himself. "Aw you'll come to the bottom of it no doubt soon."

I pulled the parchment towards me upon which the children had been scribbling.

"Your garden, eh?"

"You've room for one here. Plenty of land around about. Why don't you begin one? I'm sure Lydia would love it."

I laughed. "I've enough to do."

"Not you personally. Get your men to build and tend it."

"They have enough to do too. The forest is my garden. One huge garden."

Percy smiled.

"Mind you. I have seen a garden, a really lovely one in Mildenhall. I wouldn't mind building one like it. It's all gone now sadly though."

I thought back to the time when I'd investigated the murder of a master mason and fondly remembered the garden which his betrothed had built at the back of her house.

"You have an orchard."

"Yes, we enclosed it a while ago. It was begun in my father's time."

"You can remodel that."

"Is that what you did?" I asked.

"Yes, added to our own orchard. You remember it?"

"I do. I spent more time at Crofton climbing those trees than I did at home when we were lads, when your father was alive."

"They were good times." Percy made a moue. "And now we hardly ever see each other."

"We must remedy that then," I said, yawning again. "And the children can spend more time in each other's company too."

Sir Percival left the next morning in a welter of kisses and embraces, thanks and promises to return and bring all the family to stay for longer. We waved them off through the gateway and watched as they turned up the road to Salisbury. The manor of Crofton lay in the forest, close to Bedwyn and some way towards Ramsbury.

Hawise watched them disappear into the trees and raised her hand as Jos turned in the saddle and waved at us.

Hal took a deep breath.

"And now might we go an' 'ave a look at this fella we found yesterday, sir?"

"Ah yes.... Oswald, that was his name wasn't it? Where did Henry put him last night?"

"In 'is office I think. "Enery went 'ome to 'is old mam."

Henry's mother lived in a large cottage on the village green close by the reeve's house.

"And Oswald's dead brother?"

"John and a few of the lads got him and put him in the mortuary."

"There he can stay for a while until we decide what to do."

Hal and I turned back through the arch and entered a small room to the right of the gatehouse.

The Knighton man was sitting on Henry's bed staring into space, an empty ale cup in his hands. He looked up when we entered and jumped up quickly, nodding his head and touching his forelock.

"God keep you, m'lord."

"Oswald, please sit." I searched around for two seats for Hal and myself. Hal found a stool and I sat in Henry's chair.

"You will no doubt have been told that my men have recovered the body of your brother. He lies in our mortuary. If you wish to go and see him, just ask. Father Crispin, our priest, will have done his best to prepare your brother's soul for his eternal rest...."

"He weren't more than a boy..."

"No, I saw that."

"He were only fifteen." He wiped a tear from the corner of his eye.

"Tell us your story and if we need to have justice for Hrodulf, I promise we shall do our utmost to deliver his murderer to the authorities."

Oswald scoffed. "Nah m'lord. That ain't the way it goes. Not with the Lord Garner."

"I promise you, I will try."

"You know, m'lord, we aren't free men?"

"I know that and to me, it makes no difference."

Oswald scrutinised my face as if it were the page of a book and he could read the words written there.

"So, tell me what happened."

The man wiped his nose on his sleeve. "It's a bad place."

"Where?"

"His manor, Whittonditch."

"Why is it bad?"

"He don't care for it like it oughta be cared for. He lets it go. That man of his..."

"Foreman?"

"He's a baddun and make no bones."

"Who drew the bow which killed your brother, Oswald?"

"I dunno. I was runnin' but I bet my next meal it were him."

"Why were you running away?"

Oswald took in a shuddering breath. "He told us to run."

"Garner?"

"Aye. 'If you want to have a chance at life,' he said, 'you better run.' "

"What were you doing which made him angry enough to chase you?"

"We was up on the plot, up by the big barn, when he found us. We got no time to do anything to our own strip on account of tending the lord's bloody garden. Pardon m'lord."

"Garden? The man has a garden?"

"Aye it's a biggun."

"The law says that you must tend your lord's land, his crops, his produce and his animals, on three days of the week. This will leave you time for your own. That's the ruling. Have you not been keeping to your part of the bargain?"

"Bargain!?" The man scoffed. "We afta do as he says, or that man Foreman says or he'll stripe our backs for us if we don't. I could show you the state of me own back." He began to lift off his tunic.

"No, no that's all right. I don't need to see, I'm sure you are telling the truth."

"So 'ave we got it right?" said Hal. "This man Foreman and his Lord Garner doesn't leave yer enough time to grow yer own crops, or yer own food?"

"That's about it sir, yes. Nearly the whole village is starving."

"But that's ridiculous."

Hal turned to me "I 'ave to say, 'e looks a bit of a skinny wretch dun't 'e?"

"Yes Hal. As did his poor brother." I noticed too that his skin was spotty and sores disfigured the corner of his mouth.

"Why does he not allow you to work on your own plot?"

"Because he wants us to work day and night in the spring and summer, in his blessed garden."

I looked askance at Hal. "Another garden, Hal. What is this fashion for flowers?"

"Aye, like the Lord Percy, sir."

"But I can't imagine Percy forcing his villeins to work on a pleasure garden in place of growing food, can you?"

"Oh we 'as to grow 'is own food," said Oswald, "just not ours - much."

"The days are long at this time of year, have you not light left, enough in the day to...."

"He don't let us. We has to stay and work. We're let out at dusk and we has to be there at dawn."

"This is a walled place, is it?" asked Hal.

"Yessir. We'm get locked in."

My man at arms and I exchanged a look.

"And what were you doing, or not doing, that the Lord Garner chased you halfway across the forest?"

Oswald looked a little shifty at that.

"We had no choice. We was so 'ungry."

"So you did steal food from him, as he said?"

Oswald jutted his chin. "We pulled up a turnip and ate it. One each."

"A turnip!"

"'Twere only a little one."

"And you were seen?"

"By Foreman."

"Aw c'mon, Oswald. No one kills a villein for stealing a turnip," scoffed Hal. "What's the other story?"

"No, you're right. It were an excuse to get rid of us," said the man winking conspiratorially.

"Why?" I asked.

Oswald licked his lips. "It were because we know what's been going on, sir," he whispered.

"And what, Oswald," I asked, folding my arms, "has been going on?"

Oswald leaned forward and whispered. "Magic, sir."

"Magic?"

"Aye. Magic, my lord."

I sighed.

"What kind of magic, Oswald?"

"Magic with plants and stuff. Things what ain't natural. That's what. 'Gainst God's good laws."

*****

We left Oswald burbling on about magic and went to the hall to break our fast.

Over a beaker of small ale and a hunk of bread filled with ham, we discussed what we had been told.

"There's good lords and bad lords, sir," said Hal, chewing, "but there's also good villeins and bad villeins...look at ol' Wegemoor. How do we know this Oswald isn't peddling us a pig cote full'a manure?"

"We don't really. But by the look on his face, this 'magic' he talks about has him really worried. He might be misinterpreting what he sees but I don't think he's lying."

"Nah. Neither do I, for what it's worth. But what I don't understand is 'ow anyone can think a few flowers in a garden can possibly be evil or magical?" said Hal.

"You know when I was a younger man and had the time, when old Quimper was alive, I used to borrow a few of the books he had."

"Aye, I remember."

Quimper was my brother's tutor and a very learned man. He had been a graduate of the University of Paris in France and was a very interesting person with whom to discourse. He had been dead these many years and was buried in our churchyard. His few books lay in a chest in the solar. Perhaps I should dig out a few and resume my reading habit. Pah! When did I get the time?

Mind you Paul, I've got the time now and I have re-read a few of them since.

"One of them I remember spoke about a Roman emperor...now who was it? What was his name? Anyway it doesn't matter. He gained notoriety when his peasants were reduced to growing roses instead of food in order to satisfy the demands of their ruler."

"What? He starved 'em ? What was he doin' with all 'em flowers then?"

"They were used naturally in perfume and the ancients, I'm told, loved perfume, both men and women - drenched in it they were."

"Ugh!"

I chuckled, "and somewhere I read that one emperor used to shower his dinner guests with rose petals; bury them in flowers."

"What for?" said Hal, a crust to his lips.

"Because he could, I suppose," I answered. "What was his name?" I scrubbed my black curly hair to bring the memory forward. It worked.

"Heliogabalus."

"I beg yer pardon sir?"

"Emperor Heliogabalus. Rome's strangest emperor."

"You reckon Old Garner is burying his dinner guests in petals then?" chuckled Hal. "Maybe 'is villeins'll be reduced to eating flowers soon then."

I laughed out loud. "No, I don't think for one moment that the Lord of Whittonditch hosts orgiastic parties and rains flower petals down on them from a false ceiling."

"That's what he did, did 'e? This emperor? They were a dotty lot weren't they? Mad as a bag of badgers! "

"Well..I think we must take this sort of story with a large pinch of salt but it's a good tale."

"Hmmm, so if 'e i'n't bathing in 'em, eating 'em or smotherin' folk with 'em, what is he doing with em?"

"We must pay him a visit, Hal and find out."

*****

Later that morning found us riding once more on the road to Ramsbury. This time, no men leapt out of the verdure to be stuck with an arrow. We rode in a pleasant breeze, through the forest and onto the London Road, across it again and up to Whittonditch. We met no one.

The fields about the manor were almost empty of peasants working, either their own small strips or those of their lord. A few cows grazed the meadows close to the River Kennet and as we neared the manor house, a herd of goats was penned in the field close by. Sheep cropped the grass of the upper downs.

We approached from the London Road up a steep sided valley which eventually opened out into a flat piece of land upon which sat the house. The whole of the back of the building was walled in with a cob wall seven feet high. In some parts the top was thatched, to shed the water I supposed.

A woman came out from the house place. She stared up at us, her hand across her brow to shield her eyes from the sun.

"Good day to you, mistress. My name is Sir Aumary Belvoir. I am the Constable of this county and Lord of Durley, Warden of Savernake Forest."

The woman, who was about thirty, curtsied and bowed her head.

"The master is away from home, sir, and the steward is away from the manor. I am the housekeeper here. I am Jeanne Dicer. Can I help you?"

I dismounted. "I've heard that the Lord Jacques has a fine garden, mistress. I was hoping we might have a look? I am thinking of making one myself at Durley." I smiled sweetly.

The woman smiled in return. "It's his pride and joy sir, though I don't have the authority to let you go in and have a look. My master would have my hide."

"A good master, is he?"

The woman looked quickly at the ground. "No worse and no better than many, sir."

"Tell me, Mistress Dicer, what do you know about the brothers Oswald and Hrodulf of Knighton?"

"Nothing sir," came back the prompt reply. Too prompt.

"I know that they are a pair of the lord's workers but beyond that..." she shrugged. "They live in Knighton, you see. I never go to Knighton. I'm a Bedwyn girl. I go to visit my old mother there but apart from that I never stray from Whittonditch."

"Ah yes...." I looked round. "Very quiet here, isn't it?"

"It's dinner time, sir. Many are at home supping and eating. Or they're out in the fields."

"I'm sure they are."

"Where did you say your lord had gone, mistress?"

"He's out in the forest...at.." She stopped and I saw annoyance on her face. "I don't know exactly where he's gone. And I didn't say, sir."

"Well then, I trust you'll have no objection to us waiting for him. Surely he'll be back soon. As you say. It's dinner time." I grinned at her.

"As you wish, my lord." She dipped her head. "Please come into the hall."

The hall was about the same size as my own at Durley though not so well furnished. The walls had seen no lime wash for quite a while. The central fire was old and cracked, its stones crumbling. The stairs, I presumed to the solar or to the private room of its lord, were wooden and in need of repair and the handrail was merely a rope driven with nails into the stone of the wall.

"Tell me, Mistress Dicer, is your lord a wealthy man?"

The housekeeper turned her back to us and went to the pot board situated at the end of the hall. She collected two pottery mugs and a flagon of ale.

"It's not my place to say, sir," she said returning to us. She placed the items on the table. It was plain ash, not fine oak as was my own. Nothing lay on it but a small pot of flowers in the centre. An odd touch for somewhere so masculine.

"Dun't look a rich place does it, sir?" said Hal, winking at her as he took his ale.

"No, Hal. It looks...run down."

"But it can't be too poor, can it?"

"Why's that old Hal?" I asked, taking a sip of ale and wondering if my guts were going to stand me drinking a whole pot.

"Well, if you i'n't got a lotta money, you don't build a garden do you, sir?"

Hal took a deep draught and I saw his eyes bulge. He swallowed carefully, looked into the pot, wiped his hand across his lips and slapped down the mug in distaste.

"It's a luxury a garden is....unlike good ale."

"Hmm. I suppose you're right." I too put down my pot.

"Mistress Dicer, the lord Garner has this manor here. Does he have another property which he keeps in better repair than this one?"

The woman's eyes flashed.

"I know that he is also Lord of Knighton."

"No, sir. This is his main home. He is satisfied that it's kept how he wishes it to be kept. It's his business, not mine. I do as I'm told."

"He spends his wealth elsewhere then?"

"You must ask him, sir."

"Ask me what, Jeanne?"

We all turned as the Lord of Whittonditch came in through the hall door.

*****

Jacques Garner stopped dead. The smile left his face.

"I thought I saw your horses outside; thought I recognised that roan beast of yours."

"My lord Garner." I bowed, though not too low. "Your housekeeper has extended hospitality to us whilst we waited for you to return."

"They wanted to go into the garden, sir...but I said..."

"Garden?"

"Yes, we heard you had a fine garden and were just itching to feast our eyes on it, weren't we, Hal?"

"Oh aye, we were. We likes a nice garden. That one what we saw at Mildenhall was a goodun', weren't it, sir?"

"And then there's Percy's at Crofton."

"Oh ah...right pretty that is."

"But I'm sure yours is a sight to behold, my lord."

Garner angrily threw his riding gloves on the table.

"You'll not see it. It's for my pleasure only. Now get out."

"Oh, and we did so want to see what magic was being done there, didn't we, Hal?"

"Oh yes, we heard that you were working miracles or something inside those walls of yours," said Hal, looking out of the window on tip toe to see if the garden was visible from the hall.

Garner paced over to the window and glared at Hal.

"Get out! You are not welcome here."

He turned a venomous stare on me, "You sending back that peasant of mine yet?"

"All in good time, my friend," I said. "Though we shall send the man Hrodulf back to Knighton for burial, my lord. That is where he was from, wasn't it?"

"Knighton belongs to me. He was my worker. You can send him there for all I care."

"He was a worker in your garden I believe."

"NO!"

"Oh, we must be mistaken then, Hal. I thought Oswald said he was being forced to work in your garden instead of on his own plot. The food he filched from you...you say he stole - it was one small turnip was it not?"

"Fifteen and killed outright for one small turnip," said Hal, shaking his head. "What is this world coming to?"

Garner grew hot in the face. "I said leave this manor now."

I sat down in his chair. "Do you know, Garner...I think I explained before, I have a writ, with the King's seal upon it. It says that I am without hindrance, I think that's the word written there..."

"Yes, it is my lord," supplied Hal "without 'indrance." He nodded.

"I am able to and have the authority to search any premises I wish. Any manor. Any house, any garden."

"Get out before I..."

"Before you what?"

Garner did not finish his sentence.

"I will go then, but I'll be back and I will bring men to search. Oh dear me, yes. Men with large boots and prying eyes, unkind fingers and heavy hands. I'll let them loose in this garden of yours just to see what you have hidden there."

"I have nothing hidden!"

"Then why are you so secretive about the place?"

Garner folded his arms across his chest. He breathed in angrily.

"Jeanne, go and find Foreman if he has returned yet. Tell him to open the garden gate."

Jeanne fled the hall in a flurry of skirts.

"That's better, my lord." I said, as I rose from the chair.

"Now shall we, like civilised men and men of manners, go down and take a look at this precious pride and joy of yours, as your housekeeper called it?"

Garner stared harshly at me and paced off to the pot board. He poured himself a measure of ale, threw it down his throat and slammed the beaker down on the table. After a couple more moments of glaring at me he left the hall. We followed and in silence went down the steps, entering the garden by the back door of the screens passage and through a gate in a cob wall seven feet high.

The place was as the Garden of Eden must have been for Adam and Eve. Plants of every hue, shape, size and texture grew in beds around the walls.

Trees were planted here and there to give shade for those specimens liking cover. Sun bathed walls threw out warmth for heat loving plants. Apples, plums and pears had been trained flat against the walls and I saw some of the fruit beginning to swell there. The central place was given over to small hedges of sweet smelling plants and herbs.

I wandered around sniffing and taking in the beauty of it all.

The Lord Garner stood at the gate with a stern expression. He had waved away the men and women working in the garden and ushered them out of the space saying "Go to your dinners now."

I saw the man Foreman smirking in a corner, leaning on some kind of stone plinth surrounded by bushes. I nodded to him. He bowed and chewed on a stalk of something.

I poked into every corner, around every plant, into every bed. Nowhere did I see any signs of evil. Nor of any magic. Well, truly I did not know what I was looking for. What was Oswald of Knighton talking about?

*****

We left the manor of Whittonditch in a bad mood. We searched diligently but found nothing with which to upbraid the lord Garner.

Finally, we turned into the manor courtyard at Durley and Hal said, "Well, if we can't tackle the Lord Garner as we'd like then we'll 'ave to 'ave another go at that man Oswald, won't we?"

But search the manor from top to bottom as we did, we failed to find him.

Eventually, our patience exhausted, Hal and I made for the hall and supper. We'd missed our dinner all together. John came striding down the steps.

"Ah there you are, sir."

"Has our Knighton man fled then, John?" I asked as he made a volte face and skipped back up the steps.

"Last I saw him, he'd borrowed the key from Henry and gone into the mortuary, sir," said John. "To see his brother. I take it you had no luck at Whittonditch."

Hal scoffed "Pah!"

"No, John. Nothing to be seen. Hal, can you see if you can find Henry and ask him if Oswald returned the key to him and when?"

"Right you are, sir."

He ran back down the steps.

"I have some news, sir," said John. "About Wedgemoor."

"Lead on then," I said.

John entered the hall and strode up to Peter who was sitting with Maxime his hound. Peter bounded upright when he saw me. Maxime came to me wagging his tail furiously.

"Sir. You were wanting to know what Bardol Wedgemoor was doing out in the forest those days when he was missing."

"Yes, Peter," I said wearily.

"I saw him striding away from Burnt Copse one day, in the direction of Whitehill. He was alone and I thought it odd. I rode level with him and caught up with him and watched where he went. He didn't see me."

"And where was that?"

"Into Whitehill Copse. I knew he had no legitimate business there but I didn't follow further. And then the whole thing slipped my mind until Pa said that we wondered where he'd been."

"So what's at Whitehill copse which is so alluring, Peter?"

Peter shrugged. "A few old trees. A little bit of meadow. Some coppiced stands of hazel and alder. Honeysuckle grows madly there and old man's beard."

"Clematis?"

"Travellers' joy - another name for it...yes."

"There's no special hidey holes for animals or birds? We have no warren there."

"Not that I know of, sir."

Hal came into the hall followed by Alfred Woodsmith, my carpenter and fine woodwork maker.

"No sir, Henry didn't get the key back. Alfred 'ere has found something. We think you'd better come and look."

I frowned. Alfred was looking a little wild and white around the eyes.

"Sir?" said Peter. "Whitehill Copse is part of the land which is disputed by that man Garner you went to see today."

"So it is Peter. Well done."

I followed Hal and Alfred out of the courtyard and into the carpenter's workshop and store which was situated at one end of the village green, away from the manor buildings and most of the houses of the village.

"We couldn't find that Oswald fella, sir...." said Hal, "because 'e's 'ere."

There, partly buried under a pile of wood which had tumbled and concealed him, was Oswald of Knighton.

"I found him, m'lord," said Alfred, "When I came to look at some wood for...."

Hal pulled the man out by the boots.

"His throat has been cut, sir," said Alfred who then ran swiftly out of the barn to be sick on the grass outside.

Chapter Five

I stared down at the mortal remains of Oswald of Knighton.

Now I would be sending two bodies back to the lord of Whittonditch and Knighton, once the coroner had seen the body of course.

"Get one of the lads to go for the coroner will you, John?" I said, sighing.

"Aye sir." John left the barn at a run. I heard his boots slapping on the hard baked chalk of the path.

"Close the doors and get...who's at home nearby, Hal?"

"Hartshorn I think. I just saw 'im."

"Ask him to come and guard the door."

"Right you are, sir."

"I don't think we need to bother Johannes. It's obvious how the man died. It's just not obvious what he was doing here."

"We'll need to look for a deal of blood where his throat was cut," said Hal, stroking his beard, "it weren't in 'ere."

"Hmm...can I leave that to you?"

"You can, sir."

Hal cleared his throat. "Sir Aumary... this afternoon when we were at Whittonditch, that man Foreman, the Lord Garner said, 'If 'e's returned can you get 'im to open the garden gate.' Where'd he been then?"

"Cutting the throat of a Knighton villein perhaps?"

"That's what I wondered. Oswald has certainly been silenced 'asn't 'e? Garner sent 'im to do it, do you think?"

"One is tempted to think so, Hal."

"But why?"

"All we got from him was the fact that he was being denied work in his own fields and that some sort of magic was being effected in the walled garden."

"Why do you need to kill a man for that?"

Alfred gingerly poked his head around the barn door. "Do you need me, sir?" I noticed he avoided looking at the body on the floor.

"No, Alf, but we'll need you as the first finder, to report to the coroner."

"Yes sir."

"Who was the last person to see Oswald of Knighton alive I wonder, Hal? Can we make some inquiries?"

"Aye, we can do that, sir."

"And before too long, we must make a trip out to Whitehill Copse. I've a mind to see this place where Wedgemoor was going when Peter saw him. I don't know how significant it is but my thumbs are pricking."

Hal smiled " Gotta go with the pricking of your thumbs i'n't you, sir?"

Jonathan Reeve, the youngest son of my village reeve Walter, came in to see me a little while later. It seemed he was the last person to see Oswald alive.

"He was up on the manor wall walk for a while. I saw him. He just seemed to be staring out over the village, sir."

"Did he speak to you?"

"Just said that he was off to find Henry to return the key of the mortuary. As it happens Henry found the key on his table a little while later so Oswald never found Henry, but must have returned it to his office."

"Did you spot him again after that time?"

"He was just wandering around. I was mending the door of the threshing barn, helping Alfred out and he passed me on his way to the river. We didn't speak but when Alf went to the wood store to get some wood for a new post - well, he found him dead."

"So it was not too long between you seeing him and Alf finding him in the wood pile?"

"No sir. A matter of a little past sext."

I nodded. "So he died just before dinner time?"

"Alf came home with me to Philly's for our dinner and when we came back to the threshing barn, the man was nowhere to be seen."

"Then Alf went for some wood and..."

"Yes, sir."

"Hal's looking for the place where the man may have been killed. It was not in the barn. Close by perhaps but where he could be dragged unseen and concealed. He might not have been found for a long time if Alfred hadn't been looking for a new post."

"The forest trees come quite close to the wood barn. Easy to catch a man there. Quiet and unseen, sir."

"Yes indeed, Johnnie."

"Sir?" Jonathan rubbed his eyebrow with his finger. "Do you reckon that Bardol's murderer and this Oswald's are one and the same?"

"I think there's a distinct possibility that it is, Johnnie," I said.

Hal came back a little while later. He had found the site where Oswald had met his end and as Jonathan had said, it was just in the trees close to the barn.

I went to look at the place, just to satisfy myself. There in the leaf litter was a deal of blood and flies were buzzing around happily. Hal lifted a frond of new green bracken.

"Splattered all over 'ere."

"Was the man just wandering around as Jonathan said and was surprised, or was he called and foolishly entered the screen of the trees?"

Hal shrugged. "I don't see as 'ow we'll know now."

"I am puzzled why the killer took the trouble of concealing the villein in the barn, Hal. Why not just leave him here?"

Hal shrugged. "Folk are walking through here from their 'ouses to get water and stuff. Maybe they'd see the body too quickly? Hidin' 'im in the barn...the killer could get away and 'ope that no one found him for a while. Cor...'e coulda' a bin as high as a month old mackerel before we sussed him out."

"Just lucky for us Alf went to the barn when he did."

*****

The next day we saddled up our horses again and taking John and Peter

Brenthall with us we rode off in the direction of Whitehill Copse.

Peter led the way and explained to us what he'd seen the day Bardol Wedgemoor left the Burnt Wood and hiked on foot the distance to the meadow and its enclosing trees.

"He kept looking back over his shoulder. He didn't see me as I kept either to the trees or in a slight dip in the ground. He was jumpy there was no doubt. Once or twice he stopped and almost sniffed the air like an animal as if he was worried someone was following. He was a large man and for all his size he got quite a clip on. He wasn't hanging about, sir."

"Then he disappeared into the trees?"

"Yes. When I got a bit closer and could see him threading his way into the middle of the coppice. I didn't take Chaffinch in because I thought the noise might alert Wedgemoor."

"And you didn't wait to see him leave?"

"I waited a short while but I had work to do. I didn't have the time to faddle about waiting for him to come out. So I left."

"No, of course not. There was no one else here? You don't think he was meeting someone?"

"I didn't hear anyone, sir," answered Peter.

We left our horses at the edge of the coppice and went in on foot.

Here was a small wood of hazel, alder and birch with a few large oaks. The trees were, as its name suggested, coppiced. This was an old and well practised method of woodland management. Many trees make new growth from the stump or roots if cut down. In a coppiced wood, young tree trunks are repeatedly cut down to near ground level. Many new shoots will then emerge, and, after a number of years the coppiced tree, or stool, is ready to be harvested, and the cycle begins again. This method gives us good straight birch poles for building, oak for building and hazel for weaving hurdles.

The young trees were sprouting new growth. Some of the coppiced trees were centuries old.

"This one was done last year," said John, pointing. " Look how much growth it's put on in a year."

Sure enough the alder stool has regrown to a height of about two feet.

Some trees were what we call overstood, where they hadn't been dealt with for many years and several trunks or stems grew tall from one bole. Up one of these multiple stemmed trees grew a curling and arching clematis, now in flower. The white, star shaped, many petalled blossoms smothered the lower branches of the oak to a height of about twelve feet.

We passed it and drove on into the trees.

"Don't seem to be much 'ere sir," said Hal, swiping at a patch of nettles with his boot.

"Go on a bit further, Master Hal," said Peter, leading us off in a northerly direction.

"We are now in the disputed land, aren't we?" I asked John.

"Yes, by about half a mile," he answered, ducking under a low hanging branch.

Eventually we came out into a glade where no trees grew and the sun shone fiercely.

I've explained before, I think, that the Forest of Savernake is an area of woods and glades with some meadows and commons between; an area made up of dense woodland, leafy glades, meadows, small streams, commons and ponds. So not just trees. Here was a patch of fertile green meadow.

John hollered from the other side of the glade.

"Sir...many feet here." He was the best tracker in the forest and was skilled in the art of understanding the signs left by man and beast.

I jogged across the grass.

John hunkered down and looked at the ground.

"Several different boot patterns. Coming and going. Some from the north, others the south."

"Where are they going?"

He stood up, shrugging his shoulders. "They all end up here in this glade. They come this way..." he pointed, "and they go that way." He pointed again.

"But where do they go and why?" I asked, chewing my lip.

"There's nothin' 'ere but grass and a few trees and a lot o' flowers," said Hal.

We looked across the grass. The white flowers of the stitchwort grew in little clumps here and there. The red campion, that native of the woodland edge, grew tall and sturdy here. Foxgloves, their purple pink spikes pushing up, stately amongst the other leaves, nodded in the slight breeze. The gentle cuckoo flower with its pale pink cup shaped flowers was almost dying down and over now.

I turned a full circle.

My nose detected a pleasant smell.

"Can anyone smell roses?"

Hal sniffed. "Aye, I can."

He turned about and waded through the knee high meadow grasses. I followed.

All of a sudden we came upon a wall of green. As tall as the dead tree up which it threaded; a wild rose with pale pink cupped flowers and a heavenly scent, ten feet wide and twelve feet tall, blocked our way.

I approached and took one of the pretty blooms in my fingers, bringing it to my nose.

"Yer don't need to do that, yer can smell it from 'ere," said Hal, chuckling.

Peter and John came up behind us.

"Nothing, sir. No further tracks. A couple of horses have stood just at the edge of the clearing but...nothing."

Suddenly from a way away we heard a voice shouting.

"My Lord Belvoir..."

"Here!" I answered, recognising the voice of Henry my steward.

"Tsoo..must be something important," said Hal shaking his head, "if 'Enry leaves the confines of the village and sits on an 'orse."

It was true Henry didn't like riding, though he could do it and had to as my demesne steward. I turned in the direction of the voice. "Here, Henry...follow the voice."

A moment later Henry's silver bright head came into view as he ducked under the low branch of the nearest oak and breathlessly came to halt, skidding on the grass.

"Sir…I had to come to find you. Doctor Johannes is at the village. He brings news."

I must have looked worried, for Henry started and said "Oh no...not that kind of news, news which will...."

"What is it, Henry?" I asked.

"It's the Lord Garner, sir..."

"Oh no, don't tell me he's turned up at Durley breathing fire and..."

"No sir. He'll not be breathing, ever again. He's dead, sir."

"Dead, Henry?"

"Doctor Johannes thought you'd like to know. The man has been murdered, sir."

*****

We sat in my study and I poured from a flagon of my best Bordeaux.

"So if I have it right..." I poured one beaker, "Garner was in town. Do we know why he'd gone there? Hungerford town is nearer to him." I poured a second beaker.

"Someone said they had seen him talking to one of the basket weavers in town," said Johannes.

I nodded. "And then he was pushing through the crowd...."

"It was market day and the High Street was very busy."

"He must've been jostled and the next folk knew, he was down on the ground bleeding?"

"That's right."

"Not dead?"

"Unconscious. They picked him up and brought him the few yards to my door."

"But he was dead before you could do anything for him?"

"That's right. He died on my workroom table. A wound, a stab wound to the body. Right through the lung."

"A chance blow or a planned one?"

Johannes shrugged. "Someone who knew that a man is unlikely to survive such a blow. But not a soldier's way, if you see what I mean. Not a knife straight up into the heart."

I sat down and put the beaker to my lips. "Meaning that it was an opportunistic meeting of man and knife and not a planned killing."

"I would say so. A spur of the moment thing."

"Stabbed in the back or...?"

"Front."

"So Garner was facing his attacker and the knife was driven in some way to catch the lung."

"And he obviously did not feel himself in any danger."

"Hmmm." I sipped again. "And no one saw anything?"

"I didn't question everyone who was there but those who brought the man to me said they didn't see what happened and the three of them were close by when it occurred."

"Was that man of his with him - Foreman?"

Johannes stretched out his large frame. "Apparently not. Garner was walking alone."

"Who were the men who found him?"

"Judd Saddler, Jonas Pyper and Henry Waulker."

"The fuller's man?"

"Yes."

"I don't know the Pyper man."

"Works for the sumpter on the High Street."

"Ah. None of them I suppose knew the murdered man?"

"They say not."

"Hmm." I rubbed my lips with my fingertips.

"Do we know where he'd been in the town besides the basket men?"

"No one took much notice. It was very busy."

"Hmm. Then we have to ask why? Who benefits from his death?"

"All his villeins by the sound of it," chuckled Johannes.

"I've no doubt someone in the family, equally as unpleasant. will inherit," I said.

"Apparently there is a son."

"See, I told you." I chuckled too and drained my beaker.

"Works in London. Part of the royal household. Married to one of the Queen's ladies apparently."

"Can't see him coming out from London to take up the reins of a small and run down manor in the middle of nowhere."

"Who knows?"

"So who hated Garner enough to kill him in broad daylight, in front of.. what..a hundred people?"

"Someone with daring, I'll say that," said Johannes. "The man would be bloodied but might be able to hide it."

"All it takes, as you said, is a jostle, a concealed knife, perhaps under a cloak... you bump into your victim, you pull the man to you. 'Oh I'm terribly sorry' you say, in goes the knife. Smiling, you pull away and walk off nonchalantly, not too fast unless people get suspicious, hiding the knife in your clothes."

"A matter of an unguarded moment."

"Like cutpurses. I've seen them operate like that," I said.

"Yes, indeed. Except this curpurse was the murdering kind."

"Do we know if Garner had been seen talking to anyone in the street just before it happened?"

"Not a question I asked," said Johannes.

"Then we need to ask it," I said. "And we need to find out where Foreman was."

"His man?"

"He may have been Garner's right hand man but that doesn't mean he didn't hate him for some reason and wish him harm."

"No, I suppose not."

"And I want to ask him a few other questions."

"Oh?"

"Yes, like where he was when Oswald of Knighton was having his throat cut near my wood barn at Durley?"

"Oh no, not another..."

"Yes, Johannes. Two deaths today. Hugo the coroner is right. Murder is following me around at the moment."

*****

Next day I jogged my fine stallion Fitzroy into town. He had been given to me by a grateful father; one who'd had a son murdered in 1204. Together Johannes and I had solved his murder and Fitz was my reward.

He was a fast racehorse with Arab blood, quick over the chalky close cropped turf of the downs but he also had a bright brain and was eager to learn new things. He became bored easily. I felt I'd neglected him of late and so a swift canter down the road to Marlborough made us both feel better.

I clopped under the gate arch at the castle, dismounted and gave him to one of the ostlers.

"Glad you're here Aumary!" shouted my friend and officer of the watch, Sir Andrew Merriman, from the gatehouse. "I fear there's going to be trouble."

"Oh?" I brushed my legs of chalk dust. "This is a castle Andrew, when is there not trouble?"

"Not that kind. This is town trouble."

"Well, that's not my job; it's..."

"Ah yes...Nick the town reeve has done his best but I think he would welcome your help."

I looked round. "What's the nature of this trouble then?" All looked amazingly peaceful in the bailey of the castle.

"Out on Southfield."

"What's that to do with...?"

Andrew chuckled. "You'll never believe it...go, go on....I think I can hear the shouting from here."

With a wave of my hand, I settled my sword at my hip and turned through the castle gate on foot. Once at the end of the wooden drawbridge, I could see Southfield, a patch of scrubby ground rising up from the river. Here was where we'd held our fair every August since 1204. John had granted us a charter in that year, allowing us to hold an annual eight day fair and markets every Wednesday and Saturday.

There were a few bothies at the top of the field and one or two huts down by the river where the local fisherman, Wat Fisher kept his boats and equipment. Apart from this, it was nothing but boggy ground.

I could see several men standing on the road which ran by the field and a few others pacing around on the grass. Voices were raised.

Nicholas Barbflet was the town reeve and the man responsible for the smooth running of Marlborough. He stood at the head of the town council and was the man deputed to speak for Marlborough on all matters. He'd been elected in 1204, the same year in which we'd had the charter granted and had been re-elected in 1206. He was a popular man; the town's master miller and my close friend.

I could see him gesticulating. His face looked pinched and angry. I'd never really seen him angry. He was a mellow chap. This was going to be interesting.

With him was another gesticulating man. He had his back to me but something about the set of his head on a thick neck and his short legged body, told me I knew him.

As I jogged up, he turned.

Indeed I did know him.

He pulled down his yellow cotte and adjusted his wide tan belt.

"Sir Aumary, my Lord Belvoir," he bowed.

"Olivier Green as I live and breathe!" I said coming to a halt before him. "God keep you. What brings you to Marlborough?"

I saw Nicholas open his mouth to speak but Olivier rode in with, "Aye, not often I get out of London. Maybe to Woodstock, Windsor or Clarendon but..."

My eye roved over the men on the grass. They seemed to be pacing it out and searching the ground."

"They lost something, Olivier?"

"No, Sir Aumary, but Marlborough is about to lose something," said Nick.

*****

I rubbed the back of my neck. "Nothing I can do, Nick," I said. "If we're up against the King then..."

"You know him, can't you explain to him? It's important to the town, Aumary."

We were now crowded into my small office in the castle wall by the gatehouse.

"Aye, I know the fair is important, has become important but..."

"If we lose the field we shall have to have it in the town and Heaven only knows what problems that will cause."

"What's wrong with the common?"

"Not close enough to town I'd say," said Gilbert Cordwainer, another Marlborough artisan and friend of mine.

"No, maybe not."

"The King has set his heart on this, Sir Aumary. He'll not be gainsaid," said Olivier Green.

I sat down with a bump on my chair. I picked up the letter which a moment before I'd thrown onto the table.

In it was outlined plans to turn our Southfield into an extension of the castle. Not for any military purpose but for a garden.

Olivier Green was the King's gardener.

He had created pleasure gardens for King Henry, John's father, at many of the royal residences. Woodstock near Oxford was, I was told, a magnificent place and a favourite of Henry's. Here, legend had it, he'd kept his mistress Rosamund Clifford in luxury, surrounded by a garden the like of which did not exist outside the paradises of the heathen lands of the East.

John's Queen, Isabella, was to come to the castle at Marlborough more often, we were told in this letter and so naturally, she must have somewhere to walk and sit in fine weather: she must have a place where she might escape the masculine rigours of the castle: she must have a garden.

The Southfield was to be walled, a decorative observation tower was to be built and a dovecote constructed for the delight of the ladies. Here there must be turfed benches to sit, trickling fountains to delight the ears, flowers in shaped beds and gravel paths for ladies to walk dry shod. There were to be trees for shade and for fruit for the Queen's delicate palate, sweet smelling flowers for the delight of the royal nose and colour to entrance her eye.

To hell with the town. Damnation to its fair. John wanted a garden on Southfield.

"Nick, gentlemen." I addressed the members of the council who had come out to Southfield that morning to oppose the plan.

"There's nothing I can do. This is John's castle. He is our master. If he wishes to take a piece of land..."

"Not his to take, Sir Aumary," said Gabriel Gallipot, the apothecary, his voice barely above a whisper.

"The whole land is his to take, Gabriel. He is the King. I cannot oppose him."

"But a garden, Sir Aumary? A garden?"

I rubbed the back of my neck again. The beginnings of a headache were starting there. I'd had this problem for a few years, ever since I'd been bopped on the head with a large branch in 1203.

"It seems there's a fashion for them, Master Tanner...Gerard. Everyone who is anyone is creating a garden."

"To hell with fashion!" said Master Giles Thatcher, his white moustache bristling, making it look like a crawling white caterpillar on his lip. "It's our field...for our fair."

"To be fair..."

Everyone groaned.

"We don't use it at any other time of the year," smiled Vyvyan Fuller, the youngest of our councillors.

"We do," said Nick.

"For our archery contests and such displays," piped up Master Fletschier the arrowsmith.

I rose and turned to Olivier Green.

"The King has asked you to survey the ground with a view to creating a garden there?"

The man stood up from his leaning position on the wall by the door.

"Yes."

"Might you find that, ahem, it's maybe too wet or not suitable, perhaps Olivier? Hmm?"

"My Lord Belvoir. If it is wet, I shall drain it."

"Poor soil maybe?"

The man tossed up his hand dismissively. "I shall import good soil."

"There are no trees!" I said in desperation.

"I shall plant them."

"Gentlemen, consider the field lost." I sat down again.

Everyone spoke at once.

"No, no we shall fight it."

"It can't be, it's not fair." I must admit, I groaned at this pun.

Much as you did just then Paul!

"We shall petition the King," said Nick eventually.

"As you wish," spat Master Green. "But meanwhile I must do my job."

He left, banging the door behind him. As he'd opened it I saw his men milling in the courtyard.

"Where are they all staying?"

Andrew had somehow crept in at the back. "Not in the castle."

"Ah. That's wise, perhaps."

"Not wise to be in the town I'd say."

"No...maybe not."

"I was thinking that they would probably want to come to you," said Andrew with a snort, "at Durley."

"And travel to the town every day to do...whatever it is they do? Not practical."

"Ah no, I suppose not."

"No one in the town will put them up," said an affronted Master Metier, the goldsmith.

"Then they must be lodged within the castle." I put up my hand to quell the protests. "No, it will be so. We must accommodate the King's men."

There was much grumbling. But Nick said eventually with a sigh. "I can take the master gardener."

"Can you ask Peterkin to arrange it with the hosteller please, Andrew?"

"Certainly," said my friend, smirking "And to think, I thought this was going to be a dull day." He too left, banging the door.

*****

Eventually I managed to placate the council. I would write to the King. I would explain how important the field was to the town. I would sweetly ask him to reconsider. I knew it was a forlorn hope. John wanted a garden. He would get one. On Southfield.

I penned a letter quickly and asked Castleman, one of the guards, to take it to be dispatched with a courier forthwith. There were always one or two lurking around the castle.

Castleman came back and reported the deed done.

"Can you go out into the town and find Judd Saddler and ask him to come up here to see me when he has the time please? It's about the man who was murdered in the High Street."

"The Lord Garner, sir?"

"Yes. Lord of Whittonditch and Knighton."

"You know I'm a Whittonditch man, sir?"

"No, Ed, I didn't know."

"Course, I left a while ago. Been in Marlborough twenty years now."

"But you knew the lord Garner?"

"Oh aye. I knew him. I was never one of his tied men but I know he wasn't liked and wasn't a good master."

"You think one of them had had enough of him and saw to it that he didn't bother them any longer?"

Castleman scratched his chin. "I reckon as there's a few would'a liked to but... I dunno. It's a hanging offence to strike your lord down."

"That it is, but extenuating circumstances...it might be possible to be lenient if it's in self defence."

"Not if the Lord de Neville was here, sir."

"Ah no...not if he were in charge."

Hugh de Neville, who was presently with the King, was the custodian of the castle and a hard man. You would get no leniency from him. I had cause to know this.

"I'll go right now sir, shall I?"

Judd Saddler came back with him.

I knew Saddler to be an intelligent and thoughtful man. If there was anything to know about this murder, he would know it.

"I was walking down the High with Pyper sir. I saw Waulker across the road and crossed to speak to him. We both did. There was quite a squeeze of people in front of the Green Man and we had to shift a bit to get past. Anyway just as I got level with the slaughter pens, I saw my friend bend down in front of me."

"Who?"

" 'Twas Pyper, sir. Jonas."

"You were walking with the other man?"

"Henry, yes. Well, Jonas cried out, 'there's a man down here help me' and I bent down to help right him. Of course I didn't realise he was wounded then. I thought he'd just tripped or maybe he'd had a skinful in the Green Man and was down on the floor dead drunk."

He sighed. "I reached under his arm and it came away bloodied. Then I knew he'd been stabbed."

"Now, think carefully Judd. Before you reached down, before you stooped, who was around you besides your friends?"

"That crowd who are always in the Green Man."

"The racing lot?"

"Yes, spilling out onto the road they were but they were all facing each other and talking."

"And?"

"I saw Gilbert's back. He was striding up the High. He had that littl'un of his by the hand."

"Yes."

Judd stared at the floor as if the flagstones might give up the story and jog his memory.

"Philbert Pyle, the turner. He was there. But he was going the other way."

"Down to the Marsh?"

"Aye. Where he lives. He'd just passed and was behind me. Erm..I can't remember anyone else."

"No one striding out quickly away from the body?"

Judd shook his head. "No one I know."

"The Lord Garner was going down the High towards the castle. The man who killed him would probably be coming up from that end. He would either pass you by or he'd walk quickly, maybe across the...."

"Yes. There was a man. In a light blue cloak."

"Ah?"

"He crossed the road in front of me. In front of us. I'm sure that Jonas would remember too."

"What did he look like?"

Judd Saddler screwed up his face and closed his eyes.

"I don't know him. I hadn't seen him before so I don't think....no. He isn't a customer of mine. He had reddish tinted fair hair, a little balding, and I think at some point his nose had been broken, sir, but I didn't see much because he was going away across the road and he had his cloak pulled tight around him. Odd that because it was quite a warm day."

"Thank you Judd." I put my hand on his shoulder. "Keep this to yourself."

Judd Saddler left as Gilbert Cordwainer was about to scratch at the door.

They nodded to each other. Judd held the door for him.

"M'lord..." said Gilbert breathlessly into the gap, "I know as you want to get your hands on that Foreman fella."

I saw Judd turn back, a frown on his face.

"He's at the fletcher's now sir. I saw him from my front door. Went in about... oooh... a few St. Anselm's ago."

I grabbed my sword belt and pushed through the door. "Thanks Gil."

Buckling it on quickly, I sprinted across the yard and into the guard room where Andrew was talking to a few of his men.

"Andrew, I need men to follow a suspect. In the town before he bolts."

Andrew nodded to the three men he'd been talking to.

"Hardcastle, you two...with the Lord Belvoir...now!"

He too reached for his weapons.

"I was going off duty and about to hand over to FitzAlan but I'll come with you first."

We all bustled out of the castle gateway on foot, followed by Judd Saddler and Gilbert Cordwainer. As we jog trotted I called out. "Minimum force. I want him alive. Bunce...no arrows. D"you understand?"

The man chunnered into his beard. " 'Twern't my fault..."

A while ago he had accidentally killed a fleeing suspect with a poorly aimed crossbow bolt. He'd never live it down.

"Where to, Aumary?" asked Andrew.

"Fletschier's. The man who was the Lord Garner's right hand man's there. I have a few questions for him. I'll catch him in town before he returns to Whittonditch. Save me a trip out there."

The High Street was heaving with market day traffic. Stalls lined the middle of the wide high street in a double layer. Here could be found everything from pans to pigs, hams to horse tack and parchment to pins.

A seething mass of people, animals, handcarts, horses and wagons blocked the street on both sides.

We wove our way along as best we could until we were about one third of the way up the High.

"No violence unless absolutely necessary," I said sternly. "This is a respected Marlborough councillor's shop and home. I want no damage."

Everyone nodded.

"Gil, might you just saunter in and see what's happening? I'd like to catch the man unawares if I can."

Gilbert nodded, adjusted his cotte and opened the door.

"Mornin' Adam," I heard him say.

"Wait a while," I whispered to the others.

I listened carefully. I could hear laughter and muted conversation. I nodded to my men. "In we go, gently."

I pushed open the door and wandered in.

The man Foreman had his back to me. Gilbert had engaged him in conversation and Adam Fletschier was standing beside a table counting money into a wooden box. He looked up. He frowned. Foreman turned. Gilbert stepped back. My men ranged themselves either side of me.

"Good morning Master Foreman," I said, "I'm glad we've had this chance to meet. I really didn't fancy another trip out to Whittonditch."

I saw the man lick his lips. He bowed, keeping his eyes on my men.

"My lord."

"Allow me to present my condolences on the death of your master, the Lord Garner."

"Thank you my lord," said Foreman though his gaze narrowed. 'What the devil is all this about?' said his eyes.

"I wonder if you might accompany me up to the castle for a short while please? There are a few questions I'd like to ask you."

I stepped sideways and gestured to the door.

As quick as a mouse evading a cat, Foreman had taken hold of the edge of the small table upon which Master Fletschier had his money box and had tipped it up.

Coins rattled on the wooden floor between us.

Fletschier hollered, "Oi!" and attempted to catch the falling table and box. He only succeeded in impeding Andrew, the closest man to Foreman, from leaping forward and grabbing the errant man by the sleeve. Foreman pushed the arrowsmith into Andrew.

He then turned and bolted through into the inner room. I heard a voice cry out quickly "Here, you can't..." and then a coughing, an expelling of air as someone was punched.

Hardcastle and I were quickly through the door after the man but just as we reached the centre of the room a door banged somewhere. One of Adam Fleschier's apprentices lay winded and doubled up on the floor. This room was the place where Master Fletschier made his arrows.

A young lad, no more than twelve pointed to another door. "There sir."

Three rooms one leading to another, up the property's garden and we were out into the fresh air of the Backs, the lane which ran at the rear of the northerly High Street properties.

Foreman was running swiftly along the lane which led to Kingsbury Hill.

We all pursued.

As we ran I managed to yell, "One of you go down Chandler's Lane and stop him from backtracking up the High."

Hardcastle peeled off.

"Ed, go down to the cross and see if you can catch him there."

Castleman saluted and was gone down Ironmonger's Lane.

Bunce, myself and Andrew followed by a determined faced Saddler and a puffing Gilbert, pelted as fast as we were able down the lane at the back of the High Street.

Foreman kept looking back. As far as I could tell, he'd no weapon in his hand. I was happy about that. I had no idea if the man was prepared to use real violence to escape. I only had the word of the dead Whittonditch villein, Oswald of Knighton, that Foreman was a killer. My men were trained soldiers but still I had no wish for any of them to be hurt.

Foreman skidded around the corner at Chute Alley.

We heard his footsteps pounding down the cobbles of the courtyard. Then suddenly there was a fierce neighing and a babble of voices. A sharp cry rang out around the buildings, echoing in the confined space. Then a shrill toned man yelled, "What, you stupid oaf..." and I heard no further clear speech but a babble again.

We rounded the corner, and kept running, coming upon the scene of the commotion a heartbeat after.

Gabriel Gallipot was trying unsuccessfully to calm his horse. One of his apprentices, James was lying on the ground. A woman - a neighbour - was screaming at a small child who had been skittering about dangerously close to the horse with a hoop, only the hoop was now bowling away down the hill. He stopped and bawled and the woman scooped him up.

Another man, whom I recognised as Roger, the elder worker of the master apothecary, was bending over the lad on the floor.

Neighbours were now exiting their houses and businesses and Gilbert came up panting heavily and attempted to help Gabriel with his horse.

Two or three women, one I recognised as Mistress Glover, had stepped out of a shop and had gone to another man on the floor.

She took off her gloves and turned him over.

I came up behind her.

Lungs bursting, I leaned over. Andrew was to my right side.

"Is he...?"

"A bad gash to the head, my Lord Belvoir," she said. "Shall we get him into the apothecary?"

I looked back at James who was now writhing on the floor, having regained his wind.

Bunce jogged over. "This our man is it, sir?"

"It is, Bunce. He's still alive but has a wound to the head. Gabriel!" I shouted, "What happened?"

Andrew took hold of Gabriel's horse and walked him back to his stable at the rear of the apothecary.

"Damned man came careering round the corner, straight into Brutus, sir. James fell off. Brutus caught the man a blow with a hoof. Oh, I suppose we'd better take him in and I'll look at him."

Suddenly his face changed. "Ah...so this is a fellow you were chasing eh?"

"Garner's man."

"Ah yes. Now I come to think on it, I recognise him."

"He tried to escape before we could take him to the castle for questioning."

"Did he now?"

Bunce took the man's feet and I his shoulders and we manhandled him through the narrow doorway into the apothecary's shop and laid him on a wide bench in the inner room. Gabriel set to, dealing with his head. He shook his own. "Better fetch Johannes, I think."

Andrew nodded and disappeared through the door.

"You say you recognise him?"

"Indeed, I do."

"He is a Whittonditch man…that's not a short distance from here. How do you know him, Gabriel?"

"Oh he comes and goes at the behest of his master. He buys regularly."

Gabriel Gallipot was parting the thinning reddish fringe of hair to get at the wound.

"What did he buy regularly?"

Gabriel looked round at me. He blinked a few times as if the question puzzled him. He went on working.

James staggered in on the arm of his mate Roger and sat down on a stool.

"Bloody bastard!"

"Yes well, we'll not have language like that in here, young man," said the prim Gabriel Gallipot. "Though I will concede, he is bloody." He tittered at his own joke.

I smiled. "You were about to tell me..."

"Potash...Sir Aumary. Potash."

I scratched my pate...

"And that is, Gabriel?"

He sighed as if I was a stupid schoolboy, found wanting at his lessons.

"Sovereign for roses, sir. Oh yes indeed. Very good for roses I'm told. But it's also used in soap making and for glass manufacture."

I looked carefully at the unconscious man.

He wore no cloak but his hair was thinning and was a light sandy red colour. Under the blood his nose had the broken look of a brawler. The knife in its scabbard was wide and no doubt wickedly sharp.

Johannes came in through the door. Gabriel stood shakily. I offered him my arm.

"What have we, Gabriel?"

"Kicked in the head by Brutus, Johannes."

"Alive?"

"Just."

I turned to Saddler.

"Recognise him Judd?"

The saddler came forward and peered at the man.

"Aye sir. It's him. The man I saw before the Lord Garner was killed."

"Everyone out then!" said Johannes. "Water, bandages...."

We left him ordering the worker about and we stepped out into the sunny day.

"So, Aumary. Why did he flee?" asked Andrew. "You only asked him to accompany you to the castle."

"Guilty conscience I'll be bound," offered Gilbert.

"His kind don't have consciences," said Andrew.

"Something to hide that's for sure," I said.

"And if he snuffs it, sir," said Bunce, wiping his nose on his sleeve "you won't know what the devil it was!"

Chapter Six

We watched as Johannes supervised getting the wounded man onto a plank. They squeezed through the door of the apothecary and made off down the hill with Andrew in tow.

"Bunce, can you arrange a guard please for the doctor's workroom? I want Foreman locked in there and guarded."

"Yes sir, I can do that." He jogged off after the others.

"Gilbert, can you ask Nick to get it cried about town that I want to talk to anyone who might have seen the man Foreman in town the day the Lord Garner died and ask if anyone saw anything of the dead man before he was killed please?"

"I 'spect you'll want to know where he'd been in town besides to the basket makers?"

"I will. And that reminds me; I shall have a word with them too." I caught Gilbert's sleeve as he turned to march off to Nicholas' house.

"Gil, where are the basket makers?"

"They have a workshop at the end of Tim's buildings. Tim Roper. They need to be by the river to wet their willows you see."

"Wet their willows...? Oh yes, I see what you mean. Keep their withys pliant."

"That's it. The wooden strips they weave with."

"I'll see you later," I said as I turned and jogged down the hill towards The Marsh.

Timothy Roper's buildings were a collection of long sheds which stood beyond the wagon yard close by the river. I entered the Ropery from Barn Street and walked up to the end. Here was a diminutive timber framed house with two small outbuildings in a fenced off yard.

I called out and a man poked his head around a door frame.

A young lad came from somewhere in the house and shouted to me "Me Da's in the weaving shed, sir," and he disappeared again.

William Maunder was the master basket maker. He was a small man in his late thirties, with strong, tanned arms sporting a rich clothing of dark hair, visible because his shirt sleeves were rolled up to his armpits. His black locks were thrown back from a lined forehead in a lion's mane and the length of it was caught up behind his ears. In order for his hair not to get tangled into his work, he wore a cloth band tied around his forehead.

"My Lord." He bowed as I introduced myself. "We haven't met before, sir, but I do know of you and of your role at the castle."

"You will know then too, that I am the Constable for the county responsible for tracking down felons, Maunder."

"Aye, sir, I do. We didn't speak but when we all had to make our oaths last year, I saw you then so..."

"Yes, I suppose you did."

All men over twelve had to swear an oath to the King in 1206, last year, and it had been my job to organise this locally.

"I'm looking into the death of the Lord Garner of Whittonditch, Maunder. I hear he was seen here, talking to you, before he walked back up to the High to his death."

Maunder carefully rested the bunch of rushes he had been holding on the workshop wall and wiped his hands on the sides of his apron.

"Aye, m'lord. He did come to talk to me. It's true. He found me on the lane."

"Mind telling me what you talked about?"

Maunder's eyes narrowed.

"I don't suppose it's goin'ta hurt. He'm being dead and all now."

"It was a business matter?"

"It was. He wanted me to weave him some large arches."

"Arches?" My voice must have sounded disbelieving for the man's eyes crinkled and he chuckled deep in his chest.

"I know it sounds daft but, well, he had this idea, see, that he wanted to put some arches in that big garden of his, sir, and..."

"Why didn't he get his carpenters to build them?"

"Oh no, these were special. See here, m'lord, come into the shed and I'll show you."

He opened the door and gestured for me to precede him.

Inside the shed it was gloomy and so Maunder left the door open and the sunlight flooded in and pooled on the beaten earth floor. On that floor was a stool with short stumps. I assumed the master would sit upon this with his legs stretched either side of his basket, to weave. Around and about were various completed baskets, baskets half made and the materials of his trade, willow strips and rushes and poles of varying widths, withys which would, I supposed, be split into smaller flatter strips. These were the raw materials of basket making. Buckets of water stood close at hand.

"See here, sir." He pointed to a piece of parchment lying on a long table. "This is what he gave me."

I looked down. On the paper was the drawing of an arch which was to be woven like a basket, almost like my men might weave hazel hurdles in the forest. This however was taller than a man, for the drawing showed such a man, crudely sketched, passing right through the arch. Either side of him were flowers trained up the side, in a similar fashion to my rose which had been encouraged to grow up the manor wall.

"I was to make six o' these. But now, well, no one else will take 'em, will they?"

"You did not begin them?"

"Oh no...as you know he'd only just left us when he was struck down. He was goin'a send his man with a deposit, to formally engage us so as we could begin weavin' 'em."

I looked carefully at the drawings. The flowers winding up the sides of these wicker work arches, by the way they had been drawn, close curled squiggles in rings, were roses.

I must have looked puzzled, for the master weaver laughed. "Aye...but I reckon they'd work. Provide a framework for his flowers to crawl up. Mind you, there i'n't anything in them that'd get a man murdered, is there, sir?"

I shook my head, thinking.

"Thank you Maunder." I strode to the door then turned back as a new thought entered my head.

"No one else has asked for anything like this, have they?"

"Bless you m'lord, no, sir. 'Twas a new thought. Well, to me at any rate. Mind you... I just might make one...see how it goes on." Then he shook his head. "Nah, what am I thinking, when do I have the time…?"

My mind drew back to that glade in Whitehill Copse where we had been recently; to the large wild rose bush growing up the dead oak tree.

Perhaps Garner had seen this and the thought had come to him, to build himself a support for his flowers which mimicked the tree.

Now I had to tie the Lord of Whittonditch to my man Wedgemoor. The Lord Garner had been interested in that meadow where lay the wild rose. Wedgemoor had been there several times. I saw again in my mind's eye the pot of flowers which had been sitting on the table in the Wedgemoor home, the day he died. Roses. There was no doubt in my mind that those flowers had come from that glade in Savernake.

Maunder was looking at me strangely.

"You alright, my lord?"

I came back to the present.

"Perfectly, thank you, Maunder," I said.

*****

I stepped slowly up the hill, pondering upon what I'd just heard and crossed the road meaning to go up to Johannes to see how our felon was faring, when, passing the High Cross which stood almost exactly opposite the alley way leading to Johannes' back yard, I came face to face with a man in a blue cloak. We bumped into each other.

"Oh I do beg your pardon… I wasn't looking where...."

"Aumary," said a voice I knew. "Well met ."

"Percy!" I clasped him to my bosom. "What brings you to Marlborough?"

"You seem rather distracted," said my old friend.

"Oh it's nothing. Just musing on these crimes of mine. Not looking where I was going."

"What am I doing here? Why, I have come to see a man about some furniture. I'm off to see the turner down on The Marsh. You?"

"Going to Johannes' in the hope of some dinner." I chuckled as my stomach grumbled. "Do you not have woodsmiths in Pewsey that you can call upon to make you chair legs?"

"I do indeed. However this is a bit special." Percy looked over his shoulder. He whispered, "I have commissioned something unusual for my dear wife's birthday. I'm keeping it away from Pewsey so it doesn't leak out. You know how tales travel. It's rather a secret."

I chuckled. "I do indeed. Trust you to plan a surprise for Frida."

"Nothing is too good for my dear lady," he said, puffing out his chest. He took my arm and turned me up the hill. "Actually I was coming to the castle later to see you."

"You were?"

"Frida and I would like you all to come to dinner next week. How does Tuesday sound to you?"

"I shall have to confer with Lydia but I don't see why not. You sure you want us all?"

"Now, now, Aumary, we said we'd get together more often and we said we'd give the children a chance to get to know each other."

"Yes, yes we did. And Lydia hasn't seen Alfred yet. Nor has she gossiped with Frida for… ooh… quite a while."

"About time they did, then."

I laughed out loud. "All right. Tuesday dinner time, then."

Sir Percival Crofton slapped me on the shoulder and turned down the hill.

"Look forward to it!" he said as he ran across the beginnings of Oxford Street, dashed between two carts and disappeared down The Marsh.

I smiled inwardly. Percy had always been one for surprises, even when we were lads. Surprises and intricate practical jokes.

*****

I wandered down the alley way and into Johannes' yard.

His diminutive housekeeper Little Agnes was drawing water from the large trough kept there.

"Johannes still with his patient, Agnes?"

She nodded.

"He's still alive then?"

She made the wavy patterned sign with her hand which signified 'almost', for Agnes was a mute dwarf.

"Hangs by a thread does he?"

Agnes nodded.

"Anyone thought to go for the priest?"

The woman assented. She planted her feet wide, took hold of an imaginary sword held at the hip, puffed out her chest and put her hand on her other hip.

"Ah... Sir Andrew did?"

She nodded a little coyly.

"I'll go in then."

Foreman was lying on the small pallet which Johannes kept in his work room, his head bandaged.

I passed and nodded to one of the castle guards, a youngish lad named Jem, whom Bunce had asked to guard the door, and stepped into the work room.

"He's alive then?"

"He is, though I don't know for how much longer. His skull is cracked I think. Andrew has gone for Father Torold."

"How long have we? Will he regain consciousness, do you think?"

Johannes busied himself amongst his equipment. "With things like this as you know, Aumary, there is no sure recovery. It can take hours or days. Either way, death or life."

"Aye, I know." My mind immediately flew back to the day upon which my first wife Cecily had been hit by a stone, flung from a catapult. She had gone into herself and it was quite a few days before she was conscious again. It had been the day upon which Johannes and I had first met.

Johannes saw through my reverie and cleared his throat... "Well, yes..let's go and have some dinner and you can tell me all about what happened."

"Surely you'll not want to leave him in this state, Johannes?"

"I'll ask Agnes to step in a while. He'll be no threat in this state and Jem is by the door, besides there's very little I can do yet."

I nodded.

The front door opened and in stepped Andrew followed by a puffing Father Torold.

"We came as soon as we could," he said.

Johannes led him to the stricken man lying on the pallet. Andrew ran off back towards the castle taking Bunce with him.

"He has a broken head, Father. I am not sure if he'll survive. However he's out of his body at the moment and so can't make a confession," said Johannes.

The priest of St. Mary nodded sagely. "Yes, yes. I'll do my best."

We closed the door on them.

We had hardly begun to put knife to meat when Agnes came bustling in and stamped on the flagstone floor for attention. This must have meant 'come quickly', a gesture Johannes and she must have agreed between themselves, for the doctor leapt up from his seat and dived for the kitchen door.

I followed a heartbeat later.

Foreman was still lying on his back, a rough blanket covering his body, a pillow cushioning his head. Now his eyes were open and they looked terrified.

"I'd barely begun when he awoke," said the priest, "but he seems not to understand me."

Johannes reached for the man's hand. He looked into his eyes.

"Foreman, can you see me? It's Doctor Johannes."

The light eyes rolled around in their sockets.

"You have been kicked in the head by a horse. Squeeze my hand if you understand me and can see me."

But there was no answering squeeze. Foreman continued to look blank but fearful. He tried to rise but failed.

Johannes pushed him down gently.

"Here is the priest. He will hear your confession...."

Foreman began to moan and a cry left his lips which sounded like 'die'.

"Indeed you might die," I said. "Best that you unburden yourself to Father Torold."

Both the priest and doctor looked at me then, as if I'd said something terrible.

"If we can get him to confess to whatever crime he has been hiding..."

"Then he will confide it in me and I shall keep that secret to my grave, m'lord," answered Father Torold. "Out, all of you...out. I shall give him absolution."

Damn, I thought. I wanted to hear what Foreman said.

Johannes, Agnes and I jostled out of the door and went back to the kitchen.

"I think he may live but...it's a bad wound, Aumary. I might manage to save him, though I have a feeling he'll be lacking in some wits from now on even if he does survive," said Johannes.

"I suppose you won't allow me to..."

"No, I won't allow you to eavesdrop on them," chuckled Johannes. "I really doubt Father Torold will get anything coherent from him anyway."

"No, I suppose not. It's just galling to have him in my grasp and then for him to be snatched away again like this."

Johannes shook his head. "Nothing we can do."

Indeed there wasn't for Foreman lapsed into a deep sleep some while later. Father Torold got nothing from him that day.

We all sat round in the kitchen in silence, rather despondent if truth be known and finished our dinner.

"Johannes, Foreman's knife?"

"I have it here," said my friend, leaning over and pulling it from the table behind him.

I drew it from the scabbard. "Might this have made the wound in the Lord Garner's chest?"

Johannes took it back. He lifted it to the light.

"Too wide. The knife that killed Garner was narrower."

"Damn."

Then came a slapping of quick footsteps up the alleyway and Bunce came into view through the open door.

"Sir! Sir! My Lord Fitz wants you at the castle. There's trouble at Southfield."

*****

I ran the length of the High Street dodging the now thinning market day crowds. The base of the tower of St. Peter's church came into view and then on my left, the expanse of meadow which made up Southfield.

I heard the chanting and shouting before I got to the Pewsey Road and pushed my way through the crowd there.

"Make way! Get out of the way." Marlborough townsmen stood shoulder to shoulder blocking my passage through.

I drew my sword and laid about me with the flat of it.

"Ouch! Whadaya do that for?" said a voice I knew.

It was Timothy Roper's apprentice Adam Williamson.

"Move away Williamson," I said severely. "And take your cronies with you."

The young man grimaced, rubbing his thigh as he grabbed another apprentice - this one was one of the wheelwrights. I didn't know his name and they backed off.

I bellowed over the noise, "Move away. The Constable orders you to move away."

The crowd surged back and parted so I could walk through.

I noticed at the very front, Gilbert and his two apprentices, Felix and Harry, trying to hold back the crowd from breaking down the church's south door. With them were three other members of the town council and FitzAlan, the other officer in charge of the castle watch. Andrew was there too pushing and shoving. I heard him cry, "Back! Get back!"

I turned to Gerard Tanner who was the closest man to me and a town councillor.

"What is all this about?" I sheathed my sword, glaring around me at the young men now milling about. I saw Timothy Roper run up, grab an arm and give his apprentice Williamson a buffet on the ear.

"Southfield, my Lord Belvoir," said Tanner breathily. "They're digging up the ground. Some of the boys and the men decided to stop them."

"Them being the King's gardeners?"

"Yessir."

I glanced towards the church door where father Columba was standing before it with his arms outstretched, a hand on each side of the stone arch.

"I take it they took refuge in the church when things got nasty?"

"They did, Sir Aumary," said FitzAlan coming up behind me. "Father Columba tried to reason with the attackers but tempers were flying high."

I looked around the crowd. There were some older men there too. A couple of the castle farriers, three off duty men at arms who often worked with the moneyer at the mint and in the treasury, some of the fullers from the cloth mill.

"Disperse and go to your homes or you will be arrested. NOW!"

A fuller, a tenterman I knew to be called Sharp, stood with his feet planted. "If we go 'ome, who's to stop them digging up the field, my lord?"

"Nothing will happen today," I said. "Go home and we shall see what can be done," though I knew that I was powerless to prevent the gardeners from eventually doing their job. I just needed to diffuse the situation and restore order for the moment.

The young men regrouped, led by one of the young sons of the goldsmith, Thomas Metier.

"It's our field, my Lord Belvoir, they can't be allowed to..."

"It's the King's field, Metier. Go home to your father now I say, or I will take you all up and have you confined in the lockup. Your fathers will be forced to pay for your release."

"Aye! " said a voice, "And I'll be the one to march you up there!" Nicholas Barbflet, the town reeve came running up to the main group.

He went amongst them slapping arms and pushing them apart. "Peter, Alfred, Wulf, Will. Go! It can do you no good to cause further trouble."

The young men parted and with one backward look shifted their feet and turned their faces to the High Street.

I saw Harry Glazer give a huge sigh of pent up breath and take his hand from the priest's breast where he had been prepared to defend him from the crowd. Father Columba nodded to him and straightened his robe. His unruly red hair stood on end in a coxcomb and he shakily drew his hands through it.

I turned quickly to glare at some of the older men from the castle.

"If you are on duty, you will be fined for leaving your posts unless you came out with Sir Maurice. If you are at rest...go back to your quarters."

There was a general muttering but the men left and tardily walked across the drawbridge close by, looking back once or twice.

The townsmen left, shaking their heads, some of them glancing at us with anger in their eyes.

Gilbert Cordwainer came up.

"I was coming home and spotted the lads grouping. I yelled to Felix and Harry and we got the gardeners off the field before too much blood was spilled, Sir Aumary," he said, looking worried.

"Blood Gil? Who is hurt?"

Gilbert shrugged. "Don't know their names but there was some swinging of spades and clashing of staves."

"I think Master Green sustained some damage to his head, sir," said Harry.

"Aye. I saw a couple of blows being traded. That was what set it alight. I saw one of the young'uns with a bloodied nose," added Gilbert.

"As long as it was just a bloodied nose... Sir Maurice...?"

FitzAlan turned to me in the act of picking up a discarded shovel.

"Can you go back to the castle and get the names of the lads who left their places, if any?"

"Aye, sir." He jogged off across the drawbridge, catching up with the slower malefactors.

"Townsmen I'll leave to you Nick. Anyone who traded blows."

"I'll find them, Aumary," and he followed the apprentices and townsmen.

"Let's open the door and see what damage we have."

Andrew stepped forward and Father Columba turned, set his shoulder to the door and pushed.

Several of the gardeners were milling about behind it and leapt forward to defend the portal until they saw the priest and backed off, lowering their staves and pickaxes.

Andrew accompanied the priest into the nave. I followed with the town councillors, Gerard, Gilbert, Timothy and Jos Glover.

"Pax, pax," shouted Father Columba to the assembled men. His voice echoed into the roof beams.

"The crowd is gone. You are safe for the moment. The Constable of the castle is here to restore order."

An older man pushed his way forward. "Tom Jardine, sir. I am assistant to Master Green." He bowed low.

"Where is Master Green?"

Tom Jardine led me up the nave to where the master gardener and designer lay slumped on the altar step.

"He sustained a bang on the head."

"It's nothing, Sir Aumary," said Green, looking up at me with groggy eyes, "Felled me and drew a little blood, that's all."

The hand which he had clasped to his head shook. A wad of what looked like a torn shirt was soaking up the blood trickling down his forehead.

"I am so sorry this had to happen, Master Green. I'll get the man responsible and he shall be punished."

I turned to Andrew. "Can you run up to Johannes and see if he can come down to see to Master Green, Andrew?"

"Again? I've been up and down today like a bloody hen with...."

"I know you are supposed to be off duty but no one runs as fast as you." I grinned stupidly at him.

He tutted genially, smiled, threw up his hands and was gone.

"Are you up to telling me what happened, sir?" I asked.

Master Green adjusted his seat. One of his younger helpers held him up at the side, perching on the step on one buttock, leg outstretched.

"We all came out early to start the work. Tom here took the band who were to begin stripping the turf and building up the banks. The builders trundled their carts out and started to dig the foundations for the wall. All went well for a while," said the master gardener.

"Then about dinner time a party of apprentices, I think they were, came round the corner house and started to throw stones at us," said Tom Jardine.

"We hid behind the carts but then suddenly more men came and tipped them over," said a shaky Master Green. "We all pelted for the church then. There was some hand to hand fighting and more stones thrown."

"Young Mitchell there was hit on the arm. I think it's broken," added Jardine. "And Tom, one of our ditch diggers, was walloped with a stave. Broke his hand we think."

"A few of us have blood wounds but nothing serious, sir," finished Master Green. "I shall however, be making a formal complaint to the town council....."

I saw the present members of that council, look at each other in dismay.

"I expect the king will want to fine them for the affray, my Lord Belvoir."

"We shall talk further about this, sir," I said. "In future you will have an armed guard when you are working. I'll have no more violence."

Jos Glover cleared his throat. "I think I can speak on behalf of the council, sir....Master Green isn't it? We are very sorry that this has happened."

Gilbert, Gerard and Timothy nodded and made appropriate noises.

"We are all of us upset that the South Field must be taken from us and used in this way but none of us would offer up violence as a way of...."

"No sir," answered Green, "I'm sure you wouldn't. Oooh." The master gardener swayed on his step. "I do feel rather nauseous I must say."

I turned to find Father Columba. "Have we water for Master Green, Father?"

He ran off to fetch a beaker.

"The doctor will be with you and your lads in a moment. Meanwhile, all those who are fit and can walk, best go back to the castle. There'll be no more digging today," I said.

Olivier Green nodded and grimaced, for no doubt his head pained him. "The garden will go ahead, sir. It cannot be stopped. It will be over my dead body."

I smiled down at him. "Now Olivier...I'm sure it will not come to that."

*****

After Johannes arrived at the church, I returned to the castle. FitzAlan was there talking to a group of soldiers. He jogged over to me.

"No men left their posts, Aumary, just those off duty who live in the town, went out in their free time and got embroiled in the fighting. I took two of the guards out with me when I heard the noise."

I nodded. "I want their names. I need to find out who struck the master gardener and the others."

"'Twas none of us sir," said an eavesdropping soldier. "I saw a man strike him, a townsman."

"Who was it, Haroldson?"

The man sucked his teeth. "I don't rightly know his name."

"Ask about. See if anyone else can help you."

The man saluted and jogged off.

I opened my study door and went in to write down everything I'd been told, before I forgot the details.

It had been an eventful day. Firstly the arrival of the horticultural experts at the town, then my conversation with Judd Saddler. Our chasing of the Lord Garner's man Foreman and my quizzing of the basket maker Maunder. Finally a fracas outside St. Peter's church.

I sighed, dusted my notes with sand, blew on it and filed it away in my chest. I left a verbal note for Andrew to the effect that if the gardeners were to be out on South Field the following day they were to be guarded. I locked my office door, had Fitz saddled and brought to me and set his nose for the forest and home.

I had a dinner invitation to deliver to my good lady wife.

*****

The following day I was up and out early. We had had a deal of rain in the night and everything was sparkling and fresh. The sun would soon burn off the moisture and once again it would be a fair day.

Evisa Congyre, my mother-in-law was also up early and was sitting on a bench by the manor wall.

She looked up as she heard my tread on the hall step.

"Good Morrow, Aumary. Hal kindly brought a bench out for me," she said, smiling up at me. "I didn't sleep well last night but I had a hankering to sit out in the sunshine and watch the early morning bustle of your manor. My, my! It's a busy place."

I eased myself down by her side and chuckled.

"We have lots going on in the courtyard itself with the farrier and stables, woodsmith and potter having workplaces here. Not to mention the comings and goings of the laundress, the cooks, John and his team, Father Crispin and his little school..."

"Ah yes...he takes some of the manor children doesn't he, to educate them?"

"He does, three mornings a week, early. It all quietens down after dinner," I said, leaning back and breathing in the scent of the morning. I looked up. There was my rose, fading a little now but some blooms were still unfurling.

"You slept badly? I'm sorry to hear it, Evisa."

My mother-in-law laughed once. "Oh it's nothing. Old women sleep badly and I'm not used to sleeping alone. That's all...."

"But you have Annie with you?"

"Oh yes...I meant...without a husband. And...." She looked away and blinked back tears,

"After over forty years, it's very strange not to have him about."

I took her hand. "It will be, but the strangeness will fade with time. I know you loved him dearly."

"Yes. We were lucky in that. Though our marriage was arranged, we loved each other from the first moment."

"To the last, Evisa....that much was obvious."

She abruptly took back her hand and swallowed hard. "Oh Aumary," she said in a sob, "You don't know what it's like..."

She sighed and sat up straighter. "Are you any nearer to finding out what was going on with the will and with that man Garner?"

I leaned forward and rested my elbows on my knees.

Cedric passed by, walking from the stables with Fitzroy and waved at me. I waved back.

"The news is that Garner himself has been murdered, Evisa. In broad daylight, in town, in full view of at least a hundred people and none saw it happen."

"No!" Evisa brought her hand up to her neck. I saw the blood drain from her face.

"No! How can he have been killed...... It wasn't...?"

"I have no idea as yet why he should be killed, save that I may have his murderer under lock and key at Johannes' house, injured and like to die. He has not and likely will not make a confession, so I am no nearer solving the mystery."

Evisa's face grew as pink as it had been white.

"What is going on, Aumary?"

"I have a man of mine murdered in his home. He knew the place and was visiting the land disputed by Garner."

"The piece of land which Toruld is supposed to have left to him?"

"The very same. One of Garner's villeins is also dead, possibly murdered by that same man who lies at Johannes'. What he knew I cannot fathom and I now have a riot at South Field in Marlborough with the King's gardener injured by a townsman." I shook my head.

Evisa's light veil lifted in a sudden breeze. I noticed her hair was still coppery but with white strands now. I looked at her carefully, not something I had been used to doing. She was an attractive woman still, upright and stately but her face had become more creased, her features drawn and there were worry lines across her forehead. It was as if she held herself in. Given the moment, I felt that she would give a huge sigh and all the life would go out of her like a pricked bladder.

"I must go to the church to pray," she said suddenly.

At that moment, Hawise came skipping down the steps.

"Hello dada, gramma. What are you talking about?"

She squeezed herself between us and we moved to accommodate her.

"Oh just the lovely day and how wonderful the flowers are still..." I said, looking up at my rose.

Evisa gave a small smile. "Are you off to your lessons, Hawise?" she asked.

"I am going to help Sir Crispin with the younger children," she said matter of factly. "My reading is so good now, I can help to teach the others," she said.

"Well, that is good to hear, I said, giving her a squeeze. "Has your mama told you that we are going to Crofton on Tuesday for dinner? So you will be able to see this garden you and Jos were drawing the other week, for yourself."

"Yeees," said Hawise guardedly. She turned to look up at me. "Are you sure that you don't want me to marry Jos, dada? It seems very soon to..."

"Hand on heart Hawise," I said. "It has nothing to do with that. We have simply been asked to dinner."

"What's this?" asked Evisa.

I slapped my knees. "You tell your grandma the tale Hawise. I have work to do." And I rose, pecked them both on the cheek and skipped up the manor steps.

I sat myself at my table and scribbled for the time it takes for the sun to pass over the manor gate. I was sure that Foreman was guilty of one, if not more, of the crimes but couldn't see how to tie him into the deaths. I drew lines from his name to others and tried to place where he had been, or might have been when the murders were taking place.

I tapped my fingers on the table top in frustration.

Henry came up to the open door and scratched on the frame.

"Sir, I'm organising your trip to Crofton for Tuesday. Will the Lady Lydia be riding with young Simon in a cart or shall Felice be coming with him separately and....."

"Ask Lady Belvoir Henry. Hawise will ride Felix and I'll take Fitz I think."

"Very well, sir." He turned to go.

"Henry, is Annot about at the moment?"

"I thought I saw her go to the hens a little while ago when I went to speak to Walter, sir."

"Ask her to come up here will you?"

"Yessir."

*****

Annot Wedgemoor came running up a short while later.

She swung her long plait across her shoulder and blew a stray hair from her eyes as she entered.

"Warm day already isn't it, Annot?" I said.

She smiled and bobbed. "I've been chasing the chicks out, sir. They really don't want to be penned too late these light mornings. And I've been collecting the eggs and delivering them to the kitchen."

She flapped her hand in front of her pink face to waft the breeze across her forehead.

"Annot, your father....I know that he was a rather troublesome man and that he had no particular friends...."

"No sir, none in the village."

"Do you know if he knew anyone from the village of Whittonditch?"

Annot blinked. "Whittonditch? That's quite a long way from here, isn't it?"

"Out towards Ramsbury, yes."

"Where the poor man who was found in the wood barn came from, sir?"

"Yes, Annot. Though I doubt if your father will have known him for he was a tied man and never left his lord's villages, but your father ranged quite far into the forest in his job. He may have met someone there with whom he struck up a friendship..."

"Friendship sir. Da?"

"Well, acquaintance then?"

"I don't rightly know. I don't know of anyone....you don't mean..." she stepped further into the room and whispered, "a woman, sir, do you?"

"Is this something you suspect, Annot?"

The girl giggled. "No sir, not really. What woman besides me mam would have put up with him?"

"Well, man or woman. Just someone whom he might have met in the forest. He was seen going into the Whitehill Copse when really he had no need to be there. There was no work going on there of which he was a part. John Brenthall tells me that your father went missing a few times when he should have been at work. Do you know where he went and why?"

Annot shook her head. "No sir. I cannot fathom why he should not have been at work. He had no one to visit. No family left alive anywhere." She caught her lip with her teeth. "I do know that Master John has had to fine him for not working properly some days. He was in a bad mood and took it out on us, on those days."

"Yes, I've no doubt he did." I passed my hand over my face. "Ah well...it was just an idea. I wondered if you'd seen him with anyone who didn't belong here at the village."

Annot was about to turn to leave when I had a further thought.

"If I describe a man to you, Annot, can you recall if you ever saw your father in his company, anywhere around here?"

"I can try, sir. I can't say as I watched my father much, especially lately when he was so bad tempered about Henry and me. I tried to avoid him as much as I could."

"I'm sure you did. The man I am trying to place, Annot, is of middle height, not weighty, balding with wispy ginger fair hair combed across his pate. He's clean shaven with a small squashed and mended broken nose and pale grey eyes. Last I saw him he was wearing a grey split cotte with a band of black stitching at the top. He also wears a blue cloak I'm told. His boots are black and he goes armed with sword and knife."

Annot looked up to the ceiling. "No, sir...I can't say that I recognise your man."

There was a slight shifting of air by the door hole and Henry came into view.

"Annot might not know him sir, but I do," he said confidently.

*****

I sat up straighter. " Eavesdropping Henry?"

Henry looked a little sheepish, "Well yes, sorry sir, but I wanted to know why you needed to talk to Annot, m'lord."

"So, you know him, Henry?"

"Well...not know him, but I have seen him and I do know who he is but I haven't spoken to him, sir. I've heard his name is Foreman."

"How do you know him?"

"I've seen him in town with his master and now and again he's ridden through the village on his way to Ramsbury."

"Alone?"

"Yes. Though I did wonder what he was doing coming this way. I knew he was a Whittonditch man. I heard them talking in Master Fletschier's place."

"No, he wouldn't come this way from Marlborough to Ramsbury, he'd go through Mildenhall....much more direct," I confirmed.

"So why did he come this way, sir? To speak to Annot's father?"

"Did you see them together?"

"Never, m'lord."

"Hmmm."

"He always looked...well...a bit shifty to me, sir. He kept looking back over his shoulder as he ambled along. Never in a hurry, always just taking his time, looking round."

"Did you see him the day Bardol was killed, Henry?"

"No, sir. I would have said when asked about strangers in the village."

"Nor when Oswald of Knighton met his end?"

Henry thought back to the day. "No, sir."

Annot shuffled her feet. "Do you think he is the man who killed my da, sir?"

"I think it's a possibility but without witnesses or a confession, I won't be able to apprehend him for it. I also think he killed the Whittonditch man Oswald of Knighton and possibly his master the Lord Garner."

"Three people!" cried Annot, her eyes huge in her face. "Oh that is very wicked."

"The trouble is, I cannot work out why. Why he should have wanted to kill your father…?"

"Wedgemoor was very unpleasant, sir, do you think it was a case of Bardol just became too irritating?' offered Henry. " And the man's patience snapped?"

"One might give him a buffet, as we know some have done in the past..."

Annot giggled, "Oh yes. I remember the time that..." She giggled again tossing her head from side to side in merriment. "He had a beautiful black eye."

"But kill someone just because they irritate you, Henry? No. It's a more serious offence I think; and why would Foreman have business with Wedgemoor? No, I can't work it out...why your father Annot, why Oswald, why Garner?"

Henry thought for a moment and put his head on one side. "Well, I can think of something they all had in common."

"Oh?"

"Gardens sir. Annot tells me that her father was bringing home flowers for a month or so before he was killed. This Lord Garner had a superb garden, didn't he, which the man Foreman guarded like the dragon guards his gold and Hal tells me that this Knighton man was set to work in the garden. Plants sir. That's what they all have in common."

I saw again in my mind's eye, the pot of roses on the table at the Wedgemoor home the day the man was found dead. I explored in my memory the walled garden owned by the Lord Garner and recalled Foreman leaning nonchalantly on some sort of pillar by the garden wall. His face had worn a smug expression as if he knew we were missing something. I remembered I'd noticed a leather flask attached to his belt. Was this the origin of the two beakers of ale?

I replayed in my head, the strange conversation Hal and I had had with the Knighton villein. It must have been important even if it made no sense to us.

"I think I need to make another journey to that garden, Henry. There's no one there now to forbid it. Not Foreman, not Garner and not his son, I hear. Yes, a further visit to Whittonditch. But first a trip to Crofton... and dinner."

Chapter Seven

Tuesday dawned misty and cool but the sun would soon burn off the haze and warm us. I led the way with Hawise and Lydia following and Felice with an exuberant Simon and a steadying Evisa in the back of a small cart. Hal drove the horses and we were followed, on their rounceys, by Peter Devizes and Stephen Dunn, my two men at arms. I kept them at the castle should I need to call upon them if the King were to summon me to war. They were part of the garrison there. The birds chirruped, warbled and whistled around us and the forest was alive with blackbird, hedge warbler and chiffchaff song. I amused myself imitating them as we clopped along and Simon, giggling at my antics, tried his own version.

Yes, Paul, I am rather good at bird calls...or I used to be. Fewer teeth now you see, with which to whistle. I must say you sound like a bird yourself with that whistling chest. Better get that seen to when you're back at the priory I think.

The manor of Crofton came into view with the family standing in the forecourt, (for this was not an enclosed and walled manor like our own). A few people of the village saw us approaching and cheered, for though Percy was their immediate lord, I was their overlord and I liked to think that they appreciated a visit from their ultimate master.

After some time of greetings and embracings and the stowing away of Peter and Stephen in the kitchen where they too would feed well, we all sat down to meat in the hall.

"This is good beef, Percy." I said, spearing yet another piece on my knife and putting it onto the plate I shared with Lydia. "You are going to tell me this is home reared aren't you?"

Percy chuckled. "Yes as you know we do raise good beef cattle here but no, this was bought specially in your honour. Master Philbert Fleshmonger in Marlborough supplied this."

"Percy deemed our own beef not good enough for you, Sir Aumary," said Frida, his wife.

"I...we..are honoured." I bowed my head. "And the sallet?"

"From our very own garden, yes."

"I'm impressed, Percy."

"Pah..he spends far too much time locked in his garden, my lord!" chuckled Frida. "We are all quite forgotten in the season. In winter we see more of him but now...."

"Oh tush, wife," said Percy good naturedly, "can a man not get away from the clamour of manor, wife and children for a bit of peace amongst his flowers?"

"I thought this was a garden created for Frida, Percy," I said chuckling. "Now I find you spend more time there than she does."

Percy harrumphed..

"We hope we shall be able to see this garden of yours. Hawise is very interested, aren't you sweetling?"

"I am?" Hawise pursed her lips, "Oh yes...I am yes..."

"And I have a puzzle to set before you Percy, which..."

"One of your murders? Oh no. I'm sure I won't be able to help you with those."

"Well, it involves a garden; plants. And you with your mind on green things might be able to throw some light on the matter."

"I doubt it...but I'll try. Shall we have the next remove Frida? Now this is especially fine, for I had this beast brought from Pewsey. The biggest boar you ever did see."

"Poaching in the forest, Percy?" I said in a shocked tone.

Sir Percival Crofton chuckled. "My own bit of land at Pewsey and my own woodland. Not yours, Aumary."

We tucked into slices of roast boar, a meat we rarely ate at Durley except at Christmas.

Percival regaled us with the tale of how he'd located and killed the beast.

Frida laughed loudly. "Every time he tells the tale, the boar gets bigger, the distance gets shorter and the spear longer!"

Percy too, chuckled. "Ah well, if a man can't tell a grand tale about how he slew a large pig, then what is to be done, eh?"

And so it went on until the late afternoon.

"We must think of returning soon," I said, "But first your garden...?"

Percival rose and gestured that we accompany him outside. His hall building, unlike our own, was all on ground level and he led us a short distance to a stand of trees behind the manor buildings.

The orchard marched away; trees in serried rows, off to a cob wall in which was an open door. I hadn't been in this orchard for a good few years. Trees which had been small when I was a lad of eleven, were stately and aged now. As we walked I told Percy of the visit of the King's gardeners and what was being done with Southfield.

"Aye, it's a crying shame that the town must lose their field, Aumary. I'll not say that a garden isn't the most wonderful thing on earth mind you, but Marlborough people, I hear, feel strongly about the field being taken."

"They do. Enough to riot and attack the workers."

"No! You don't say? I had no idea."

I told him about the fighting and how the gardeners had taken refuge in the church.

"That bad, eh?"

I was waved through the door, which was studded with nails and as sturdy and thick as our manor house door.

"I have seen another much like this at Whittonditch - the garden of the man Jacques Garner...do you know him, Percy?" I said, running my hand along the oak.

"Garner? No. Heard of him of course. Whittonditch isn't so far away that I don't know of him. He too has a garden, has he?"

"He did. It's masterless now. He was murdered in Marlborough High Street in front of dozens of people and no one saw the deed."

Percy shook his head. "My, oh my! We live in such dangerous times. No one is safe. Not even with folk like you in charge eh? What was it, a theft gone wrong, a brawl...?"

"That's just it, I don't know. I can think of no reason why the man should be singled out."

"Here we are then," said my friend as he pushed the door further back into the green space.

The garden stretched away with gravel paths and raised beds surrounded by small wattle fencing. Different shapes had been created in the soil and turf benches were raised by the wall for sitting on. I wandered to the middle.

"All this in - how many years, Percy?"

"I started it seven years ago but it was obviously much smaller. I am learning as I go along for there are few to teach what you need to know."

"You should go into Marlborough and speak to Master Green, the King's gardener. I'm sure he is a veritable treasure chest of knowledge."

"I'm sure he is," said Percy as he turned away to the right. I followed. Frida with Lydia, came after us, nattering and Hawise and Jos brought up the rear. Evisa had chosen to stay in the house with Simon, Alfred and Felice.

Hal was dawdling outside the door looking at the trees in the orchard. He remembered them too, as infant saplings.

"Come, let's walk this path," said Percy.

I stared about me in amazement. Beds of lavender punctuated others of flowers I had never seen and of which didn't know the names.

"What's this, Percy?"

Percy stooped and picked a yellow daisy-like flower and crushed it in his fingers.

"Smell....have you never smelled this in preparations that your good Doctor Johannes or maybe Gabriel Gallipot has made?"

"What is it?"

"Calendula or Mary's gold."

He dropped the crushed petals into my hand. "Smell."

I dipped my head. "Yes indeed. I've smelt it in preparations for skin ointment, made by Gabriel."

My eye was swept upwards by a tall plant, twelve feet high with huge blooms growing up the stem. The leaves were large and lobed and the flowers the colour of the wild forest strawberry, a dark pink, thin and like soft vellum to the touch.

"What on earth is that?"

"*That* is a holy hoc....don't ask me how it got its name. I'm told it comes from the Holy Land so maybe that's why it's so called. They flower forever and are such lovely plants. So easy to grow."

I strode away to the wall. "Ah now that one I *do* know. That we find in the forest don't we, Hawise?"

"Foxglove," said my daughter who had come up to me and put her hand into mine.

"And this one dada... Columbine."

"Yes, that's a forest flower too."

I turned about, "As are the roses. Mind you they aren't as magnificent as these. The flowers mainly just have single petals."

"The first crusaders brought this kind of rose from the Holy Lands," said Percy, cupping one of his pink specimens in his hand, "They've crossed with the native flowers to produce different kinds of roses. This one has a lavender rose scent. Smell."

Hawise bent to smell. "Ooh yes." Her eyes rose to the wall. "And this one... ooh this one is huge. Much bigger than the rest."

"Yes, as I said the crusaders brought new versions for us to grow and look at. This one is one such. It's known as the Rose of Damascus. The Damascena rose."

"Isn't that what perfume is made of, Uncle Percy?"

"It is indeed, my knowledgeable and clever young lady."

"Are you going to make perfume then?" she giggled.

Before Percy could answer, Hal came up and grinned. "No, 'e's goin'a cover his dinner guests in petals, i'n't 'e m'lord."

I laughed out loud at him and then, of course I had to tell the story of the Emperor of Rome who, it was said, had done just that.

As I told the tale, we wandered to and fro.

Hawise ran off. “Look! I think this one is a lily.”

“Mind it doesn’t stain you, little one,” shouted Percy. “It’s used as a dye and the colour is a devil to remove from clothes.”

“I won’t touch,” said my daughter, pointing. “Where does that go?”

Another door, smaller than the main entrance was set in the side wall.

“Oh that’s the boring bit, my girl!” said Percy lifting Hawise from her feet and swinging her round. “That’s where I keep the rubbish! Shall we throw you over the wall so you land on my plant midden? It’s just about there behind the wall.”

Hawise giggled as he swung her round again. “Noooo.”

Hal tried the door. It was locked.

“I have tools and poisons to destroy vermin there, Hal,” said Percy, setting Hawise down. “I keep it locked just in case.”

He took Hawise by the shoulder and ran with her up the gravel path.

“Now how about a plant you can eat...plucked straight from the bush eh?”

Hawise laughed in delight as they stopped in front of a little bush no taller than my knee.

Percy grabbed a handful of the little white flowers and stuffed them into his mouth smiling all the while; Hawise did the same, grinning.

“Hahaha,” she laughed. “It’s anise. I know that one.”

We left them tasting other plants and crushing them in their fingers and wandered off, Hal and I, to the end of the garden wall.

The path turned and to my amazement there across it, was an arch.

An arch made of basket weave. Several of them at intervals marching in a row across and down the path.

I stood underneath the first one.

Roses of a dark pink variety spiralled up the side.

“I’ve seen these before, Hal,” I said in a serious tone. “At the basket weavers in Marlborough... only as drawings but nevertheless, the same. Master Maunder told me he’d made none like them and yet here they are....”

Hal parted the greenery. “Yep. Made like a basket would be.”

"Maunder swore he's made none and that they were a new thing to him. Garner brought him the drawings the day he died."

Hal looked confused. "Maybe he'd seen the ones here?"

"Percival says he didn't know Garner."

"Well then…."

I raised my voice over the babble of my daughter and my friend.

"Percy...these arches? Who made them?"

He came ambling up the path then, with Hawise in tow.

"Ah, my own design, these. The man in Pewsey made them. Good aren't they?"

"I've seen the like before."

"No, no, my friend, you can't have done," said Percy, chuckling, "I drew these out with my own fair hand and got the basket man in Pewsey to make them...oh about four years ago I'd say."

"Four years ago?"

"You can tell they 'in't new, sir," said Hal, rubbing his hand along the upright. "They'm wearing a bit with the weather."

"Took four years for this rose to clamber up to this height, Aumary," said my friend with a puzzled expression.

"And yet I saw the same thing in the basket makers in Marlborough not a few days ago. A drawing like you made, no doubt. Did your man in Pewsey perhaps pass on your idea to The Lord Garner?"

"I'd have his head if he did," said Percival, folding his arms across his chest. "It's my design and my creation."

"And yet Garner went to ask the weaver to make something similar.....nay exactly the same, the day he died."

Sir Percival Crofton's face creased in puzzlement and he shook his head.

"Maybe he saw them at the weavers. Though I asked him to make none for anyone else, I paid him enough to do that too. Pah! I'll have words with him when I see him next."

I sighed. "It's a mystery but I suppose you're right. The man couldn't keep it to himself." But my brain said silently 'Why go to another weaver to have them made up and why wait four years?'

"It's of no matter now since they'll never be made." I didn't tell Percival that Master Maunder had said he might have a go at making one just to see how it might turn out.

*****

We wandered a little further up and down the beds of flowers and then we made our way out of the main door and walked slowly down the orchard.

"You may not have heard, Percy, but Garner's man Foreman, lies sore hurt at Johannes."

"What happened?"

"Kicked in the head by Gabriel Gallipot's great horse."

"Ah, unfortunate but from what I hear, it's no more than he might deserve."

"Aye, he's not a man that one could grow fond of."

"A bully, I've heard, responsible for more than one or two beatings."

I nodded.

"Will he live?"

"It's unsure and if he does, it's likely he'll be a cripple for the rest of his life."

"God works in perplexing ways sometimes."

We walked on.

"Tell me, Percy, why would a man like Garner who wasn't particularly interested in the forest, visit a glade over and over and try to wrench the land from the Belvoir estate by foul means or fair? I told you one of my tied villeins was seen visiting the same coppice when he'd no need to go there. This place seems to draw folk to it like a bear to honey. Any ideas why?"

Percy strode down the avenue of fruit trees.

"What's there then, Aumary? Someone found gold there eh?" and he laughed, his voice echoing around the trees.

"Nothing but a wild rose, some twining woodbine and few coppiced trees. I can think of nothing special."

Percy threw his arm over my shoulder. "Then no doubt, there is nothing. Maybe your peasant was meeting a woman there. Wouldn't be the first to couple in the wild open air, eh? And Garner, well.....he was, I've heard, a strange one. Wouldn't put anything past him."

"Like magic?"

"Magic?" Sir Percival Crofton laughed till he grabbed his sides and said they ached. "Magic? Well, if it was magic, he's gone to the devil now," and he drew off laughing on the path down the avenue of trees, my daughter and his son skipping gaily behind him.

*****

All the way home I mused on the arches at Percival's. Was this just a case of independent creation? Had two men interested in gardens come up with the same idea, individually, four years apart? I bewailed the fact that I hadn't asked Percy if he still had his drawings. Were they the same that were supplied to Master Maunder? Had Garner, unbeknown to Percy, stolen them somehow? Had Foreman obtained them?

We reached home just as supper was about to be served and I fell gratefully into my bed replete and tired, and I dreamed of flower gardens and arches made of tall men leaning across paths their arms clasped and full of roses.

Next day Hal and I journeyed to yet another garden. The housekeeper of Garner's estate made no demur and with a stony face fetched the keys for the door in the thatched wall. She said nothing but her look said, 'whatever do you hope to find there? Foolish men.'

We pushed open the door and stood in the entrance. Today no one was working here. It was oddly quiet and just a little ghostly, knowing that the man whose creation it was, was lying in the church crypt in Marlborough awaiting transportation to his burial place at the church in Ramsbury. Hal strode into the middle of the five paths which radiated out from the central bed and circled, keeping his eyes trained to the eight foot wall.

"Just the same as it was....only some plants are dyin', sir."

"Yes, Hal. There doesn't seem to be much difference. Let's walk around the wall like we did before."

"One difference."

"Oh?"

"We 'in't got that Foreman chap grinning at us like a gargoyle."

"No indeed. Speaking of Foreman, we must go to Johannes' and find out if the man still lives."

"There's the same plants here that Sir Percy has in his garden."

"Bound to be Hal. I suspect they all come from the same sources." As I said it, my mind lit up with the thought, 'where do they all come from?'

"I must ask Master Green where the plants come from. He will know."

"Some of them are different. I di'n't see this one at Crofton," said Hal.

"Ah. That's Fennel. I know that one. I've seen Matthew Cook pound the seeds to a powder."

We walked slowly around the walls. There had been no removing of the dead flowers for a while since Garner had died. The roses were looking a little forlorn as they came to the end of their flowering.

Hal looked up.

"Has that plant escaped then, Sir Aumary?"

"Hmm?"

I looked up where Hal pointed. A prickly stem waved about in the breeze at least a foot outside and over the top of the wall.

"It's a briar, Hal. In the wilderness beyond. Nothing to do with the garden."

"Then what's this?"

Two feet from the wall stood the stone plinth upon which Foreman had been leaning as we toured the garden the first time. We had totally missed the low narrow door which had been hidden by his body, the bushes and the stone work.

Hal took a step back. I tried the door. It was unsurprisingly, locked.

Although it was small, no more than five feet tall, it was sturdy and again with the iron nails driven into the surface. Why would anyone want a door like this to a garden? It wasn't a fortress.

"Allow me, sir," said Hal as he flexed his leg and kicked the door. It rattled but stayed firm.

I saw my old friend's face as he hopped back in pain. "Damn door.....beggin' yer pardon, sir."

"We need something to lever it with, Hal."

"Wait!" he said as he fiddled in his purse. "This looks big enough to take this one. There's two keys and they 'in't the same. I thought they were, but no."

The second key, one very similar to the main door key, was inserted into the lock. It was harder to turn but turn it did and we heard it click as the lock fell. It was accompanied by a strange twanging sound.

What made me take great care before bowing my head and entering the space beyond I will never know but before I did, I took hold of a discarded log from one of the partly dismantled beds and slowly pushed open the door.

Immediately there was a swishing sound and an axe came falling blade first, to embed itself in the log.

Hal whistled. "We 'in't supposed to go in 'ere are we?"

"No, and keep your eyes open for any further traps. You never know."

I picked up another log and ran it around the door space. No further weapons came out at us and eventually, courage up, we stooped and entered the hidden garden.

I turned and looked at the space above the doorway. A weighted device had been installed on the wall. As the door was pushed open, it tripped a wire attached to a block of stone and down came the axe. Anyone with their heads through the door would have been decapitated.

The space, about thirty feet square was a walled enclosure tacked onto the large rectangle of the main garden. Here there were benches with pots; troughs of soil and cisterns of rain water; various tools for the gardeners use. Here too were wooden poles driven into the ground and plants trailed up them which were held with strings wound round nails much as my own rose in Durley was trained up the manor wall. Twelve feet tall, they looked like crucified men with their arms outstretched. I shivered.

I say plants. All these plants without exception, were roses, but roses without flowers.

"What's this then?" said Hal, looking round. "Why's these gotta be away from the rest? What's so special about 'em?"

"I don't know Hal. Carefully. Don't touch anything. Watch where you step." We walked further into the space.

In some of the small pots, tiny plants were growing, just a few leaves, others had shrivelled and died. One benchtop was covered with those red pods of the rose plant, hips. Many of these were split in half, some were empty of seeds altogether. Many were dried up and mouldering.

Two small curved knives lay on another bench top. Pots, some full of some strange powder littered the shelves. A midden of discarded greenery was piled up in the nearest corner. Weeds grew up the legs of the benches.

"Doesn't look like this was for show does it, sir?"

"Quite the contrary, Hal, a secret space. But for what?" I picked up a few rose centres; just the middles denuded of their petals which had been tossed away on the bench.

Hal shivered "Magic sir? Like Oswald said?"

I smiled. "No...not magic. I don't think anything magically sinister was enacted here. Do you know, I have an idea that Master Green should see this place. He will be able to tell us what goes on, I think."

Hal had made his way to the discarded plant pile. Layer upon layer of rose petals, browned, dried and crinkled littered the top of the pile.

"Why would anyone want to throw away the 'eads?" asked my old man at arms. "I thought that's what flowers was all about. The pretty 'eads." He let the fading blooms trickle through his fingers.

"I don't know, Hal. Come. Let's go, there's nothing more to see."

Suddenly and with an echoing clang, the door to the little garden shut with force and the key was turned in the lock.

Hal had left the key in the keyhole on the further side.

In two strides we were at the door but I knew even before I tried it that it was shut fast.

And that we were locked into this eerie and mysterious space.

*****

Hal quickly looked around for another door.

"No other way in or out, sir."

"Now, who has followed us here, Hal, and why?"

My man at arms shrugged. His eyes raked the top of the wall. I knew he was looking for an enemy with a bow or crossbow. Here we were totally vulnerable for there was no cover, nothing behind which we might hide. Even if we had upended the benches, they were only two feet deep and wouldn't afford us much protection, even if we lay flat on the ground.

"I reckon as we'd be safer up by the further wall, sir," said Hal, gesturing with his arm. "If I remember right, the plants on the other side are thick and prickly and it won't be too easy to 'oist yerself up fer an attack."

We backed quickly to the wall which divided the main garden from this space, watching the wall top above us for an attacker, but none came.

We waited.

"Think we're safe, Hal?"

"Aye I reckon he's gone." As if for confirmation we heard the main gate bang shut.

"I still got the key. Even if he locked it with another key, we can get out the main plot."

"The only way out of this garden, Hal, is up and over the wall."

Hal was peeping through the keyhole of the diminutive door. "'E's left the key in the lock."

I looked round at the benches.

"Right, let's drag this one to the wall and clamber up. It's tall enough to get you over the top."

We pulled the nearest bench, which was waist high to the wall's edge and hoisted it on edge. I gave Hal a leg up and onto the bench end and unsteadily he clambered up and over the wall. I heard him slither down and jump the final few feet. There was a rustling, a curse, then the door rattled.

"Hal?"

"Oh 'tis all right, Aumary," came his disgruntled tones, "Just a bloody great prickly bush the other side."

The key rattled in the lock and we were free.

We raced for the main gate and threw it open to see a figure in blue rounding the final set of trees of the orchard. He didn't look back but ran on at a pace.

As we came out onto the main road through the village, we heard a horse being ridden away at a frenzied speed, though we could see nothing round the bend. He had been too far ahead of us.

"Damnation!" I shouted out in frustration.

"Beezulbub's balls!" yelled Hal, squirming to right and left. "I reckon I got an arse fulla arrers."

I turned in alarm.

There in the seat of his braies were several large thorns of the blackthorn bush.

"I expect Johannes will have a salve for that, Hal," I said laughing.

"Well, it 'in't funny. How'm I supposed to ride 'ome with an arse fulla prickles?"

*****

Ride home we did with Hal grimacing at every lump and bump of the road.

I'd managed to get most of the thorns from his rump but he would need Johannes with his tweezers to extract the final ones. I knew what blackthorn was like. It would quickly fester.

I remember the last thing I said to him as we parted, was that he should go to his room in the manor wall and I would go up to the hall.

"Well, we know one thing at least?"

"Oh..?"

"Our follower cannot have been Foreman, he's lying in Johannes' sickroom with his head bandaged, unless he's made a miraculous recovery and managed to jog to Whittonditch on his horse."

"I doubt it."

"No. So who was it, Hal?"

"I dunno. But when I get 'old'a 'im, 'is backside'll be red raw so it will and that's a promise!"

*****

Thursday saw us travelling back to the town to check on Foreman.

Once in his workroom we told Johannes the tale of the strange enclosure at Whittonditch. He took pity on poor Hal and extracted the final thorns from his backside and salved it.

Foreman was still lying on the pallet. He was alive, said the doctor, but he reiterated that he would never quite be the same again. The man had been kicked at the front of his head. He was lucky to survive at all, said Johannes, but he no longer seemed to perfectly understand what was said to him. He looked puzzled at the things around him and could not seem to organise his movements correctly. His facial expressions were blank as if he had lost the ability to show how he felt.

"He flails around when trying to eat, for example," said Johannes. "The finer movements seem difficult for him. Wee Agnes has to feed him still. Like a baby."

"And you say he doesn't understand what you say to him?"

"He seems to understand some things. He did manage to make a confession of sorts and has had absolution from Father Torold."

"How, if he cannot speak?"

"He can speak slowly in monosyllables, not always intelligible and I think that there was a lot of prompting from the priest, lots of yesses and nos."

"Will he walk again or be able to do those things he once did?"

"With practice perhaps, but as I said, I doubt he'll truly be the man he was before. He is, after all, lucky to be alive."

I looked over at the sleeping man. "I suppose rest is the thing he needs most."

"That and a helpful person to do for him those things he can't. He sleeps a great deal, it's true. But when he wakes I set him to small tasks which I think might help him to regain a few skills."

"Such as, Johannes?"

Johannes gestured to a pile of cloths sitting on the table. "I get him to sit - that is difficult in itself, his balance doesn't seem to hold him up for long but I prop him up on pillows, then I ask him to pick up those kindling sticks and move them from one pile to another. And I got him to fold these cloths over and over."

"He finds that difficult?"

"At first, as I said he flailed around and he had no idea of the sequence involved. Then as time progressed he seemed to be able to concentrate and make a fist of doing it, though he can't fold straight. It's very interesting. It's as if he is relearning those things we take for granted. He was like a small child grabbing with no finer movements. Now he manages with effort to concentrate on using his fingers but he is still poor at it."

I bent over the sleeping man and peered at the bandaged wound. "So the bit of the head which was staved in has something to do with his fingers?"

"I wish I could tell, Aumary," said Johannes coming up behind me. "Damage there nearly always results in poor movement and confusion about things. I've seen it before. That's if the person doesn't die of course. They mostly do."

I looked back at Johannes, "So why didn't he?"

The doctor came closer to me and whispered. "Because I lifted the bone from the brain beneath so that it did not press on it and drained the fluid building up there. But you didn't hear that from me."

"You can do that?"

"I have never done it before, but I have seen it done and, yes, it saves lives. It saved him."

"My ears are deaf, Johannes, you know that," I smiled. "And you know that Hal is as deaf as a dead man."

Hal grinned at me.

"Foreman won't remember. He was out of his body."

"And Little Agnes will say nothing...even if she could," I added.

Doctors like Johannes had to be very careful, for some of their practices were considered devilish. Were it known that he had performed surgery such as this, he could be at best drummed out of town, at worst stoned to death. In fact physicians such as he, were not supposed to perform surgery at all. That was to be left to the barber surgeons.

"Watch it, sir," said Hal quickly "The devil is opening his eyes."

Foreman did indeed open his grey eyes. He blinked and yawned feebly, like a kitten and then focussed on me. There was no recognition in the look. The face was blank now, no fear or terror in the expression as there had been at first.

"Sir Aumary Belvoir, Foreman," I said slowly. "How do you feel now?"

The eyes roved around again, took in Johannes' face. Ah, yes! Here there was recognition.

The man's mouth opened but no sound was uttered.

"Can you sit?"

Foreman blinked and slowly he tried to raise himself. The movements were jerky and uncoordinated. I eased him up with a hand behind his shoulder and he managed to swing his legs from the bed. Once upright, he fought to stay there, wavering and swaying until he almost toppled sideways. Hal pulled him back upright. Johannes stuffed a pillow to his side.

"I think he will regain balance one day but when, I can't say."

"And walk..will he walk?"

"He might. Again with practice. I don't have the time to devote to his practising, Aumary. Soon he'll have to be moved somewhere."

"Back to Whittonditch?"

"If that's possible, I suppose. It is, after all, his home."

"It seems there's no one there who misses him. In fact I think if he were to be returned there, folk would see to it that one dark night he disappeared without trace. He's not popular there at all."

"Ah no."

"Will the priory not take 'im in, sir?" said Hal, "jus' till he gets on 'is feet and stuff."

"I suppose it's a possibility," I said. "They have an infirmary and lay staff to care for the sick and infirm."

"I'll ask Prior Alexander," said Johannes. "He's helped out before."

The Priory of St Margaret of Antioch lay with its front door on the High Street. Gilbert Cordwainer lived in a house which abutted their northern wall. Their grounds were extensive and took up a whole swathe of land from Figgins Lane almost to Crooks Lane and was bounded by the River Kennet on its southern border.

"Let me know Johannes." I slapped him on the back. "We're away to the castle now."

I turned in the doorway.

"And thank you and… well done," I smiled.

*****

We walked our horses back to the castle and Hal took them to the stables.

"All quiet, Maurice?" I asked the duty officer.

"Yes, Sir Aumary. The gardeners are out on Southfield with a contingent of my men to protect them as you requested. There's been a bit of jeering as folk pass by but nothing sinister."

"Good."

"You have a visitor. He's waiting in the guardroom.

FitzAlan roared, "Bunce! Where's the Lord Belvoir's visitor?"

"Here sir," said a voice. I furrowed my brow in puzzlement as I turned from unlocking the door to my office. I recognised the tones.

Into the sunshine, beams of which were slanting through the wide opening of the castle gateway came a bearded figure wearing a blue cloak. The man looked as if he hadn't slept for days.

I squinted against the sunlight.

"Congyre!"

"Yes, m'lord." The man licked his lips. "I can't stand it any longer. My mind is made up. I have come to make confession to you," he said.

Chapter Eight

I took in his words but they didn't register until I had fully unlocked the door and ushered him into my room.

"Confession, Congyre?"

"Aye, m'lord. It's been playing on my conscience. Keeping me awake at night."

"Confessions are made to priests, Congyre. I cannot..."

"I have already made my confession before God, sir. I need to let you know.... what...what it is I have done." He seemed to screw up his face behind his long beard. "It was a wicked thing to do and I must pay the penalty for it."

"Come. Sit and tell me what you want me to know." The man looked so worried that I feared he would burst into tears.

I closed the door behind him but not before I had seen Hal come back from the stables and begin to engage the guard Bunce in conversation outside the gatehouse. He caught my eye and I swivelled my gaze to Congyre nodding once in his direction. Hal understood me perfectly and jogged up to the door to position himself outside to listen and to prevent disturbance.

I looked Congyre over. His whole body shook as if what he was about to say was eating into him.

"Sit down, Sherwyn."

The man groped for the seat in front of him and lowered himself onto it.

"I am sorry, sir, that I was so obstructive when you came to see me that day."

"I did know that you hadn't told me the whole truth, but I felt your story was better coming from you in the fullness of time. You aren't a bad man; of that I'm sure. You are my father-in-law's brother. He was a good, good man. The acorn does not fall too far from the oak, Sherwyn."

"No sir. You're right. I am not a bad man, but I was led astray by one...."

"Garner?"

"How did you...?"

"Whittonditch and Chilton are not that far apart that you cannot have known the man, Sherwyn."

"No sir. Just three miles. We are....were....almost neighbours."

"So..." I leaned back in my chair and crossed my ankles. "Are you here to tell me that you killed Garner or to confess to the killing of your brother?"

Sherwyn Congyre paled. "I..."

I shook my head. "No, I think not, Congyre. You don't have it in you. Of that I am sure."

Congyre crossed himself. "As Jesus died on the cross and rose again on the third day, I swear to you, I could not kill in cold blood, in that way."

"It's obvious, I think, by your speech that you know that the Lord Garner is dead?"

"Yes, m'lord. The whole of this part of the county must know it by now. The story has raced through the forest and over the downs like a wind fanned fire."

"Murdered in Marlborough High Street by a knife to the chest."

"Yes, sir." He looked down at his hands clasped tightly in his lap. "I swear to you I did not kill him."

I leaned forward. "Do you know who did?"

"No, m'lord."

I leaned back again. "So make your confession. I'm listening."

The man moistened his lips. "I knew the Lord Garner for many years. He was an avaricious and cruel master, a man who ruled with the sword and lash. There are many tales of him..."

"I've heard the stories. I know what sort of man he was."

"Then you will know he is not the sort of man to be..." He stopped and searched for a word, "to be thwarted, my lord?"

"I can imagine. He was a forceful man. I met him but twice and he struck me as the sort who ruled by fear. He was, I think, the kind who threatened and intimidated. Did he threaten and menace you, Congyre?"

"Not the man himself but his crony..."

"Foreman?"

"Aye, him. The Lord Garner would send out his bully with his men to frighten and coerce folk into thinking his way."

"I have Foreman under lock and key in Marlborough, Congyre. He'll no longer be a threat to anyone."

Congyre visibly brightened. "He burned down my barn last spring. He and his bullies. He threatened to burn down the house should I refuse his request."

"Hmmm. Do you have witnesses who can testify to this, Congyre. Reliable men?"

"I do, m'lord. Both to the threats and to the burning."

"Go on."

"He had heard that my brother was failing and he knew about our quarrel."

"Did he know Toruld well, Sherwyn?"

"I hadn't seen Toruld for ten years, sir. I don't know if they were well acquainted or not, but I cannot think that Toruld would countenance such a man...as a frie...."

"No. The Toruld I knew would have sent him packing, threats or no threats. He would have sought redress in the law."

"But he did know him for Garner came to Chilton himself one day and told me that should Toruld call for me in his last hours I was to go."

"So Toruld had told him in passing that should he be coming to the end of his life, he would wish to be reconciled with you, his brother?"

"It appears so, m'lord. However I have a feeling it was another's work. This telling."

"So why was Garner so interested in you and your brother making your peace?"

Congyre licked his lips again. "I was to take a document to the house. I was to remove Toruld's will which the Lord Garner told me was kept in a chest by the bed and substitute it with a new version..."

"One of his own making"

"Yes, sir. One naming him the beneficiary of certain areas of land in the forest."

"Why? Why did he want this land so badly, Sherwyn? How did he know where the will was kept? My father-in-law was not a loose tongued man. He would be especially guarded with such a creature as the Lord Garner."

Sherwyn Congyre looked down at his hands once more. "Why he wanted the land I do not know, but I have a feeling sir, that it was, forgive me m'lord, his own wife. The Mistress Evisa. She may have said more than she ought. I think it was Mistress Congyre who may have unwittingly let out the fact that Toruld wanted to see me and that the will was kept close by my brother's bed."

I nodded and wiped my hands over my face. "That is perfectly possible. Women gossip with women. I think I know a woman with whom she might have chattered. There was one at Garner's manor who visited Bedwyn often. I can see her passing on information. These things seem innocent at the time but...." I sighed. "Go on, Sherwyn."

"However it was accomplished, the facts were known and I was threatened with harm and my family and servants too if I didn't do as I was asked."

"And I suppose it seemed a small thing to do to avoid disaster?"

"Sir, if they burned us down, how would we recover? How would we manage? The farm is my life, sir. My family is my life. I would do anything to protect them."

"As would we all, Sherwyn."

"You cannot imagine how I agonised over it and when the summons came, I took the document with me and, wicked man that I am, I...." He put his head in his hands. "I left the new will and took away the old one."

"Where is it now?"

"I gave it to Foreman the next day when he came calling. Shortly after you did, my lord."

"And he will have given it to Garner. Hence his absolute assurance that day, when I met him in the forest, that the land belonged to him."

"And now he too is dead, sir. I swear to you...it was not I who killed him."

"The blood and hair we found under my father-in-law's nails Sherwyn... was this yours?"

"Yes sir. Oh, I am so ashamed." Once more he covered his face. "I spoke with my brother for a short while and gave him the kiss of peace. He lapsed into sleep and I thought it a good time to search for the will. It was not where the Lord Garner had said. The chest was empty. I panicked and began to search the bed. Suddenly with a surge of strength my brother reared up and grabbed me. I am unsure if he understood what I was about but he caught me here...."

He turned his face to the side and lifted his beard. There on the right hand side of his neck was a long scratch, healing now.

"He fell back and when next I looked, he was dead."

"No Sherwyn, he wasn't dead. It was shortly after you left the room that my father-in-law met his end."

Sherwyn's eyes grew round "I was not the cause of his death?"

"No, it was not you."

Tears filled his eyes then. "Oh Jesu...I had thought that my action had ended my brother's life. I had not meant to kill him sir, but...."

"You did not, Congyre."

He crossed himself again. "Thanks be to God. I could not live with that thought, my lord."

I stood and paced to my window. I looked out over the castle moat. "The will was lying on the table I'm told."

"It had been knocked to the floor and so I dropped the new one where it had lain, took it and tucked it in my cotte and fled the room."

I turned back to look at him and nodded. "That is where it was found."

"It will be somewhere at Whittonditch I suppose, now," said Congyre absently.

"It matters not," I said. "Garner will not and never would have profited by his actions. And as you say, now he is dead. You didn't kill him. Foreman did not kill him..."

"Are you sure of this sir?"

"As sure as I can be."

"So who did kill him, m'lord and why?"

I shrugged. "I have no idea - yet, Sherwyn."

I smiled at him and raised my voice, "Hal!"

The door bounced open and Hal stood there, steely eyed.

"Take Master Sherwyn to Harold the scribe, Hal. Get Harold to write down exactly what he has told me and then accompany him to his horse and see him off, will you?"

"Right you are, sir."

"And send a party of men to Whittonditch to look for the will of my father-in-law. It'll be there somewhere, if not destroyed. Minimum force but if they have to break open a chest or two....."

"Aye, sir."

Sherwyn looked up at me with liquid brown eyes. "You will not punish me for my part in..."

"You have punished yourself enough, Sherwyn," I said, "What agony can I put you through that you have not already visited upon yourself? You will bear this weight to your dying day. Go. Go and be with your family. As I said, you are a good man. I don't punish good men."

Sherwyn's Adam's apple bobbed as he swallowed back tears. He nodded into his beard, turned and pushed past Hal standing in the doorway.

My old retainer sighed.

"Another dead end then, sir?"

"Not quite, Hal," I answered.

*****

I turned once more and stared out at the moat. I could just see a corner of Southfield through my narrow window. Men were busy with barrows and pickaxes. The scrubby bushes to the edge of the field up at the back of the buildings facing Figgins Lane were being grubbed up. I saw Master Olivier Green, his head still bandaged and leaning on a stick, waving his arms about, whilst a young boy, the same one who had held him up in St. Peter's church, stood behind him watching carefully and holding a large piece of parchment.

Snatches of shouted conversation came up to me but I couldn't hear properly what was being said.

Sounds from the bailey of the castle filtered in through my open door. I yawned. My belly grumbled.

Yes, I must eat some dinner and then I would go out to Southfield and talk to Master Green about visiting the garden at Whittonditch as I'd planned.

A body passed the door quickly. I yelled. "Jem, can you see if you can get me something to eat from the kitchen?"

The youthful soldier whom Bunce had set to guard the door of Johannes' workroom whilst Foreman was recovering, trotted back a few paces.

"Aye, sir. What might you like?"

"Oh, I'm not fussy. Just not their black bread, it's only fit for pigeons. Oh and no stew...I cannot stand any more gristly stew."

Jem chuckled. "Yes, sir."

As he prepared to leave I asked, "Jem, who is guarding Foreman now, if you're here?"

"I was relieved by Edouard Picot sir. He was at a loose end and said I could come back for some shut eye."

"Yes of course. You deserve it. You slept on a blanket in the corridor, I hear?"

"I did sir. Should the felon wake in the night," answered Jem. "If sleep was what I did, sir."

"Good man."

Jem danced off and was shortly back with four boiled duck eggs, some bread and two thick slices of mutton. Two small red and wizened apples and a flagon of ale completed the repast.

Jem laid the tray down on my table.

"I got enough for two, sir. Master Hal will be back in a moment, won't he?"

"He will, yes."

I sat down with a sigh and broke the bread in two.

"Thanks Jem, that will be all. Go now and get some rest."

Jem ruffled his curly dark hair and swayed uncertainly from foot to foot. "Sir..I..."

"Yes, Jem?"

"I know that you wanted to catch the man Foreman and question him but that..."

"He was injured before we could speak to him, yes?"

"You didn't get him to say anything, did you, sir?"

"No Jem, I didn't. Why?"

I took a bite of bread. My stomach grumbled again.

"It's just that....that night...when Father Torold was there..."

"He came again?"

"I was asleep in the corridor as I said, sir."

"And...?" I chewed.

"In the workroom, Foreman started to yell and scream." Jem came closer and lowered his voice. "There were no words I could understand, sir. Master Johannes, he came down the stairs in his shirt and unlocked the door and went in."

"Yes, Jem." I swallowed the bread.

"I stayed alert in case I might be needed."

"Good man."

"Then Little Agnes came and Dr. Johannes asked her to run for the priest."

"So Father Torold returned? What happened?"

"The doctor left the room and that was when Father Torold gave the man absolution, sir."

I put down the bread I'd been holding.

"And you heard what was said?"

"Yes sir....it wasn't what Foreman said...it was what Father Torold was repeating and trying to get out of Foreman. You know how loud his voice is, sir?"

I chuckled. "I do indeed. He is renowned for his booming bass voice, Jem. Everyone knows Father Torold's powerful tones."

"Sir...should I tell you...I'm not sure?"

"Tell me...?"

"What Foreman admitted to, in confession, sir?"

I shifted to the edge of my seat.

"That is up to you lad. I can't make you tell me. You know that a priest cannot tell anyone what his sinner has confessed to."

"I'm not a priest, sir. And it would help you, wouldn't it?"

"It would....it would greatly. But might it not be on your conscience? That you had confided a secret such as a dying man's confession to his priest? Hmmm?"

"But he isn't dying now, is he, sir? Doctor Johannes saved him. Oh he isn't a whole man, never will be, but it would be good if you knew what he said."

"If you feel you can tell me Jem, then that's good. If not..." I shrugged, "I will understand."

The lad squared his shoulders.

"This is how it went, sir," he said.

*****

July came in blustery and wet.

Some of the work on Southfields however, continued on boggy ground, amidst squelching mud.

Foreman continued to improve and with help began to totter around the work room at Johannes' house, clutching at the furniture. Soon he would be well enough to move to the priory. Even though it was still a struggle for the man to walk, Jem and Edouard by turns, guarded the room to make sure the man did not attempt to flee, nor anyone get to him. He was still to be charged with his crimes.

The swallows' young left their nests in the barns and buildings at Durley from the early part of July. We saw them in groups, twittering on the branches of the elder tree growing up the wall of the manor.

The berries had begun to form and Hubert Alder, our resident farrier, eyed them jealously, for he always made a sort of wine from the pressings.

The blackbird, with his sharp, bright yellow ringed eye, watched Hubert and judged when to make his swoop for it was always a contest between the two; who would get to the berries first, man or bird.

The rose growing up next to the elder began to form its hips. These were always eyed up greedily by the local thrushes and finches. Lydia did battle with these birds, for she liked to collect them and make a syrup of them which soothed the sore throats of winter.

Thinking about these two plants made me recall the glade which the Lord Garner and my villein, Bardol Wedgemoor had frequented. Naturally my inquisitive brain began to form questions again. Why was it so important? What was there in that meadow significant enough to break the law for? I must ask Master Green the gardener to come out there with me and tell me what he thought.

One miserable day in July when a watery sun was trying to break through the grey clouds, Hal and I rode late into Marlborough to meet with the King's master gardener.

He had dispensed with his bandage but still leaned on his stick, his faithful young acolyte by his side.

We found him standing on the road to Pewsey directing a party of men unloading stone for the walls of the garden. A small square shed made of planked wood had been erected on the south westernmost corner of Southfield. Here, I'm told, Master Green had his office and here he stored his plans and equipment.

Across the field, I saw my friend Percy clopping along between Southfield and the church on his nag Pebbles. I raised my hand and he saluted me and rode on.

"Master Green, Olivier. How goes it?" I asked, striding up the road, my eye on the overloaded cart.

"Ah, Sir Aumary. Good day to you. It would go better if these idiots could learn to pile stone a little more carefully."

"Ah yes. I see you've had a spillage."

"No one hurt but..."

"Frustrating for you."

The man chuckled. "Oh it's the least of my worries, I can assure you."

I looked back towards the castle.

"No more trouble with the townsfolk or apprentices?"

"No indeed. Thank you for your guards. They have made our task much safer."

I nodded once. "I think now you have come this far, there will be no further resistance."

Master Green looked towards the Heavens. "We now just need the weather to be on our side and we can move on apace."

"Sadly, sir, I have no control over that."

We both chuckled and for a while then, watched in silence, the building going on.

"Olivier. Might I ask you a favour? If you are feeling well enough, might you accompany me to a glade in the forest. I would like your professional opinion of it...."

Green's eyebrow flew up. "You wish to build a garden, Sir Aumary?"

"Oh no, nothing like that. The glade was frequented by two men who are now dead - murdered. I cannot for the life of me see what drew them both there. You, with your gardener's eye, might see something I have missed for both of these men, it seemed, were taken up madly with flowers and gardening."

"I suppose I might..."

"And then there is a strange garden belonging to one of the dead men. At the village of Whittonditch. Entirely encompassed by a wall, much like you're building here but with a secret space partitioned off from the main rectangle."

"Secret, Sir Aumary?"

"So secret, Olivier, that it was guarded by a trap which if Hal and I had not had our wits about us, would have taken off our heads with one swipe of an axe."

Master Green's eyes widened. I saw Hal pass a hand across the back of his neck as if he felt the bite of that axe.

"Oh my! This I think I must see."

"It's been used for some arcane practice or other, but for the life of me, I cannot fathom its use."

"Tomorrow then, if the rain holds off?"

I bowed slightly. "I will meet you with mounts and men, sir, shall we say at the second hour of the day, in the castle bailey?"

"That would suit, m'lord. I hope to have this situation under control by then and I'm sure my men can be left to continue without me for a short while." He looked round at Master Jardine who was red facedly trying to put some order into the mess that was the tumbled stone.

"Yes sir," said Jardine, "I'll bang a few heads together. That should do it."

And we all laughed together amicably.

Master Green put his hand to his head. "Oh... I think I might go home early. I do feel rather queer. Can you accompany me Alfonse?"

The young lad nodded.

"Till tomorrow then, Olivier," I said.

"God willing," he replied.

*****

Next day early I was walking back from the privy to my office at the castle when a cry from the main road by the end of St. Peter's church drew my attention. I peered through the opening of the gatehouse.

"M'lord.... Sir Aumary...!"

"It's Roger, Master Gallipot's apprentice, sir," said Hal, who was lounging in the guardroom doorway with a pot of ale in his hand.

"Journeyman now, I think, Hal," I answered, for Roger was now past his twenty first birthday and out of his apprenticeship as an apothecary.

"Ho Roger! What can I do for you?"

The man came puffing down the lane and slid on the loose chippings and mud of the road surface, churned up by the delivery carts travelling from Master Firmin's stone yard to Southfield. I made a grab to steady him.

"My master asks you to come quickly." He swallowed and took a huge breath.

"Something is happening at Doctor Johannes' house. It doesn't look good, sir."

My heart lurched and began to pound. "Injury, Roger?"

"I didn't see any to my master but I don't know for sure who is injured."

My heart failed to return to its normal place and pace.

"Lead on."

We ran up to the High Street and dodged the traffic going up and down the road. More than one fist was raised to us as we dashed between carts and round the rumps of horses.

Master Philbert Fleshmonger had several casks of goods before his shop and we swerved round these carefully so as not to upset them Finally we made the space by the slaughter pens and slowed.

I regained some breath. "Roger, is it safe to go straight in?"

"Master Gallipot is in there, sir."

"Alone?"

"Aye, sir. He sent me to you."

"Where is Doctor Johannes?"

Roger shrugged. "I don't know, sir."

"Little Agnes?"

Roger shrugged again.

I loosened my sword and took out my knife. Hal did the same.

"Roger, stay here."

Carefully I opened the front door. All was quiet.

I called out, "Gabriel?"

I was answered by his voice coming from just inside the workroom door, which was partly open. "Here, M'lord Belvoir."

I swung it towards the wall slowly, peering through the rather badly fitting hinges where there was a gap of at least half an inch. Nothing to be seen. No one was behind the door.

"Are you alone?"

"Sir Aumary. Here."

I looked back to Hal who nodded at me.

I took the door at a leap and threw myself into the room.

Gabriel was struggling to get a man onto Johannes' pallet in the corner.

"What's amiss, Gabriel?"

The apothecary turned. The front of his cotte was covered in blood.

Hal touched me on the shoulder. "Blood sir, all the way through here from the kitchen door."

"Gabriel, are you injured?"

The apothecary shook his head. "No. No...not me but..." He gestured to the bed.

Even though I knew by the lack of height and bulk that the man who lay there was not Johannes, my heart lurched again.

In two strides I was by the bed.

I looked down at the waxy face of my castle guard Edouard Picot. A huge red stain disfigured the front of his cotte.

"Foolish man," said Gallipot shaking his head. "Oh silly, silly man."

"What do you mean, Gabriel?"

Hal took the shaking and aged apothecary to a stool and seated him slowly.

"I came in to see Johannes about something," said Gallipot. "I found him. Slumped by the kitchen door. I think he must have opened the outer door."

"And Foreman gone?"

"No Johannes or Agnes."

"Agnes might be out at her marketin', sir," said Hal

"That is perfectly possible," I said.

"Can we do anything?"

"Oh no, Sir Aumary, there's nothing to be done," said Gabriel Gallipot. "Sadly, he's well and truly dead."

Foreman was nowhere to be seen.

Chapter Nine

I sighed and then ran my hand over my face. It came away sweaty and damp.

"Hal, can you check the rest of the house? I'll do the kitchen."

"Right you are, sir."

He turned on his heel and I heard him clomping up the stairs and travelling across floors.

"Gabriel, stay here. Don't move."

The old man took one of the folded pieces of material which Johannes had given to Foreman as a practice exercise and which had been lying on the table and mopped his brow. His shaking hand was bloodied. Picot's blood, but it had dried now.

I carefully moved to the kitchen. Hal was right. There was a trail of blood all the way from the kitchen door to the workroom door and beyond. Blood had sprayed out onto the whitewashed wall between the kitchen and the stairwell.

I carefully opened the door and looked in. It was deserted.

There were two empty bowls of food and two ale cups on the table.The back door was open and as I poked my nose out into the courtyard, I noticed the back gate was also open.

I checked the stable. Titus, Johannes' horse was still there - so he'd not ridden out on him. Mary the mule was close by.

I shut and locked the back gate and did the same with the kitchen door.

Hal came back into the kitchen.

"Not a soul. As empty as a spendthrift's purse, sir." He helped Gabriel from the workroom to a kitchen bench and went to pour him some ale.

"Agnes is no doubt out in the town. Johannes may have been called out on foot to see a patient."

"We 'ope so, sir."

"Do you think that Foreman struck down your guard, Sir Aumary?" asked

Gallipot, a little more colour coming into his face. He sipped the ale gingerly, still shaking.

I furrowed my brow.

"I know not what to think, Gabriel, When I last saw the man, he was just about able to put one foot in front of the other and stay upright. Holding a knife and thrusting it into Edouard's chest was not something I thought him capable of."

" 'E can't have gone far," said Hal. "Not with 'is gimpy legs."

"Why did you have him guarded, sir, if you thought him incapable of harming anyone?"

"For his own safety as much as anyone else's, Gabriel. He isn't the most popular of men. Someone might have taken it into their heads to get even with him, in his weakened state."

"So you think someone might have spirited him away?"

"To kill him? I doubt it. They would just have run a knife into him as he lay incapable on his bed here."

"And scarpered sir," added Hal.

"Yes Hal. And fled."

"So where is everyone?" asked Gallipot shakily.

"No one is in the yard but the back gate is open so someone has gone through it either to the road, through the alleyway or into the churchyard. We should have seen anyone coming through the front door onto Kingsbury Hill."

"I most certainly would," said the apothecary.

"Want me to 'ave a look out the back, sir?"

"Gabriel, can you stay here? If Johannes returns let him in. Or Agnes. Hal and I will be out in the churchyard."

It was then we heard a deal of shouting and yelling.

Hal cocked his head. "Coming from the church, sir."

We unlocked and raced out of the back door, unbolted the yard gate and rushed out into the alleyway which led to the churchyard of St. Mary. There we stopped to listen.

"Not Torold's voice," said Hal.

"No. It's not him. Where the devil is it coming from?"

"Not the church neither."

"I do believe it's from the tower, Hal."

As quickly but as carefully as we could, we entered the darkness of the church, through the western door. I called out to Father Torold but received no answer.

The noise above us continued unabated, dulled by the tons of stonework piled on top of us. I could make out no one's voice in particular.

We took the tower steps two at a time. This tower was taller than that of the church at Durley and it seemed an age before we exited onto the roof. We climbed higher and higher, holding our swords away from the stones of the wall.

When at last we came out into daylight, the sight that met our eyes was strange in the extreme.

To the eastern side of the tower roof and half lying, bleeding onto the tiles was Sherwyn Congyre.

Flattened to the southern edge of the parapet and bleeding heavily about the midriff, was my good friend Percival Crofton.

Above him and weighing him down was our man Foreman. Percy had hold of his upper arms.

With a huge gathering of strength, a fainting Congyre grabbed a piece of iron; it looked like a crowbar, which was lying on the rooftop and flung it at Foreman. His aim was poor, his strength ebbing. He fell back unconscious. The iron bar clanged ineffectually on the roof tiles.

Almost at the moment we entered the roof, Percy struggled to free himself from the grasp of Foreman. He swivelled around and off balance, the Whittonditch man wavered, flailed his arms and with an unholy and inarticulate scream, fell head first and backwards over the stonework at the top of the tower.

Percival wavered there too until I leapt over to him and grabbed him by his blue cotte.

He slid down to a sitting position on the tiles, his back to the stone parapet and slumped sideways.

"Aumary..."

"You're hurt. Where are you hurt?"

"Stabbed, he stabbed me."

I pulled up his cotte. There was a knife wound to his chest. The knife lay on the roof tiles somewhere near the door we had entered.

"Come. Lean on me. We'll get you to Johannes' though God knows where he's gone!"

I risked a look down to the ground.

Foreman lay in a confused mass of limbs. His head was cracked like an egg; brain and blood splattered the flagstones of the lane to the church door. I remember thinking. 'Johannes will not be able to mend that damage by lifting the bone from the brain matter now.'

As yet no one had reached the dead man.

I swallowed down bile and then tears sprang unbidden into my eyes. Not for Foreman of Whittonditch, but for my young son Geoffrey, the progeny of my first wife and myself, killed in his fifth year, nay murdered, by masonry flung from the gatehouse at Durley. I stepped back.

Hal looked up from his search of Sherwyn Congyre.

"This one's in a bad way too."

"Can you bring him Hal, or must we have help?"

"I can carry 'im. 'E's only a stick."

"Good man. Down we go."

*****

It seemed to take an age to get the wounded men down the church tower.

We exited the building by the southern door so as not to become tangled in the mess at the west wall that was Foreman of Whittonditch and staggering, we made the alleyway which led to Johannes' home.

At last Father Torold had been located and he raced around the tower in a flapping of black robes to the place where Foreman had fallen. I saw the priest and his sexton approach the body.

Struggling to open the kitchen door, I tipped my friend Percy onto the rough floor and ran for pillows and blankets. I grabbed what I could from the bed in the workroom, apologising to the shade of Edouard Picot as I rummaged underneath him and sped back into the kitchen.

Hal was placing the insensate Sherwyn Congyre onto the floor as I entered. Gabriel was bustling about getting water and fetching cloths.

Breathing heavily from our slipping and sliding lurch down the steps of the church tower, I called to Hal.

"Can you go out and find Johannes, Hal? Also get father Columba if you can, to come up from St. Peter's. On your way, tell Roger at the front door to go and find Nick. Once Father Torold has finished with Foreman, can you get him to come here too."

"I'm yours to command, sir," said the deep voice of Father Torold coming in behind us at the kitchen door. "The man you call Foreman is beyond help and I have left folk covering his remains. Until we know what is afoot here, he can stay where he is."

"Thank you, Father. We have two men here in need of your spiritual help."

Gabriel Gallipot, now much recovered and busily professionally engaged, was cutting away the clothing surrounding the wound of Sherwyn Congyre.

"I think this one is most in danger of his life, Sir Aumary."

I turned to the priest of St. Mary "Then sir, please, do what you can for him. I will see what I can do for my friend here."

It was a little more than a hundred heartbeats before Johannes came rushing in the back door.

"Roger found me, Aumary, outside Nick's. What's going on for goodness sake?"

I took a deep breath to answer him but found that I had no answer.

"Johannes, in all truth, I have to say, I have no idea what has been going on."

*****

Nicholas Barbflet organised a cart to take Picot to the church at the other end of town and Hal went up to Chantry Lane to tell his wife that he was dead. Father Columba had come up from St.Peter's as I'd requested and ministered to Picot who was part of his flock. Then he accompanied the cart back to the castle. Gallipot had long ago gone with Roger back up the hill to his house and shop.

Johannes dealt with Congyre in his methodical and capable way and laid him down on the pallet where Foreman had recently lain. Little Agnes who had now returned from town sat with him for a while.

Sir Percival Crofton was accommodated in the front room on a mattress.

"He's very lucky. Yes, he lost a lot of blood but the knife didn't pierce any organs nor catch his lungs, like Garner, for example."

"Will he live?" I asked, my heart in my mouth.

"I think so, with care. The other man, Congyre..." he shook his head. "I'm not so sure."

"Please do what you can for him, Johannes. He is my father-in-law's brother, as you know."

"What were they all doing up on that tower?"

"I have no idea. Perhaps we'll get answers when Percy regains his wits."

Johannes scratched his head. "I am really puzzled as to how Foreman managed to get up the tower. He could barely stagger around the workroom."

"And how could he overcome Picot? Oh yes I know he was a normally a dangerous man but as you say, things were strange to him, he no longer had his strength. Picot was an idiot - God rest him; but in that state Foreman could not have subdued him, I'm sure."

"You think Foreman stabbed Picot, fled to the church, met Congyre on the way and stabbed him too and then Percival? No, it doesn't seem right."

I shook my head. "Perhaps he was feigning more hurt than he had?"

"In order for us to let down our guard?"

"Perhaps."

Johannes considered this for a moment.

"No, I don't think so. Folk with wounds like Foreman sustained behave exactly as he did. Unless he's seen someone in that state and was copying, how would he know how to behave?"

"Besides, before you intervened, he was for certain death."

"And why pin yourself in the church tower? No way out but…down," said Johannes. "Even in his confused state he wouldn't go there, I'd have thought. Maybe try to claim sanctuary at the frith chair in the chancel but not the church tower?"

Johannes took the leather thong from his queue and let his shoulder length hair free. He shook it, ran his hands through it and retied it, as if by shaking it, he could order his thoughts more clearly.

"No. It doesn't make sense to me."

Father Torold came in from the front room.

"He is sleeping comfortably now. I have done my bit. Do you want to come and see the man who fell from the roof, doctor; this Foreman? To satisfy yourself of...well I don't know what. I've sent for the coroner. I hope you don't mind, my Lord Belvoir?"

"No not at all," I smiled, "One less job for me."

Johannes sighed and picked up his medical pack.

"Lead on father. We'll have a look at our flattened Foreman."

*****

Hal returned a little while later.

"How was she?"

"'Ow d'you think?"

I laughed. "I know they didn't get on but..."

Hal took off his sword belt and sat down. He reached for the ale jug. It was empty. He grimaced and rose to find another supply. I waved him down and gave him my cup. I wasn't in the mood for ale.

"Bit like our old Widow Wedgemoor. She'll make the best of it. Mistress

Picot's got a lad of nearly twelve to 'elp and a girl of sixteen who works as a weaver, livin' at 'ome. They'll be all right. Besides she's a good lookin' woman. She'll find another man soon as wink."

"And Picot died in the course of his duty so the funeral will be paid by the fund and there may be a post mortem stipend from the King."

"Pah! If it gets paid."

I grimaced "As you say... if it gets paid."

I stretched out.

"How's Sir Percival then?"

"The wound isn't a mortal one, Hal, he'll live."

"And Congyre...?"

I shrugged. "It's in the lap of the Gods."

We sat in companionable silence for a while until Johannes returned. He looked in on both his patients and then came in to us, his face severe.

"Gallipot is with the coroner now," he said, "reporting on Picot. The coroner will go down to St. Peter's to look at the body."

"No amercement for moving the body?" I asked.

"Naturally, but I'll pay that."

I nodded.

"So... Foreman?"

"A mangled mess." Johannes threw back a beaker of water. "Limbs broken, head smashed at the back. Spine broken. Internal organs no doubt mashed."

Hal screwed up his nose. "Well and truly dead then?"

"Aye, Hal." Johannes rubbed his nose and closed his eyes. "Perhaps it was for the best. He would have been a mess for the rest of his life anyway, I think. He would probably be reduced to begging at the priory door. God obviously willed it."

I leaned forward. "He killed Bardol Wedgemoor you know."

Johannes' eyes snapped open.

"How do you know that?"

I sat back and smiled.

"Ah....Jem... Jem Chadwyk?"

I nodded. "He felt it his duty to tell me what he heard that night. The night Foreman managed to make a confession of sorts to Father Torold.

Johannes chuckled into his chin. "You wily ol'..."

I shrugged. "I now know that Foreman killed Wedgemoor...I don't know why. I also know he killed the Knighton villein, on instruction from his master, Garner. He did not, however, confess to the killing of Garner himself."

Hal put down his ale cup noisily. "Can you believe that, sir?"

I shrugged. "Jem could only tell me what he managed to hear Hal, and Foreman didn't confess to it. Neither did he confess to the murder of my father-in-law."

"But if 'e killed all the rest, 'in't it likely he did the job especially with Garner too?"

"Foreman didn't follow us to Whittonditch, Hal. We must look for another felon there. It isn't likely *he* killed Garner?"

"But why?"

"That is the mystery, Hal."

"And another mystery..." Johannes went to the pot board and took out a jug of wine. He poured two cups.

"Foreman was a mass of bruises as you'd expect when you fall from such a height. However, there was the distinct mark of hand prints, bruising on his upper arms. As if he had been grasped tightly there."

"Percy had him firmly by the arms when we saw him."

Hal nodded. "Tryin' a stop 'im pushin' 'im over the edge. Foreman had Sir Percival by the arms too."

"Ah, of course," said Johannes.

"Though to me it looked as if Percy was trying to pull Foreman away from the edge. Away from danger."

"Didn't work, did it?" said Hal.

We all sat again in silence.

"Right!" I said suddenly. "Hal, you take this part of the High Street and I will go up Kingsbury Hill as far as Silver Street. Ask everyone you see if they saw

Foreman coming out of Johannes' house in the company of anyone....or even alone. Someone must have seen them."

"Would you like me to ask around here, Aumary? Folk who live around the alley and down Oxford Street?" asked Johannes.

"If you could. Someone somewhere must have seen them even if they don't recognise it."

But we drew a blank. No one had seen the three men anywhere.

*****

We met for supper at Johannes' house that night and chatted long into the evening. I said I'd bed down with my friend Percy in the front room, Hal would sleep in the workshop with Sherwyn Congyre.

I lay down on my mattress, my tired eyes gritty and with a headache coming on. No sooner had my head moulded to the pillow than I was asleep and dreaming, it seemed.

I was in a very strange place, like a bird rising above the ground. The view was that of the top of the church tower of St. Mary and the surrounding area. Three men came down the alley way by Johannes' house making for the church. They were drunk and singing. They all disappeared into the church and in my dream I knew that they were climbing the tower.

True enough, in the time it took to spit, and it took much longer in actuality to climb up the steps, the men appeared.

It seemed they were very friendly in their drunkenness, pushing and shoving and laughing. Then suddenly one of them let out a cry.

I awoke with a jolt. I looked over to the wall. Percival was missing from his bed.

I jumped up and was out of the door, into the next room before I'd fully realised I was awake.

Hal had let out the cry and it had not been in my dreams.

Congyre was still asleep in his bed, quietly breathing. Hal was standing by the table watching, his hand held out to me.

Percy, staring straight ahead but not seeing, was in the middle of the room, immobile.

Hal whispered to me. " 'E's walkin' in 'is sleep, sir. I think I told you once I 'ad a sister who used to do that. You'd just 'ave to take 'er arm and lead 'er back to bed all quiet like. You'd ask 'er the next day what she'd thought she'd been doin' but she never knew. Never remembered."

I nodded. "I suppose this business has upset his mind, Hal. I don't remember him doing this when we were boys."

"That's the way of it, I s'pose."

Hal moved forward gently. "Come on now, Sir Percival, you come along'a me and we'll get you tucked into yer bed again, nice and snug."

Johannes appeared in the doorway, his face creased in sleep. He yawned and rubbed his eyes.

"What's..."

"Sleepwalking, Johannes," I said "it's not a problem. Hal was woken up by him in the room but I..." I chuckled "I was gripped in the arms of Morpheus. I never heard him get up."

Johannes nodded. "The syrup I gave him might make him a bit disorientated, yes."

He leaned past me to look at his other patient.

"Sleeping. Good. I'll bid you goodnight again then."

I lay on my mattress hearing the rise and fall of Percy's breathing. A tawny owl hooted somewherein a tree or on a rooftop close by. I heard the tramp of the two men employed to pound the streets at night and look for trouble. They rattled a door across the road to make sure it was locked and then, muttering to each other, they stomped off and their voices receded. I was now wide awake and tossed and turned until I decided to get up and sit in Johannes' chair.

I idly played with some of the things on his table, many of which I had no idea of the function.

A faint dawn was now creeping through the shutters.

I lit a candle and drew a book towards me, which Johannes had open on the table top. It seemed to be all about treating wounds. There were many ink drawn pictures, all of them horribly gruesome.

The page which was open seemed to me, relevant to poor Percy's wound, for the drawing was of a man stabbed in the chest but just below the ribcage on the left hand side.

The medical Latin was beyond me but I understood that this was probably not going to be a fatal wound and shut the book with a snap.

I looked over at Percy. His eyes were open and he was looking at me.

"Are you awake?"

"I am alive then?" he said groggily.

I took a cup of water to him, lifted his shoulders and allowed him a few sips.

"It's dawn soon. I'm sure Johannes will be up early and he'll come to look at you. He did tell me though that you were likely to recover with time."

"Praise be," said Percival quietly.

I eased him back onto his pillow.

"So are you able to tell me what happened?" I dragged the stool closer to the bed. "If you'd rather wait till you feel better..."

"No, no." Percy swallowed, "It matters not."

Suddenly he looked up at me with wide and alarmed eyes. "Oh, has anyone thought to tell.."

"A message was sent to Crofton and to Pewsey. We were unsure at which manor Frida would be."

"Thank you."

"She will no doubt be here tomorrow, fussing and fiddling."

Percival laughed and it cost him dear for he moaned at the pain of it. "Aye she will. She'll probably bring a cart in which to get me home."

"Johannes will not let you go anywhere until you are fit...wives or no wives."

Percival smiled and closed his eyes. "She cares about me, that's all."

"I know. We are both very lucky in our wives."

There was a little silence as Percy shifted to a more comfortable position.

"The man who went over the edge...he's....?"

"Aye he's dead. He stood no chance."

"What was his name again?"

"Foreman."

"Ah yes. I did know him. Seen him about but I didn't recall his name."

"So what were you doing with him up on the tower?"

"I was on my way down to the Marsh to check on my birthday present for Frida when I saw the man dragging himself along the alleyway by the side of this house. I was attracted to the place because just before I'd seen him, I heard a cry."

"You saw Foreman?"

"Yes. I'd heard, of course that you had tried to take him up for the murder of his master...."

"Ah no. That isn't strictly true but gossip will probably have it so."

"Well, whatever I heard, I thought it odd that he should be looking so furtive coming along the alley." I let Percy sip the water again. "And he'd come out of the back of the house after the cry."

"That was probably poor Edouard Picot breathing his last."

"I just thought it wasn't right. He saw me, turned round and made his way back into the alley and towards the church."

"How did Congyre come to be at the top of the tower with you?"

"Is that his name? I don't know him."

"He is my old father-in-law's brother."

Percy nodded. "Well, I saw him coming the other way, down the lane from the church. Foreman approached him and I cried out for I was sure that he would injure him."

"Sherwyn Congyre was injured..."

"Yes I know. I saw him. That was what made me go for the bastard!"

"Foreman?"

"Yes. He grabbed your man Congyre and pulled him into the church. I followed. I couldn't find them. It's damn dark in there. Then I heard another cry coming from the steps to the tower, I think. It's all a bit of a blur now."

"Let's take our ease and talk of this further another time then."

"No, no." Sir Percival's eyes grew large. "He'd taken him up the tower and stabbed him. I emerged out on the top just as he lay slumped by the wall. I ran to him to see if he was badly injured. Foreman went for me. I managed to turn him away. I went for my sword but it was easier to take out my knife, grappling as we were."

"Your knife was found on the rooftop."

"Aye. Once he'd got me, it fell from my hand."

"We saw you trying to pull Foreman away from the edge."

"I swear he was mad. He was trying to jump off and fly, Aumary."

"It looked to us as if he was trying to get you near to the edge to tip you over."

"As it was, he went over instead." Percy closed his eyes. "Horrible...it was just horrible. What was he doing, my friend, what was he doing?"

"Trying to get away I suppose. Though he wasn't in his right mind. The earlier blow to his head had made him confused and disorientated. Maybe he did think he could fly."

Percy shook his head. "Is the other fellow alive still?"

"Only just I think. He hasn't regained consciousness yet."

"Ah."

Percy's eyelids were falling.

"Sleep, old friend. It's the best thing for you. Johannes will be in soon."

And I left him to his rest.

*****

I went into the workroom. Hal was snoring on his back. Sherwyn Congyre had not moved. I leaned over him. He was still alive-just, but looked deathly pale. I must ask someone to go to Chilton to inform his family that he was here and injured. Hal awoke with a jolt and a snort.

"Oh, it's you."

"Aye. Our man still lives."

"Good."

"I've spoken to Percy and he told me what happened." I then told Hal everything Percival had explained to me.

Hal scrubbed at his hair, disordering it even further after his sleeping. He rummaged in his purse, took out a comb and ran it through his locks. He then ran the same comb through his long grey beard, carefully unplaited the two ends which he wore in peaks and twisted them until they stood separate.

"Foreman grabbin' Congyre?"

"Aye, that's what he said."

"Don't seem possible. But then, we did see him fightin' with the Lord Percival and our man Congyre did try to 'elp 'im by throwing summat at 'im."

"I think Foreman must have been stronger than we believed possible, Hal."

*****

A little while later I walked down alone to the castle, unlocked my office and wrote down everything I had seen and everything I'd been told. For some reason, I felt uncomfortable, something niggled me. As Hal would say, my thumbs were pricking.

I broke my fast and set off to the stables to get some mounts saddled, for a trip to Whitehill copse and to Whittonditch with Master Green. On the way there I asked one of the grooms to go out to Chilton and inform Master Congyre's family of his condition.

"Oh, and Hobler..."

"Yes sir?"

"Don't tell them anything...just that he's injured."

"I don't know nothin', sir."

"No repeating gossip then."

"No, sir."

Then, I waited in the bailey for Master Green.

And I waited. I marched up and down.

Finally, I strode out onto the drawbridge and looked across at Southfield. The gardeners were there, digging, barrowing soil here and there. Builders were raising the walls; other men were taking off the meadow turf from the lower pasture by the river.

Master Green was nowhere to be seen.

I spotted his assistant Tom Jardine and cupped my hands to my mouth.

"Master Jardine!"

He turned, saw me and came jogging up the bank.

"Sir? I thought you'd be out with the master by now."

"So did I Tom. Do you know where he is?"

"I haven't seen him this morning but then I knew he'd be going out with you so didn't call for him at his lodging."

"Where is he staying?"

"The rest of us are in the castle, sir. Master Green is staying with Alfonse in a rented house on... erm...The hill that goes down to the main road....is it Kingsbury Street, sir?"

"Where?"

"Quite close to where your doctor lives. The house belongs to the town reeve I believe."

"Nick's house. Yes, I know it."

It was indeed, three doors down the hill from Johannes' house and opposite the town lockup. Nick rented it out but the old occupants had recently moved out.

I must have looked worried, I know that I was biting my lip.

"Why sir...do you think there is something wrong?"

"Come with me, Tom and we'll go to the house. It's probably something and nothing."

We jogged along the High Street, once again avoiding the shopping matrons and delivery carts. I met Gilbert Cordwainer as I passed his house and he jogged along with us.

We passed the Green Man alehouse and at the blacksmith's we crossed the road and laboured up the short hill to Nicholas Barbflet's rented house.

I banged on the door. There was no answer. Then I tried the door. It was open.

Jardine gasped. "Master Green would never leave the door open, sir. He is an absolute stickler for locks and bars."

"Alfonse is the young man who is always with him....might he have gone out and left it open?"

"Oh no, sir. Master Green would never allow it."

I pushed at the door. It stuck on something just behind the panel. I got my hand in and felt cloth.

"Jesu!"

I pushed the door harder and managed to get an arm and shoulder through the gap. I grasped the cloth and pulled it backwards away from the door. Jardine and I then managed to push harder on the portal and I slipped through.

Master Green was lying behind the door, his head to the inside of the house. He was stiff and it was extremely hard to move him. There was a bloody wound to the side of his neck.

Jardine cried out and I saw tears spring into his eyes. "No! No, it can't be."

"He has been dead for some time. Gilbert, can you run just three doors up and ask the doctor to come?"

He nodded and turned on his heel.

Jardine looked at me and tears silently tracking down his leathered face, he said, "Where is Alfonse?"

"Is there anyone here?" I shouted as I stepped over the body of the dead gardener. I was worried that the further I travelled into the house the more bodies I'd find.

It was only a small house, like Johannes' but even narrower, with a corridor serving two rooms, a kitchen at the rear and a stair going up between the two front rooms. One larger room upstairs served as a bedroom, partitioned off and there was an attic for servants.

I put my foot on the bottom step of the staircase. I swear I heard an indrawn breath.

I waited; there was no further noise.

I searched the house but there was no other apparent occupant dead or alive.

As I came down the stairs. Johannes was just entering the front door with Gilbert. He stepped gingerly over the body, trying not to stand in the pool of blood which was congealing on the flagstones of the corridor.

"Another one Aumary!" he said "The coroner was right when he said..."

"Yes, yes I know what he said."

"Master Green the King's gardener?"

"There will be hell to pay for this. John will have my neck."

"It's not your fault."

"Nevertheless..."

"Looks as if someone tried to stab him in the upper chest but that he turned at the last minute and was hit in the throat."

"How long ago, Johannes, do you think?"

"In the night or perhaps late yesterday afternoon or evening by the stiffening. The weather is warm and it always..."

"Yes, yes, I know. Warm weather speeds up the onset of the rigor."

I turned to Gilbert standing in the gap in the doorway. "Gil, can you go and get Nick please?"

"I think he'll be at the mill," he said and plodded down the hill.

Master Jardine sat on the bottom step of the stair, his head in his hands.

"This is terrible...just terrible."

"Can the work continue without him, Tom?"

The gardener wiped the sweat from his brow and sniffed.

"I'd like to say no it can't, but to be honest, once Master Green has drawn the plans and...." He sniffed again. "There is nothing he could do that I can't."

I nodded in assent. "Then go, take over. Keep the work going. Do it for him."

Jardine stood and he said resolutely, "Aye sir. I will."

"And watch yourself. Someone is determined this garden will not be built."

The horror on Tom Jardine's face was palpable "Oh no! Surely not....not... murder sir? Not to stop the garden going ahead?"

I shrugged. "Once more we shall have to call on Father Torold."

Johannes got up from his knees and dusted himself off. "I'll go, there's nothing I can do anyway."

Johannes took Jardine's arm and the two men exited together.

I was left with the corpse and silence.

"Alfonse!" I shouted. "It's the Constable, Sir Aumary Belvoir. Don't be afraid. You can come out now."

There was a strangled cry. It came from what seemed like the stairwell. I passed up the side which for a few feet was open sided. It had been enclosed with a heavy curtain and formed quite a good storage space in this tiny house.

I drew back the curtain. There was a scrabbling as Alfonse shuffled back into the corner to make himself as small as possible.

"Come on out, I will do you no harm."

Alfonse, who I realised was no older than about ten or eleven, but tall for his age, shook his head violently.

I reached in and grabbed an arm.

"Come on, let's have you out."

Alfonse screamed then, high pitched and terrified. I dragged him snivelling into the kitchen out of sight of his master's blood and sat him on a stool.

He cried and shivered, all the time watching me carefully.

"I mean you no harm. I am the law, Alfonse....."

"I didn't kill him," he hiccoughed.

"I am not saying you did." I modified my tone. "Look here, have a drink. You must be very thirsty, not to say hungry."

I pushed a beaker of ale into his hand.

"Have you been there all night?"

His hand shook as he upended the beaker. "Aye...all evening and night."

"You hid when..."

"When the man came in and...and ..."

"Yes?"

I looked around the kitchen. "Is there anything to eat?"

The young boy shook his head. "I always go out first thing to get something for us from the baker on the High Street."

"We'll get you fed and...."

"Sir, I need to go to the privy."

"All right then. I'll come with you so that you will be safe."

The boy's eyes widened. "You'll feel safer with me near you, hmmm?"

Naturally my accompanying him had nothing to do with his safety. I was just making sure he didn't scarper, as Hal would put it.

We came back from the privy in the yard out at the back and Alfonse was a little more steady.

"So, you hid when the man who killed your master left?"

The boy nodded.

"He didn't know I was here. Master went to answer the door and I was in the kitchen. I heard Master cry out and peeked through the crack in the door. He was staggering and fell. I didn't know what to do. I waited a moment and then when the front door closed, I went out and saw...."

"Yes. Did you see the man who stabbed him?" I reached for his shoulder and gave it a squeeze.

"I saw his blue clothes."

"Ah."

"But I know who it was and I hid because I thought he'd come back. He came back you see, he came back to kill the master after he had argued with him."

"He did?"

"He came earlier and they stood in the hall and they argued and he wasn't very nice to the master and he pushed him and he said that..."

"Yes?"

"He said that if he had to kill to stop the garden being made, he would. And he did sir...he came back and he did!" He began to cry again.

"Who was this man,Alfonse? Do you know his name?"

Alfonse wiped his nose on his sleeve. “No, but I know what he does. He’s a roper and he has a little bit of his finger missing.”

I remembered the day that the gardeners had been attacked by the apprentices and had fled to the church.

“Adam Williamson,” I said.

Chapter Ten

I spoke with Alfonse a little longer, then I heard the front door open and Nicholas Barbflet and with Gilbert Cordwainer entered the kitchen. Gilbert's eyes widened when he saw the lad but he made no comment.

"He was hiding under the stairs."

Nick whispered to me, "Did he see anything?"

"Aye he did. He heard Adam Williamson, the roper's lad, arguing with Master Green. He says Williamson came back later with a knife to finish what he'd started."

"Adam is often in trouble but..."

"Aye I know. He's not usually the one giving it out."

"He was there that day on the field when the gardeners were attacked and he was mouthy."

"Yes. I remember it." I sighed, "Can you find him and bring him in, Nick?"

"No weapon found?"

"No. You might like to make a search for one."

Nicholas nodded and disappeared through the kitchen door.

"Well, my lad. What are we to do with you?"

Gilbert caught my sleeve and pulled me away to the corner and whispered.

"Sir... do you think... the lad might be in any danger?"

"He saw the murderer you mean?"

"If Nick can't find him and he's loose about the town?"

"Or if it isn't Williamson as Alfonse thinks ..."

"You think he may be wrong...?"

"Mistaken perhaps?"

"Adam's a bit of a, well… he's an idiot and gets into scrapes. He has a loud mouth and it gets him into trouble but murder?" said Gilbert shaking his head.

"Aye I know. Maybe the situation just got away from him...It happens."

There was an authoritative knock on the front door. The coroner and his scribe had arrived.

"I'm the first finder, Gil...wish me luck. I'm sure Sir Hugo already thinks I set up these murders myself so I have something to do with my time!" I smiled.

Gilbert nodded at the young lad Alfonse. "In truth he's the first..."

"I know, but we'll keep that quiet shall we?"

*****

Gilbert left to warn Grace that we were coming and Hal came trotting up as the coroner was leaving.

"Where've you been?" I asked, my arm around the lad Alfonse's shoulder.

"Ah, I've been talking to Harry." Hal gestured his thumb at the boy.

"'Oo's this then? The gardener's lad? I heard from Gil that summat has happened to ol' Master Green."

"That summat, Hal, is murder."

Hal's mouth fell open. "No. Now that's a shame. I liked 'im. 'Member when we went to Windsor and we all...."

I cleared my throat, "Yes, Hal, I do remember." I squeezed the boy's shoulder .

"I am going to drop Alfonse off at Gilbert's for some food and then I'm off to Southfield to see Master Jardine again. I'm not wasting a day. What was it you were going to tell me about Harry?"

As we walked to the Cordwainer house, Hal told me that Harry, who had been at the front of the fracas by the church, remembered he had seen something.

"We'll get it from the horse's mouth then when we get there."

We deposited the young Alfonse into the arms of a matronly and clucking Grace Cordwainer and turned to our work. Harry, as usual was in the back room, bent over his last. He knocked the last of his pins into the sole of a shoe and stood up.

"My Lord Belvoir," he bowed.

"Good Morrow Harry. How goes it?"

"Well sir. Remarkably well. And yourself?"

"People are falling around me like ninepins, Harry, but I am well. Hal here says you have something to tell me."

"It may be nothing at all."

"I'd rather hear it and it be nothing than miss it and it be important, Harry."

We sought seats and we all sat down.

"I've no ale to offer you, sir..."

"No matter, Harry...go on."

"It's about the day when you came to quell the rising on Southfield."

"I never did ask you what happened. That was remiss of me. I was more concerned with assuring the gardeners' safety."

Harry smiled. "You were busy, sir. I didn't bother you but the more I thought about it, even though I knew it was awkward, the more I was convinced I'd better say something."

"And then 'e came upon me in the street and..."

"Yes, Hal. What did you see, Harry?"

"As you know I was at the front of the crowd with the priest. Along with Felix and Gilbert."

Now that Harry had achieved his journeymanship and was no longer an apprentice, he had been allowed to call his master by his first name. They were as close as father and son anyway.

"Gilbert saw the apprentices gathering by the end of the church, just by the chandler's old house, sir. He watched for a while and came in to fetch us. He said he thought some mischief was afoot and we were to go and watch with him. He could send one of us fleet footed to the town reeve if need be."

"He's a good man."

"He is my lord. I saw the group move off and start chanting. They picked up some stones from the road and I thought, 'Hell,' begging your pardon sir, 'they're going to stone the gardeners.' In the end there was no time to run for the authorities."

"No, I don't suppose there was. However, someone must have gone for

Nick later."

"Gilbert got to the gardeners first and told them that it would be best if they went to the church. That Master Green said it was all right, they weren't afraid of a few young lads but when it came to it, it was more than a few lads."

"Yes, in the end there were about thirty people all told, I think."

"I saw the person who was stirring them up, sir."

"I saw young Metier. He..."

Harry shook his head.

"Williamson was...."

"No it wasn't an apprentice. It wasn't a townsman. He came from out of town. He had a fine dappled horse and he rode up and spoke with the folk when they were gathering on the High."

"Where did he ride from, which direction?"

"The Pewsey road. He rode the whole length of the northern Southfield border, watching carefully. I saw him. Then he jogged onto the High and spoke with the rioters, m'lord."

"Did you hear what he said?"

"No, sorry. By then I was with Master Cordwainer on the field. But I saw him throwing his arms about. He seemed to be inciting them to pick up stones and throw them. One lad asked him something and he mimed what looked like pushing over a cart, which is what they did, sir."

"They did indeed."

"So this man had a dappled horse. How did he look?"

"Small, dark haired with a straight dark moustache. He wore spurs and a sword. Oh, and he wore a blue cloak over a blue cotte, I think."

"You don't know him?"

"Yes, sir, I do." Harry looked at Hal and licked his lips.

"Come on lad," said Hal. "The constable i'n't goin' to beat yer jus' cos you tell the truth."

"He's a gentleman, sir. He comes to us for his boots, from Pewsey. It was the Lord of Pewsey sir, Sir Percival Crofton, as I live and breathe."

*****

I felt as if I'd been punched in the chest.

"Harry, you are absolutely sure?"

"I am sir."

"Thank you. Will you do me a favour and get it all written down? Bring your account to the castle and give it to either Andrew Merriman or Maurice FitzAlan. They will keep it for me. I am off to see if I can solve the mystery of the Whitehill Copse. Then I shall be at home for the night. Keep this information to yourself save for writing it down. Gilbert will help you."

"Yes, sir."

"I'll be back in the castle tomorrow. If there is anything else you remember, seek me out there."

"Yes m'lord."

"And don't look so terribly worried. I know that you know Sir Percy is a friend of mine but I am sure there is some ordinary innocent explanation for all this."

"There must be, sir. I cannot think that such a gentleman would be involved in....he is always so pleasant and kind when we see him."

I smiled, though the stone in my belly was still pressing. "I'll ask him what he was about, Harry. We shall get to the bottom of it."

"Gil said he was injured last evening, sir."

"He was, badly. He lies at Dr. Johannes' recovering."

"It can't be anything then can it, sir?"

"Not what it seems."

"Like young Williamson 'in't what it seems either then?" said Hal with a glint in his eye.

"Perhaps that too, Hal." I said. "Look after the young lad Alfonse for the moment will you Harry and then will you return him to the gardeners at the end of the day?" And I exited the shoemaker's shop.

I stood for a while outside the door staring into space.

"You all right, lad?" asked Hal.

I turned to look at him but all I could see was the dream I had had the previous night. I stared through him.

"C'mon, let's get goin' and see what we can find out. I take it in place of Master Green you're going to ask Jardine to come out with us?" said Hal.

"That was my plan, old friend."

Hal looked up at the sky. "Fine day for a foray into the forest."

*****

"It'll rain later or I'm a Frenchman!" said Hal, looking up at the clouds.

Master Jardine, looked up also.

"Nah Hal... those are fair weather clouds. They might be dull but..."

"Here we are," I said as I threw my leg over Bayard's ears. "The garden is just over here. Hal, the key."

Hal fished in his purse and brought out the two keys.

We had reached Whittonditch in good time, travelling fast along the Ramsbury road. Master Jardine had agreed to accompany us and we told him of the secret garden off the main place made by the Lord Garner.

He furrowed his brow. "It sounds to me like the man was trying to grow his own plants but we'll know when we see it."

He had needed no persuasion to accompany us, for the death of his master had dragged his mood down and a trip away from the town where it had happened was just the thing to lift the spirits.

Hal opened the gate.

Jardine whistled through his teeth. "This hasn't cost just a penny."

"No, I would say that the Lord Garner spared no expense on this, his pastime Most monies went into this and not into the upkeep of the manor, I'd say."

"It will need an army of gardeners to keep it up together. It's no small task to mow and hoe and weed a patch this big in the season and keep it up to standard. Never mind build it in the first place."

The gardener wandered into the middle where the five gravel paths radiated.

"It's absolutely beautiful. Plants here from... well... all over."

"Where do plants come from, Tom? Where do you get them from?"

"For the King's garden we shall bring plants from his other gardens, ones we have grown ourselves. We also buy from reputable sources. For example if the owner of this garden offered us some of his cuttings..."

"Cuttings, meaning small parts cut off the main plant?"

"And grown on, yes. Mind you, it's an exact art. With plants like this one for example...." and he bent down to lift a small clove scented gillyflower in his fingers. "These have to be grown from these spikes here. Take one of those and put it in some earth and it'll take. Try the stem and you're lost."

"Come, let us show you the secret garden."

Hal put the key into the lock and turned it. As before, it was stiff. Then we realised it was already open.

The door was pushed open and I stood with my arm outstretched.

"This was where we met the axe which fell as a trap, Master Jardine." I bent double and looked up just in case. There was no axe now.

We ducked and entered the space.

The whole place had been turned over. The tall poles upon which the roses had been trained were splintered and felled by axe blows. The benches which we'd previously noticed full of small pots and seed pods were turned over, smashed and broken. The pots had been ground to powder under a heel.

The plants were scattered here and there, scythed in two and three and even four or five pieces as if someone had taken a sword to them and sliced them in anger.

"Oh," said Tom Jardine as his gaze raked the secret space, "Who could do this to such plants?"

"Looks like someone was in a frenzy over this, don't it?" said Hal, picking up a discarded piece of prickly rose stem no longer than eight inches.

"You say these were trained up poles and on these ropes?" asked Jardine.

"Many rose plants, none with flowers that we could detect."

He nodded. "And these..." he stooped to pick up a handful of toppled hips, "These were split you say and emptied of their seeds?"

"Yes, we noticed that some had been planted in small pots. Some had died, others were showing small leaves."

He nodded as he strode to the wall. "Here's one that escaped."

We followed him.

Like the rose in my manor courtyard this one had been trained up the wall of the garden and had been secured by strings coiled around nails driven into the stone. It had no blooms now.

"They were all roses?"

"I think they were, yes."

Hal picked up the handful of rose heads he had seen at the heap on our first visit. "Just 'eads, all 'eads. Dead and dried up now."

Jardine shivered. "I know what has been going on here, sir. Can we leave now? I do not need to see more. It's abhorrent that someone would do this to such beautiful living things."

"If they can murder a man or two, Tom, they can murder a few plants."

He nodded sadly.

"I'm glad that my master didn't see this. It would have made him very angry." He looked up at me with a moist eye. "It's wicked. A wicked thing to do."

Hal shuffled his feet. I think he thought it more wicked to murder a man.

We regained our horses just as the housekeeper came round the end of the house. She had been feeding the chickens it seemed, for she carried a bucket of scraps on her hip.

"You... Come to turn the place upside down again…m'lord?"

"We are leaving, good lady," I said. "You will find that someone has been into the garden and destroyed part of it."

"Destroyed...it?" said Jeanne Dicer absently.

Then she seemed to collect her thoughts and with a venomous eye she stared up at me, atop my horse.

"What have you done with Foreman, my lord?"

"I sent a message to you to say that he was injured mistress, but it is now my duty to tell you that Master Foreman is dead. He fell from the church tower in Marlborough yesterday. His body will be returned to Whittonditch."

"Dead?"

"You may have him interred where you wish."

"That will be for the new master to say, sir."

"Ask him to come and see me at Marlborough castle. I will explain it all."

As we rode away, I heard her laughing, loud, long and joyously.

*****

Whilst we rode, Master Jardine explained to us what had been going on in the small garden.

"You asked, my lord, where we got our plants from? Well, we have a lot of plants all over the kingdom in the King's gardens and when we know that we are to create another garden, we start to make some new ones. We grow our own and then plant them out."

"Like the cuttings you were speaking about?"

"Some plants are made from cuttings of old ones, some are grown from seeds. With others we do what we call grafting."

"And that is, Tom?"

"Grafting and budding are the horticultural terms for when we join parts from two or more plants so that they appear to grow as a single flower. In grafting, the upper part, which we call the scion, of one plant is made to grow on the root system or properly, rootstock of another. In the budding process, simply a bud is taken from one plant and made to grow on another. That is in part, what was going on in your secret garden, sir."

All this was accomplished with hand movements and physical explanations.

"So the Lord Garner was making his own plants?"

"His own roses, sir."

"Why roses in particular?"

Jardine looked surprised I'd asked.

"Roses, sir, are the queen of flowers. Beautiful sweet creatures with petals as soft as a maiden's skin and as blushing too. They are the gardener's crowning glory."

"How very poetic, Tom," I chuckled.

"And as prickly as women too," said Hal.

"You say he was growing them. What you mean is, he was trying to make a particular rose?"

"That's right. He was crossing the one with the other."

"Why?" said Hal and I together.

"It's like this," said the master gardener. "You have to decide what you want your rose to look like. You then take two roses which have those qualities which you desire in your new rose."

"For example, few thorns?" I asked.

"Exactly, sir. Then you take one to be the male and one the female...."

"Oh no!" said Hal, "don't tell me that even roses have conjugal..."

Jardine laughed. "All plants have male and female Master Hal, you just need to isolate those parts."

"No, don't tell me any more. I don't want to know," said my man at arms putting his hands to his ears.

Jardine chuckled again."You need a seed parent and a stud...rather like when breeding horses."

"Ah, I see," I said.

"The pollen from the male which is the stud, is introduced to the female which is the seed part and if you are lucky you'll get it to take and if all goes well, a seed head will form..."

"A rose hip?"

"Yes, that's right. Then you halve your pod."

"We saw 'alf pods in that place when we were there before," said Hal, once more paying attention.

"And you scrape out the seeds."

"And plant them," I finished.

"Well, I'm making it sound simple. It's not quite so easy, but yes, essentially that is what you do."

"You should, if you are lucky, get the rose you wanted?"

"You'll have to do it time and again to get exactly what you want, m'lord. It's rarely done in one go," said Tom.

"Needs a lotta patience then?"

"A great deal Hal."

"Hmmm. I i'n't got that amount of patience."

"It's rather like wooing a fair lady, Hal," laughed the master gardener.

"Aw well, that's why I i'n't ever bin married, see," answered my man at arms.

*****

We approached Whitehill copse much later in the afternoon. The sun had disappeared behind the clouds and, leaving our horses at the edge of the copse we went, as before, into the trees on foot. We ducked under the lowest branches and swished through the dead bluebells which had carpeted the floor some two months before.

"Here Tom, is our glade. It's simply a meadow with wild flowers. A few coppiced trees, some overstood older ones. A few are dying and dead and we shall fell those soon, I expect."

"And you want to know why it should be so special m'lord?"

"Why did two men keep coming here? They are both of them dead. What is there here which is so amazingly desirable that one man would forge a will to get his hands on this small piece of ground and then be killed before he could profit from his perfidy? What is so special that Bardol Wedgemoor, one of my woodsmen, was drawn here over and over, neglecting his proper job and at peril of being disciplined for not working where he should? What got him killed?"

"I can't see anything that..." Tom Jardine circled the glade. "No, there are plenty of ordinary plants. Those we find anywhere."

"Aye, foxgloves, woodbine. There's a large rose over there. It's nice but it's nothing to get a man killed over."

Jardine picked his way over the meadow grasses, now rippling in a light breeze.

"Yes, I can smell it. It's a late flowerer."

He rounded the few trees and the dead oak came into view with its burden of pink roses.

"Oh yes, it's lovely. Heavenly scent. That's one of the things that plantsmen always want to breed into roses, a stronger and stronger scent. The old roses and the wild ones usually have very little."

"So in order to do that you'd still have to breed together two plants which were highly scented?"

"With roses, I suppose you'd want scent, colour and longevity of bloom…."

Jardine had rounded the oak and was now out of view behind the trunk and the curtain of leaves and trailing stems.

"Oh merciful Heavens!" We heard him say.

"Tom?"

Hal and I looked at each other and with worried expressions we followed in his footsteps around the oak and stood at the other side.

There stood Tom Jardine, a look of rapture on his face.

"Well, sir. You asked me what was here?"

His gaze drew our own gazes upwards.

On the other side of the tree was yet another rose. One we'd missed on our first trip, for it was well hidden and was smaller than the first, only six feet tall and about five feet wide. This one was still flourishing, despite the lateness of the season, with bloom after bloom weighing down the stems. The scent was powerful and heady. The blooms were many petalled, curled and packed into roundels with a deep centre. This in itself was wondrous but the thing which took away our breath was the colour.

This rose was not pink, nor white as were its companions. It was not even a mixture of the two colours, making it a paler pink.

It was a striped and blotched rose. A pale pink body with markings of darker pink striping and blotching it here and there. I had never seen the like. It was as if someone had painted it.

"This would be the sort of thing I'd kill for, my lord, if I were the killing sort."

"Oh?"

"Aye...this would make you a deal of money should you be able to reproduce and sell it."

We all stared up at the rose and marvelled at God's creation.

Rosa Mundi.

*****

Master Jardine cleared his throat.

"Someone has been looking after this plant. You can see it's been pruned and dead wood taken out. It's been trained. If you look at the other one, the pink rose, there are a lot of whippy stems and it's a tangle of briars."

"So this is not a creation of nature?" I asked.

"Oh yes, I think it's a natural plant. Or it was once."

"You mean it just grew this way?" asked Hal.

"The colouring is a result of the crossing of several roses, though how it was achieved here I have no idea. I think it will be able to be reproduced by taking cuttings. You notice it has no hips forming? I am by no means sure but I think it might be easy for this rose to revert."

"Revert?"

"Go back to the way one of the parents looked, sir."

"Ah. So you think this is what Garner was doing with those small plants in pots and this is why he wanted to acquire the meadow?"

"And someone wanted to stop him, sir," said Jardine.

"Well, I would have stopped him," I said "But I would have done it by legal means. I would not have killed him."

"Someone did, sir," said Hal thrusting his thumbs in his belt.

"Hmm. And Foreman kept an eye on the place? Maybe recruited Wedgemoor to tend it? Someone who had legitimate reason to be out in this part of the forest."

"Aw sir," said Hal, "the Wedgemoor I knew wouldn't 'ave done that out of the goodness of 'is 'eart. He would have wanted payin'. "

"No doubt. And perhaps when he became too troublesome or they had no further need of him..."

"Foreman stuck a knife in him," finished Hal.

We looked up at the rose once more.

"I bet he jus' got too greedy."

"That's probably it, Hal," I said.

"Makes sense now, what Oswald of Knighton was saying?"

"What's that Hal?"

"That magic was being performed in the garden. To 'im, something like this, growing a rose from nothing, locked away in that little garden, tinkering around with little pots o' this and snippets of that....well it would seem unnatural if you hadn't any idea what was really going on."

"The brothers certainly knew something and Garner wanted them silenced."

Master Jardine was looking at us strangely.

"We believe that the Lord Garner had a couple of his villeins murdered because they knew about his playing around with nature, Tom."

"Aye, there's many people who think that fiddling with God's creations is unnatural and shouldn't be done. It's against God's Law. God is right when he creates what he does and men shouldn't be trying to better him."

I laughed and my voice echoed around the glade. "But it won't stop them breeding a bigger pig, meatier cattle or a faster horse!"

"Or a more beautiful rose."

I looked up at the sky. "If we are to reach Durley before nightfall, we had better be going. You will stay with us won't you Tom, and return to town tomorrow?"

"That would be most kind, my Lord Belvoir." He bowed low.

I slapped him on the back. "Thanks for your help."

We began to make our way back to our horses.

"Tom..?"

"Hmm, sir?" He turned back.

"I don't need to say that until we can see the bottom of this mystery, this must stay a secret, but when our problem is solved, I give you permission to come out here and take whatever, cuttings, wasn't it, that you might need, for the king's garden."

The huge smile that the master gardener bestowed upon me, lit up that dull and sunless meadow.

*****

We reached Durley just as the sun was setting. Henry took a tired Master Jardine to one of the guest rooms and I asked him to come up to the hall for supper once he had washed off the dirt of travel and made himself comfortable in the room.

Lydia rushed up to me and took me up to the solar.

"John was in town and he said he heard that poor Percy has been injured. Is it true, Aumary?"

I pulled my gambeson over my head.

"Aye it is. A knife in the midriff."

Lydia sat down with a bump on the stool by the bed. "Oh no. Poor Percy. Will he live? Has Johannes seen him? What had…"

"He'll live. Johannes tells me the knife pierced him just where there are no major organs or blood lines. And what he was doing...well....he tells me that..."

"You have spoken with him?"

"Early this morning. He said that he saw that villain Foreman..."

"The man kicked in the head by Gabriel's horse?"

"Yeees... Foreman," I repeated. "He saw him go up the tower with Toruld's brother at knife point. He ran after to prevent Congyre being injured but he was too late."

"Not Congyre too?"

I nodded as I pulled off my boots with a grunt.

"Foreman jumped him and Percy sustained the knife wound. We arrived on the scene just at the moment when Percy and he were grappling by the tower parapet. Foreman went over and was smashed to pieces." As I told the tale to Lydia, the same feeling of disquiet washed over me; that same feeling that I had felt when walking alone down to the castle that morning. I dismissed it as tiredness.

"Oh," said Lydia, her hand in front of her mouth.

"And we took Congyre and Percy immediately to Johannes."

I lay back on the bed. My wife sat by me.

"Does Frida know?"

"Aye, I sent a message." I yawned. "I think I'll just take a short nap. I was up in the night and didn't sleep past the fourth hour of darkness."

Lydia ruffled my hair. "Sleep then. Matthew Cook has prepared your favourite for supper."

"Ah...a pie. That will be nice. I have lived on castle fare for two days, or simply on fresh air."

"Did Johannes not feed you?"

I smiled, "When I had time to eat. Yes. But it wasn't much."

"I'll wake you when supper is served."

*****

Wake me, she did.

Matthew paraded the pie around the main table and folk clapped and whistled. Matthew stood in front of me, placed the pie on the table and handed me the knife. I took it handle first and stood looking at it for a moment as if I had no idea what to do with it. I saw Lydia looking at me strangely; Matthew looking worried as if there was some fault to be found with his pie. Something had just come into my mind and was gone as soon as it had entered.

I smiled and plunged the knife into the hard pastry.

"Ah...mushrooms and chicken...goodness Matthew, you have outdone yourself. Does Annot know she has one chicken less?" We didn't usually eat chicken on a weekday or for that matter, much at all. They were too precious for their eggs.

Matthew grinned. He scratched his cheek, "Erm well sir, it's like this. One of the dogs took a liking to it...."

"Don't tell me...Hubert's little terrier, Aura?"

I saw my farrier trying to make himself small on the lower table. This was impossible for he was over six foot and folk around were nudging him and laughing.

"The very same...and although Annot rescued it and it was all right, later it keeled over and so we thought it best to put it out of its misery and stick it in the pot, sir."

"Nothing going to waste eh?"

Matthew bowed, smiling.

"Nothing seemed to be wrong with it, no blood, no wound, the dog hadn't even pierced the fowl. Just had it in her mouth."

My memory pricked me. No, it had gone again. Ah yes....another thought, mushrooms....

As I ladled out the gravy I asked Matthew to remain.

"The mushrooms which I believe you wanted to gather in the forest... when Bardol Wedgemoor warned you off, Matthew?"

"That was some time ago. For your table m'lord. Good large horse mushrooms for a soup."

"Aye, I'm sure. Where were they growing?"

"In a meadow by Whitehill Copse. Oh, I know it's a long way to go but I was returning from Ramsbury with the wife sir, we'd been to see the goodmother. We took a short cut and 'twas then I found them. I picked a few that day and meant to return and search round a bit further but Wedgemoor, blast him, got wind of where I'd been and said that if he heard that I'd gone anywhere near there again he'd break my arm. Last year it was, sir."

Hal tutted.

"Thank you, Matthew."

Yes. It all made sense now. I was sure that Wedgemoor was guarding the site and was perhaps, with his knowledge of woodland plants, nurturing the beautiful striped rose, for money.

I sat down to my pie, thinking how fine it was we were rid of such a man as Bardol Wedgemoor. I swallowed. I'd have to acknowledge that thought and speak to Father Crispin about it when I next made confession.

*****

I slept beyond the dawn and rose a little dull in the brain. I plunged my head into some cold water, washed my hair, scrubbed my teeth with salt and dried my wet skin with a rough towel. I ran a comb through my curly and tangled black locks. Then I felt fit to greet the day.

I was on my way to the room which we'd given to Master Jardine for the night when I heard raised voices. I stopped outside Henry, my steward's office.

I heard Henry say. "Oh Ancie, give it a rest will you."

"But it isn't you who will be ..."

"You're not with child are you?" he said anxiously.

"No, but if it goes on any longer..."

"All right. I'll see."

"Oh Henry, don't be cross with me. I know you think it forward of me to...."

"He's probably just forgotten. He's been very busy this..."

"Can you speak to him Henry…please?" wheedled Annot. "Bevis Joiner says the house will be finished this week. It's been long enough since my father died."

Damn. I had forgotten all about asking Father Crispin to find a day to arrange to marry Annot and Henry.

"Yes. I know," said Henry.

"Oh Henry, you do still love me don't you? You do still want us to be married? You don't think me too bold? If you didn't I don't know what I'd do..."

I backtracked a little way and began to whistle as I re-approached the open door of the office.

"Ah, Henry, just the person I wanted. Oh, and is that you, Annot? Well, what a fortuitous meeting."

Henry rose from his desk and bowed and Annot turned and curtsied low.

"I meant to tell you both that I have asked Father Crispin..." I crossed my fingers behind my back, "if he will marry you. You need to go and set a date. Both of you."

"Oh sir," said Annot, her face splitting into a grin; the freckles dancing on her nose.

"Thank you, m'lord," said Henry, looking at me strangely.

I cleared my throat. I was never a convincing prevaricator.

"Sir," Annot lifted her face to me. "Does this mean that you have found out who killed my father?"

"We thought, sir, that you would not allow us to be wed until you'd discovered the truth about Bardol's death," said Henry.

"And why would I not allow it, Henry? I have said I would and that is that."

"Well, when time passed and the mourning was over, we thought..." said Annot

"We thought perhaps, you..." Henry looked down at his feet with an uncertain expression. "Thought it was us after all, sir."

"That we'd killed him because we wanted to..." Annot's face was suddenly pale and her freckles had disappeared.

"No, no, my lad and lass," I said, smiling. "Your innocence was never in question."

Henry heaved a sigh of relief. "So we can do it sir. Soon?"

"Yes indeed. And to answer your question, Annot. Yes I have found out who killed your father. It was indeed that man Foreman. He killed him because he was going out to the forest, to Whitehill Copse to be precise, to be the guardian and gardener of a rather spectacular rose which the Lord of Whittonditch coveted and had discovered growing wild there. I have a feeling, your father being the man he was, he was demanding more money to do the job and Foreman killed him to stop his mouth."

Annot took in a sharp breath.

"Annot?"

I looked at her quizzically but Henry supplied the answer.

"Sir, when Annot's Ma was cleaning the cottage, she found a lot of money stuffed under a loose stone at the edge of the hearth. We were going to tell you when we saw you...but..."

"I know..." I rubbed my forehead. "I haven't been much at home."

"I have it here, sir." He made to leave his table and go to one of the chests secured by large iron hasps.

"No, no, Henry. I don't need to know about it. You keep it."

"But sir, there's quite a bit of coin...by rights it should come to you."

"A gift. From me, Henry. A wedding gift. Keep it."

Henry looked aghast at Annot. It was more money I suspect than they had seen together in all their short lives.

What's that Paul? How much? I never knew. I didn't ask. Annot and her three sons are still alive and in the village and well, let's say they are wealthier than many a resident of Durley.

Annot recovered first, she curtsied again. "Thank you, m'lord."

I nodded, smiled and as I walked away, I heard Henry say, "Well my girl, we shall have everything we need. No need for hand me downs, this will buy us anything we need for the house."

When I thought I had walked nonchalantly far enough across the courtyard and couldn't be seen, I gathered speed and pelted up the steps to the hall. I sped through the lower end and up the stairs to the chapel where I knew Father Crispin would be at this time of day. This lay above the buttery, pantry and my small office, on the mezzanine floor.

"Crispin. Two things... no three... Henry and Annot want to be married, will you set a date to do it please... soon? Notify the village."

His brow furrowed. "Yes, I know."

"And I have two things to confess."

"Can it not wait till confession at...?"

"I lied to the happy couple about asking you. Can you, without lying yourself, pretend that I asked you a while ago?"

Crispin laughed.

"And, oh yes. I was glad that Bardol Wedgemoor was dead. Very glad."

"Well!" said the priest. "You aren't alone there. That's no sin. Even I have given thanks for his demise," and he winked at me.

Chapter Eleven

The next day was rainy. Very rainy. Hal, Jardine and I sloshed our way down into town and even with our waterproof cloaks were soaked and miserable by the time we gained the castle drawbridge. Master Jardine peeled off to his infant garden and met to talk with his builders who were sullenly standing under a hastily erected tarred cloth.

It seemed no building would be done today.

The horses stowed and a report of sorts taken from Maurice FitzAlan, I unlocked my office door and took off my wet cloak. The hems of my cotte sleeves were soaked as were my chausses where they had been pushed into my boots. I pulled off my wet footwear and changed into ankle high boots, which I'd left in the office. Then I yelled out of the door for someone to bring me a brazier for warmth.

Castleman, who was leaning out of the guard room looking up at the leaden sky, saw me.

"Do you want Barty to come and light the fire for you, sir?"

"It's July, Ed, not December! We can't light the fire in the summer."

He laughed. "No, sir."

He looked right and left to make sure there was no traffic coming in or out of the castle and trotted across the entrance.

"Sir, might I have a quick word?"

I beckoned him over and ducked back into the room just as a shower of droplets fell from the stonework.

Castleman followed me in shaking himself and shivering.

"Straight down my neck that went! Bloody chilly for July."

"One moment boiling the next cold and damp. What can I do for you, Ed?"

"You remember the nasty to do in Southfield when the apprentices tried to get at the gardeners? Haroldson said he saw someone laying about him. Not sure who it was though."

"I do. I think I told him to ask around."

"Well, he did."

"And?"

"Turns out it was someone from out of town."

"We know him, do we?"

"Oh yes, sir. We know the little sh…shirker, sir," said Castleman, a chuckle in his voice. He folded his arms and planted his feet wide.

"We've had him here in our gaol," he nodded in the direction of the castle keep. "You once wanted to hang him, sir."

"I did?" I sat down slowly at my table. "Ah...yes.....Wouldn't be that miserable little apology for a man - Glanville Lovell? And I mean little, would it?"

Glanville Lovell was an extremely small man who only came up to my chest but he was big trouble.

"The very same, sir."

"He loves a fight, does Lovell."

"Especially with drink inside him, Sir Aumary."

"Been in the Green Man, I suppose."

"With the rest of his racing cronies."

The Green Man was a relatively new drinking establishment where ale was brewed every day and available to drink on the premises from morning till curfew. The crowd who raced their horses up on the downs would collect there and do business.

"Right Ed, send someone to find out when he might be at the Green Man again. Glanville lives out at Oare and comes into town when the whim takes him. We might need to keep an eye out. I'm not going to send someone out to fetch him in if he'll come to us."

"Yes, sir."

"So, it was he who struck the master gardener, was it?"

"According to Haroldson, sir. With a length of timber."

I nodded. "Ask Nicholas Barbflet. Get all in the town to keep an eye open for Lovell. Anyone seeing him, get the officer of the watch to send out a party to fetch him in. He won't come quietly. You'll no doubt have to subdue him but please, don't kill him."

"Yes sir," said Castleman laughing.

Castleman turned to leave, his hand on the door latch, and looked back. "And the fire, sir?"

I looked down at the ring of wet fabric circling my calves and pulled down the soggy cuffs of my cotte.

"Ah yes..get Barty to light it, Ed, please."

*****

The rain continued. I worked through a few parchments. The room grew overly hot but at least I'd dried out. Hal came in from the guardroom where he had been gossiping with his pals.

"God's Cods, it's 'otter than a 'olyday in 'ell in 'ere," he said, pulling the shirt from his neck.

"Damp the fire, Hal, there's a good man." I said, sending my castle scribe away.

Hal looked round. A most fastidious man, he looked for something with which to pick up the turves to lie over the wood burning fiercely in the fireplace. He shrugged and took out his knife, speared a turf, held it up and laid it carefully over the flames. He then repeated the action.

I watched him with the knife and a thought sprang into my mind, gone as soon as Hal said,

"Ed tells me it was Lovell hit poor Olivier Green."

"According to Haroldson, yes."

"Reckon it was 'im what did for 'im in the end?"

"Has he a finger missing?"

"Aye, he 'as."

I threw down my pen and scrubbed my face.

"I forgot...yes he does, doesn't he? Left hand, little finger."

"And Williamson's is right 'and, little finger."

"He hasn't been found yet. The town has been searched. His master says he didn't turn up for work. He hasn't been home to Master Roper's."

"This 'in't a big place. 'E'll turn up somewhere," said Hal.

"I suppose his friends have rallied round, given him a bolt hole."

"Want me to ask about, sir?"

"Start with the Green Man. He's there with the racing crowd often enough. Find out who he's pally with."

"Right you are, sir."

"If the roper's apprentice has run and gone into the forest or to another town, we might need to make searches further afield but not in this weather, Hal."

"If the lad's got any sense..."

"By no means certain, my old friend."

"Ah no...'e is a bit empty in the top larder 'in't 'e? Well, 'es gonna lie low in this weather."

I got up, opened the shutter and looked out of the window. "I think it will rain for a few more hours yet."

"No work on the garden then, sir?"

"They can't lay stone in this weather, they tell me, and digging flower beds is just a matter of moving mud from one place to another."

"Aye, it looks a right mess."

Hal had joined me at the window.

"Why would Lovell hit Olivier, Hal? He had no quarrel with him that we know of."

" 'E don't need a quarrel. If 'e sees there's goin' ta be a fight, 'e's there with 'is tongue 'angin' out."

I chuckled and shook my head. "I remember when I took him on."

"Cocky little bug....beetle," said Hal "Flashing 'is knife everywhere, like it was some kinda tumbler's clubs."

I blinked. I'd remembered the thing which had been niggling me now for quite a while.

I turned to Hal.

"Hal. We found Percy's knife didn't we?"

"Aye we did. It had skittered somewhere up by the stair door." He looked at me with a puzzled expression.

"And Congyre's?"

"His knife was still in his scabbard. 'E din't get the chance to use it."

"So, where was Foreman's?"

*****

Morning turned to afternoon and we dined…

If dined can ever be the word, Paul, for what is served up at the castle...I'm told it's no different nowadays…

...on pork stew and bread which tasted like straw.

Then with the rain slackening off, we walked up to the doctor's house to check on the two injured men.

Congyre was much as we had left him. Sleeping on his back, breathing shallowly.

Johannes told me that he was probably one of those people who when given a drug to keep them pain free, would sleep and sleep until the drug wore off. Some people were like that, more sensitive to the medicine. Some were like this with alcohol, said the doctor. He was sure he would come to, eventually.

Percy was sitting up with a pained expression and was being fed soup by a worried looking Frida.

After our cordial good afternoons, I sat on the edge of the table and dangled my legs. Hal stood by the door.

"How is the poor fellow next door, Aumary?" asked Percy. "Is he sensible yet? Johannes told me he was still out cold this morning."

"No, not yet. But it won't be long. Johannes was very worried that he might die but he's made of tough stuff is Congyre."

"And Johannes is a very good doctor."

"Yes, yes he is. He stitched you up nicely."

Percival gently patted his left hand side. "As neat as a housewife's hem."

Frida smiled and spooned more soup into Percy's mouth.

"Thank you, Sir Aumary," she said. "If you hadn't arrived when you did, well, I think Percy would be the one that they are digging that grave for in the churchyard."

"Oh. Foreman's being buried here, is he?"

"No church at Whittonditch, sir," said Hal. "And no one wants 'im."

"Ah, no."

I shifted, a little, uncertain how to begin my next round of questioning.

"What was all the shouting we heard at the top of the tower before we came up, Percy?"

"Shouting? Was there shouting? Ah yes. That was Foreman. Yelling and screaming at me, I think. God knows what he said. I just made for Congyre and ignored the noise the man was making."

"We found your knife."

"On the roof, by the door to the tower," added Hal.

"And Congyre's was still with him."

"Aye. I don't think he had any time to draw it in order to defend himself," said Percy. "Poor devil."

"So did Foreman strike you both with his own knife?"

Percy grimaced as he sat up straighter, waved away the soup and thought for a moment.

"Aye, I think so. He got both Congyre and me with it."

I nodded to Hal, who slipped around the corner of the table and reached up onto a shelf by the door. He handed a knife to me.

"This knife maybe?"

Percival screwed up his eyes. "Aye, maybe that one."

"And then again, maybe not. This is Foreman's knife. We took it from him when he was first injured. It's lain here the whole time untouched."

"Well, then, it must have been another," smiled my friend.

"Where is it?" I said baldly.

"Where? If it isn't on the rooftop then it must be over the parapet with him."

"We came upon you as you and he grappled, Percy. Foreman had no knife in his hand."

"But he must have done. How else could he have struck both Congyre and me?" Percy looked completely perplexed.

"All right. We'll make a search." I nodded to Hal. "Get some lads from the castle and search the yard behind Johannes' house, the pigs next door, and the surrounding ground in the churchyard, in case it was flung, Hal."

"Right you are, sir. Is this before or after I go to the Green Man and look for..."

I smiled "The ale at the Green Man can be your reward, Hal."

Hal made a moue. "That'd be torment then," he said.

The ale at the drinking establishment was not noted for its superiority.

Hal left and closed the door. Frida went into the kitchen to wash up the soup bowl and to take some sustenance herself.

I jumped from the edge of the table and stood looking out of the window. The rain had stopped.

"You've been in town a few times lately, Percy?"

Percy lay down slowly.

"I met you on one of those days. I saw you the day you were hurt, clopping along to town on the Pewsey Road. You were seen another day, the day of the riot on Southfield."

"No, I don't believe..."

"You were seen."

Percy's eyes met mine. There wasn't a trace of guile in them.

"Why were you here then, Percy?"

"Checking on my present for my dear wife, I suppose. Shhh, no word about it now."

"You were seen with the crowd of rioters."

"Ah yes..... I remember now. I stopped to have a word with the apprentices."

"A word about what?"

"They looked like trouble. I told them it would be best if they dispersed."

"Hmm. What did you say exactly? I can have the apprentices fetched. I know who they were. I can question them...."

"What is this all about, Aumary? First you question me about a knife, now the apprentices?"

"I am just trying to establish the facts, Percy."

Percy ran a shaking hand over his forehead.

"The apprentices were obviously going to cause trouble. I think I said something like, ' you aren't thinking of throwing those stones are you?' "

"You were seen miming the action of throwing."

"Maybe I was. Perhaps I just pointed at the ringleader."

"I shall ask."

"The scene on the rooftop, Aumary, is very hazy. All I can say is that when I grappled with Foreman he'd already stabbed Congyre and he caught me too before going down."

I nodded.

"I don't know where the knife went."

"If it went over the parapet, we'll find it, though I don't know where he will have obtained it."

"Does Johannes not have knives in his room? Foreman must have had something with which to strike at your guard. Father Torold tells me that he killed him too."

"All right, Percy. We'll leave it there. Let's see what happens."

I turned to go.

"You don't believe me, do you? For some reason you don't believe me."

I did not turn back to look at him.

"For God's sake, Aumary. Why would I kill Foreman? I hardly knew the man."

"I'll see you later," I said and I closed the door.

I went and sat for a while in the work room to think; the room where Congyre was lying peacefully . Oh, how I wished the man would regain his wits.

For some reason Percy had feigned not to know that there had been a fracas on Southfield. I had told him the day we'd visited Crofton. Now, he admitted to being there at the time. What was going on?

I looked again out the window, opening the shutter and letting in light. The rain had completely stopped and the sun was coming out again.

I saw the High Cross which stood almost in front of Johannes' house. A few people were standing on the steps chatting. With one more glance at Congyre, I left the room and locked the door, taking the key with me.

As I entered the kitchen, Hal was coming in the back door smiling from ear to ear.

"Rain's stopped."

"Good, makes your searching easier," I said.

"Well, there's one thing I don't 'ave to search for."

"What's that Hal? Have you found the knife?"

Hal chuckled. "Nope. Not yet. But you can come and 'ave a look at what I 'ave found."

I sighed.

"No, honestly. You'll like it, I promise."

"I will?"

Hal turned about in the doorway and I followed.

We exited the yard at the back of Johannes' house and turned left up the little alleyway which led to the church, its graveyard and the houses at the back of Oxford Street. The lane eventually led out onto the road which ran up the hill, travelled through the forest and ended up in London.

Hal scurried along, chuckling.

He turned left again and walked through the gap in the churchyard wall and out to the back of the chancel.

Here were a few of the castle guards; those he'd collected to help him search for the knife.

They were all milling around at one spot and they parted as I drew up.

"Sir,"

"Sir"

"M'lord," said another.

"What is it, Bunce?" I asked.

'Well, sir, it's like this. We was searching around and poking the grass and such. Not wishing to disturb the dead too much but still getting on with the task when..."

"Bunce..."

"Yessir." The portly man at arms put his thumbs into his belt, "And we was a swishing the grass about like you said, well it were awful wet..."

"Bunce!"

"Yessir. Sorry sir. When we came upon this newly dug grave."

"Yes, the sexton has dug it for Foreman, the man who fell from the tower. He'll be buried here, later today."

"Well, sir, if he's buried in this 'ere 'ole, he'll have company," said Bunce.

He nodded to a couple of the younger men and they lifted the planks which had been laid over the hole dug in the churchyard.

I stared down into the pit.

I smiled.

"Hello Williamson," I said. "My, my, you do look terribly wet."

*****

Adam Williamson was pulled up the side of the grave and two men kept hold of him though he made no struggle.

"Portman, can you go down to the mill and see if Master Nicholas can come up? Adam is a townsman and I'd like him to be there when we question him."

"I can do that, sir."

Williamson flicked his wet and muddy hair from his eyes.

"I ain't done nothin."

"No. I don't suppose you have. What were you doing in there?"

"Nothing."

"Nothing sir!" said Bunce leaning into the young man and shouting into his face, "beggin' yer pardon, m'lord."

"Adam. I'll ask you again. What were you doing in that open grave?"

"I wasn't 'idin' "

"No?"

"No, I fell in."

"I reckons as that's true sir, cos..." Bunce turned and fiddled behind him, "This was partly dislodged from the 'ole. Looks a mite gimpy to me." He held up a plank which was rather rotten at the edges and which had lost a big chunk from the middle.

"I reckon it gave way..."

"It was dark," whined Williamson.

"And you were running I suppose?"

Adam hung his head. "Before I knew it, I was on me arse in the bottom of that 'ole."

"You didn't cry out for help?" I said, trying not to smile.

"I figured if I could stay there till it was a bit light I could climb out. It were bloody cold and wet but I managed to get into a covered corner."

"And then the little shite fell asleep, sir," said Bunce. "A bit the worse for the drink, I think," he mouthed.

"Why did you run, Adam?"

The young man's eyes peered at me from under a sodden fringe. "I heard you were looking for the man that killed that Green gardener man."

"And was that you?"

"NO!"

"So why run?"

"Cause you'd say it was me."

I closed my eyes and sighed.

"All right. We'll get him to the town lockup in a moment. We'll wait for his master and Master Barbflet. Then we'll ask more questions."

"I'd beat him about the head a bit, sir," said Bunce, grinning "He'll tell the truth then."

"Or he will tell us what we want to hear to stop the beating, Bunce."

"Aye sir, but we'd have him then, wouldn't we?"

"And what if what he told us was an untruth, Bunce?"

"You threatened to beat me once before," said Adam suddenly. "I don't reckon as you would. I heard things about you."

Hal cuffed the young man round the ear.

"Don't be too sure of that, Williamson. If the Constable wants you beating, it'll be in a place where it don't show. You won't sit down for a month. If ever. And I'll do it an' you can be sure o' me."

"Pearson, can you go down to the ropery and tell Master Roper that Adam has been found alive and.....muddy. Ask him to come to the churchyard please."

Pearson nodded and ran down the path, vaulted the stone wall and disappeared down the slope.

I looked up at the sky, now bright blue but with a few wispy clouds.

"We'll get you cleaned up a bit first, shall we?"

*****

Before we even got him to the lockup Adam Williamson protested his innocence, though the idiotic young man did admit to going to the gardener's lodging and threatening him.

"You are twenty years of age you clod! "said his master Tim Roper, his white moustache bristling with fury. "Not three! One more year and you are out of your apprenticeship. Now I shall have to consider whether I keep you on till then, or not. Think, what a waste. Oh!" he threw up his hands in frustration.

"Why did you go and shout at Master Green, Adam?" I said putting a placatory hand on Tim's back. "You have no interest in Southfield beyond the ordinary."

Williamson shuffled his feet.

"It were a dare."

"A dare?" shouted Tim Roper. "That's the sort of thing a child does, man!"

"I weren't goin' to be..."

"Adam. This dare, who was it asked you? How did it come about?"

"Just a few of us were out on the street."

"Where?"

"At the front of the Green Man."

"And?"

"Someone said that someone ought to go and put the shits into the old man!"

"Master Green?"

"Yeah."

"Yes sir!" shouted Tim. "I am so sorry sir, for this apology of a roper."

I smiled at the poor artisan. He was a quiet, gentle man, kept himself and his family to themselves and ruled his apprentices tightly. Not tightly enough perhaps.

Nicholas Barbflet, the town reeve looked up, his arms folded sternly before him.

"Williamson, for every time you are disrespectful to the constable you will receive further punishment from me, over that which he dictates for you. Do you understand?"

"Yes, sir."

"Who said that you should be the one to do this, Williamson?" I asked.

"I dunno...sir. I was drunk."

"Were you so drunk that you didn't know what you were doing?"

"No, sir."

"That it all got out of hand and you went back, after perhaps fortifying yourself a little more with drink..."

"No, sir. I di'n't go back."

I looked over the young man. "Adam." I said in a quieter tone. "You were seen. In the clothes you wear now. Blue hose and blue tunic," (if a little less muddy, I thought.)

"You were seen threatening the gardener. You said that you would kill him if the garden making carried on."

"No, sir."

"My witness lies?"

"I dunno, sir."

"You say you went but once. Shouted at Master Green and...."

"He were alive when I left him."

"Was this a bet?"

Adam Williamson looked shifty.

"Adam...did someone bet you that you wouldn't do it?"

Williamson swallowed, squirmed a little and then nodded.

"Speak up, Adam," said Nick forcefully.

"Aye sir. It were a bet."

I grabbed the young man by his collar and dragged him to the graveyard wall.

"About here wasn't it, Tim, that Mistress Williamson was laid?"

"Just there, m'lord," he pointed.

"Tell me truthfully. Upon the soul of your recently dear departed mother whom I am told you loved greatly, did you return and kill Master Green?" I asked.

Adam pulled up his head and I saw agony in them and tears in his eyes.

"You are now standing upon your mother's grave, lad. Tell the truth."

"No sir. Upon my mother's soul."

I nodded a few times.

"Who dared you, Adam?"

"It were a fella I didn't know."

"You did the bidding of a man you didn't know?" said Timothy Roper in disgust. "You idiot."

Adam hung his head.

"What did he look like?"

"I dunno."

"Why?"

"I don't remember, I was drunk."

"In the lockup with you. We shall keep you there until we are certain of the whole business," I said.

Then I turned to his master and took him away by the shoulder.

"Tim. I do think he's an innocent in this and has been used. He's obviously desperate for the approbation of his peers. Keep his place for him, please. I think this will be the turning of him. I can't compel you but I am asking."

Tim caught his lip with his teeth. "If I wasn't a friend of his mother's." He crossed himself. "Bless'er heart, I'd lay him out cold meself. But...I'll look to him as you say, sir. Jack will keep an eye on him."

Jack was Tim's own son and a fine young man.

"Nick," I turned to the town reeve. "Shall we keep him here for what...four days? Short rations? No admittance to anyone at all, except those I specify. In leg irons I think."

"As you wish, Aumary." He took me aside. " Are you concerned that someone might try to get at him?" he asked quietly.

"I'm not at all sure, Nick. Best we take care I think."

Nicholas Barbflet nodded. "The place is guarded anyway, as you know when we have malefactors in there." This was the job of the nightwatchmen who lived in the very end house on the hill and opposite the lockup. "I'll make sure we are extra careful."

"If it wasn't Williamson and..." I shrugged. "I see no reason why Adam should want to kill the master gardener; frighten him yes, but not kill him, then we have another felon abroad."

"Lovell?"

I shrugged and turned to leave. Hal caught my eye.

"Oh sir...sorry to say..."

"Yes, Hal?"

"We i'n't found a knife, sir. Not yet. We looked everywhere. Even in places where it can't have been. It's gone into thin air, so it has."

Thank you, Hal," I said wistfully.

Chapter Twelve

The day was now muggy Hal and I traipsed back towards Johannes' house.

"What I can't see..." said Hal in a musing mood, "is how that knife can 'ave done the damage to Congyre and Sir Percy, then gone from the top of the tower and we can't find it. It's not as if there's anywhere it can 'ide up there."

I turned off and made up the path to the west door of St. Mary's.

Hal followed.

"Aw no, not up there again!"

"Yes Hal, up there again. I want to look around once more. See if there's anything we've missed."

"Ow can we 'ave missed anythin'? There was you, me, Congyre and Sir Percival and a fallen Foreman up there. One iron bar… well, I don't know what that's doing there, and nothin' else."

"Let's be certain, Hal."

We laboured up the steps again. By the time we reached the top we were perspiring heavily.

Hal stepped out onto the roof and scanned the tiles.

"Nothin'. Just the iron bar."

I picked it up. "What is it doing here?"

Hal looked over my shoulder.

"Sort o' thing you use in the stoneyard, I think. I seen them there."

"Perhaps it was left behind sometime when they did some repairs to the stonework?"

"Mebbe. It's heavy. No wonder Congyre had a hard time with it."

I laid it down where Congyre had been felled.

"Let's go through it again. You stand there and be Congyre for the moment. I'll be Foreman. According to Percy, Sherwyn Congyre was dragged at knife point up the stairs."

"Right. Struggling?"

"Perhaps not. He only had the one wound to the chest. If he'd struggled we might expect further, lesser defensive wounds. So up they come. "

"Why here?"

I looked round. "Maybe Foreman thought he could talk himself down with a captive and bribe his way to freedom?"

"Nah, he could just as well a' stayed in the church for that."

"Hmmm. So I make for you with the knife. You have no time to go for your own..."

"No?" Hal's knife was in his hand and he was grinning.

"Hal, you are Sherwyn Congyre. He's a farmer. You're a soldier," I chuckled

Hal grinned. "Oh all right then." He re-sheathed his knife.

"I make for you with a knife...stab...down you go onto the tiles."

Hal slid down the parapet and lay as we'd found Congyre.

"Ah! It's still a bit wet!" he moaned.

"Now I'm Percy. I come bounding through the door."

Hal opened an eye. "Yer knife in yer hand."

"Yes. I make for Congyre to see if he's alive."

Hal sat up. "But you 'aven't time to really look before Foreman is on you."

"Get up and be Foreman, will you, Hal." Hal jumped up.

"So, you and I are fast coming up the stairs. Foreman, according to Percival, is shouting and screaming."

"We heard two voices."

"Aye we did. Well, Congyre isn't unconscious yet. We saw him throw the bar at Foreman. Maybe he was yelling."

"'Watch out'...or 'be'ind you' or summat?"

Hal did a very good impersonation of Foreman staggering about as we'd seen him do in Johannes' workroom.

"Or maybe Percy was shouting at Foreman?"

"There was a good deal of shoutin'. It were more than that I reckon."

"Yes. I agree. More words were spoken," I said.

"I come for you with me knife."

"I've no time to draw my sword. I swipe you, you lunge and catch me here. Maybe I don't feel I've been stabbed."

"Well, you know that, sir. Sometimes you don't, do you?" said Hal.

"No, not till later."

"I go for you." I grabbed Hal by the arms. "We tussle.....not too close to the edge, Hal...we don't want this to end in the same way. Foreman can't use his knife again for some reason."

Hal grinned again. He swung me round.

"S'like dancin'."

I laughed and then we changed places. "And over you go. Then I, being Percy, slide down the parapet and sit, saying.... 'Aumary....stabbed, he stabbed me."

"I'm at Sherwyn Congyre's side by then," said Hal, going to the other side of the tower.

"Hmmm."

We both looked down to where Foreman had fallen.

We stared at each other. "So where is Foreman's knife?" we asked each other.

We searched again at the top of the tower. We looked along every ledge up and down the tower in case the knife had lodged on a stone projection or the lintel of one of the two windows in the stone faces of the building. We pulled at the tiles to see if the knife might have become trapped. As we climbed down we checked the stone work.

"Father Torold was the first to see 'im on the ground. Maybe 'e knew where the knife went?" said Hal as we descended the tower.

"The man who helps the priest in the churchyard was also quick on the scene, I think, Hal."

But when we asked them, they both said that the man had had no knife, either in his hand, or on his mangled person. Nor was it thrown free as his body hit the flagstones.

The knife had indeed disappeared.

*****

We returned to the doctor's house.

The door to the workroom was fully open and Johannes was seeing to a man who had a bad gash on his hand.

Percy was sitting fully dressed on the edge of the bed.

"Well!" I said "You're looking better."

"I am trying to encourage him to stay here a little longer, Aumary, but the foolish man will go home."

"I *feel* better," said Percival, smiling. "The wife has brought Pebbles and I can ride home like a warrior, and not be carted home in the back of a wagon like a weakling!"

"Riding already?" I said.

"It'll be a slow journey but...."

"Best to stay till tomorrow then and set off at first light. The day is too old now, Percival."

"Nonsense, it's nine miles, that's all."

"Nine miles which might be the undoing of you. Wait till tomorrow - please. You can't ride as fast as you'd wish," I said.

Percy sighed. "I suppose you're right. I just want to be at home," he said in sulky tones.

Johannes sent off his mended man with a slap to his back. "See you tomorrow Peter. We'll see how it's going then."

He turned to his other patient.

"You will mend better, Sir Percival, if you take a little longer here," said Johannes, his tone of voice almost an order.

"One more night then. Can you put up with Frida and me one more night, Johannes?"

The relief on Johannes' face was appreciable.

"One more night will make no difference to me and it might make all the difference to you. As Aumary says, it's late in the day to set off, even though it's light till late. The weather today has made the roads treacherous. Best you stay, sir."

At that moment, Little Agnes' face peered in at the door. We all turned. She flapped her hands at Johannes.

He was wanted elsewhere. He quickly wiped his hands on a cloth and was gone through into the next room, saying, "Back in a moment."

"Ah, has our friend Congyre regained his wits then?" said Percy.

"Maybe. He has been asleep for a very long time. He should surely be improving by now," I answered.

"I'm glad," said Percy. "He seems like a good fellow."

"Aye, he is," I said. "And he was one of those who'd been tormented by the Lord Garner and his bully man Foreman."

"Had he now? Well, maybe that's why Foreman went at him with such venom eh?"

"It may well be."

I turned in the doorway. "Hal, I am away to see how he is."

*****

Johannes was re-dressing the wound in Congyre's chest as I entered. Sherwyn's eyelids fluttered.

His eyes focussed. "M'lord," he said.

I smiled down at him.

"We thought you'd gone, Sherwyn. Welcome back."

"You are a very lucky man, Master Congyre," said Johannes. "An inch to the right and half an inch up and the knife would have had your heart."

Congyre, though weak, smiled at Johannes. "Not my time to be gathered to God, eh doctor?"

"No indeed. I had thought that the knife had penetrated your gut. Then there would be very little I might have done. But no. The knife passed into the area known as your diaphragm. Somehow, it managed to miss your major organs and barely nicked it seems, the muscles lining your chest. Neither did it catch your lungs...."

"As the Lord Garner was killed, Johannes?"

"That's correct. However, you might have a shortness of breath for a while. We'll keep an eye on you until we are absolutely certain what's going on inside."

Congyre closed his eyes.

"I feel very tired."

"Aye. You are one of those people very susceptible to the liquid I gave you for the pain and have slept for hours. That's no bad thing. However, you must now take some water...."

I turned to go but then thought to ask him a question. "Congyre, I must ask you, what were you doing up on that tower?"

Sherwyn Congyre shifted his head on the pillow, took some water and lay back.

"Tower, m'lord?"

"You were fetched down injured, from the tower of St. Mary's by my man, Hal of Potterne. We found you there and someone had gone for you with a knife."

I saw the man's hands convulse under the tight covers which Johannes had replaced after he had helped him to the sip of water.

"Tower… I can't remember rightly. I was walking up the lane....and I saw a man....he was running down the lane and he had... oh... I can't remember."

"Leave it, Sherwyn. We shall speak again soon. Sleep."

Johannes let out a relieved sigh. He never liked me questioning his patients when he felt them vulnerable or too weak.

"Tomorrow, Sir Aumary," he said with a smile.

*****

I stepped out onto the roadway outside Johannes' house where it bellied out towards the High Cross. Hal followed me.

"Where to now, sir?"

"Back to the castle, I think, Hal. We can do nothing here yet. I don't wish to go back to Durley...well yes...I'd like to but we have too much unfinished business here."

"Another supper at the castle then?"

I chuckled "Another bowl of gristly stew and hard bread."

"I wonder if Pete is off to his cousin Philly's tonight. Maybe we could tag along?"

Peterkin Gayle had a cousin recently moved to the town who was an excellent cook. He went out on a Friday night to sup with her and often brought back food with him, to last him a few days until he'd be off to her house again.

This thought kept us happy until we reached the cordwainer's shop. I'd not seen Gilbert since we'd discovered the body of the master gardener.

We were almost past when Gilbert came hurtling out of the front door.

"Sir! Sir Aumary."

"Whoa, Gilbert. You'll do yourself a mischief leaping around like that."

"Your man. Skulking about by the river," he said breathlessly.

"Which man?"

"Lovell. I've just been out the back to the river to fill up the buckets for....." Gilbert put his hand to his chest and heaved in a great breath. "I saw him. He was skulking around on the river path."

"Now what might 'e be doing there?" asked Hal.

"Where was he going, Gil? Which direction?"

"Up the mill way."

"Have you Harry and Felix in there, Gil?"

"Aye, I have."

"Can you send Felix to the castle to ask his father to fetch some men? Ask Andrew to get together a party of five. That should do it. Can you ask Harry to follow, on the river path? He isn't to intervene, just watch where he goes. We'll run back the way we came and go the main roadway. We might be able to catch him between us."

We turned about.

"Gristly stew or not Hal, looks like we shall be missing supper."

We ran down Crook's lane, past the corn mill and made for the small riverside path which led to the back of the priory. As we reached the mill side we saw Glanville Lovell walking nonchalantly along, his thumbs in his belt, his face up to the sky. He was whistling quietly through his teeth.

We ducked back behind the wall and watched as he passed.

"Where's 'e goin' then?" asked Hal at a whisper.

"My guess is he's visiting the Green Man and will go up Angel Yard to get there. Watch. If he ducks up the lane we follow."

Sure enough Lovell turned off at Angel Yard where the tanners and fullers had their premises. The Green Man was situated on the High Street very close to where this lane exited. Lovell would be seen by few as he entered the backyard of the ale house.

We noticed Harry following at a distance and waved him over.

"Can you go and tell Sir Andrew that Lovell is in the Green Man, Harry? We'll go in and then Andrew can wait outside the front. The back door also needs watching in case he makes a run for it."

"I can do that, sir."

"When you have delivered your message, Harry, and you're not to do it alone. Do not engage him. He's a dangerous man, for all his size," I laughed. "The lady Lydia always says the smaller the animal the more feisty they are."

" 'Tis true of tiny shrews, sir," said Harry, laughing. "They are fearsome beasts. Weasels too."

"Aye, but gert big plough oxen, like our Milo and Dundas at Durley are as mild as babies," said Hal.

Harry pivoted and ran back the way he'd come. We saw him loop up Crooks Lane to the High to see if he could head off Andrew and his party.

We tightened our sword belts, freed our knives in their scabbards and entered the back door of the ale house.

It was dark inside after the light of the afternoon and we squinted into the front room. There was Master Green, the brewer and owner of the house, going about the tables, smiling and chatting with his customers. He turned to his barrels which were positioned on a plank at the back of the room. Then he caught sight of Lovell.

" 'Ere, Lovell. I don't want any nonsense now. You just take your drink and be quiet about it or I might be forced to bring in the town reeve to evict you."

"Well, that's a fine way to talk to a good customer, Green, I must say," said Lovell. "Here I am, only just got me ale in me hand and there you are telling me I gotta leave."

"No, I ain't saying that...yet...but I know what you were like that other time you came in."

"I heard about one of those times I think," I whispered to Hal. "The man was brawling with one of the fullers and Green here threw them both out into the dirt of the road."

Hal nodded. "He i'n't related to ol' Bardol Wedgemoor is he?"

I chuckled, "Not as far as I know."

Lovell sat on his own in a corner. He took a huge gulp of ale and noisily ordered another from the young man serving. His eyes were everywhere but not once did he glance out of the exit where we stood, partly screened by the door.

The front door opened and Hardcastle, his head stooping to miss the lintel for he was as tall as me, entered the alehouse.

Very gently his eyes raked the assembly. He made no movement towards Lovell but collected an ale mug and sat opposite on another table. He noticed us in the doorway and very slowly and unobtrusively lifted his hand in a gesture of recognition. I nodded. Now it seemed our men were in place.

Hal and I came in through the back door.

I saw Lovell stiffen as he spied me but then his body relaxed and he smiled.

"Master Constable, m'lord," he said with a slight sneer. "How are you today?"

"Not too well, Lovell," I smiled. "Not too well at all."

"Aw that's a shame that is. Why's that then?"

"He's got to look at your ugly arsed face, that's why," said Hal.

Lovell deliberately put down his mug of ale. "There i'n't nothing wrong with my face, my good man," he said, smiling.

"What are you doing in town, Lovell?"

Glanville Lovell, who had not risen from his seat, looked up at me. "Why I'm havin' a quiet drink that's what, i'n't I?"

"When was the last time you came into town for a quiet drink then?"

The smile left Lovell's face. "Oooh that mighta bin...February maybe?"

"So you didn't come in here a few days ago when you were in town?"

"I weren't in town a few days ago," said the man, shifting his feet. "I been very busy out at Oare. Ask Master Green 'ere, he'll tell you."

"I ain't lying for the likes of you and getting my license revoked, Lovell," said Green, fingering his right ear. "Yes m'lord, he was here a while ago, shouting his mouth off."

Hardcastle stood up; leaving his ale he stretched languidly and came to stand by me.

"You were seen, Lovell," I said.

"Doing what?"

I leaned over him and put my knuckles on the table. I could see him shifting very slightly towards the table edge. I knew that manoeuvre, grab the table, tip it up, floor the person in front of you and jump over them and out, before they had a chance to breathe.

"Sir...please...m'lord..." said Master Green, "I don't want no trouble here inside again. Can you take the little runt outside and..." He had obviously seen the same thing happen before.

"Come on Lovell. Let's go outside and finish our conversation. Poor Master Green has only just recovered from your last spree in here."

Lovell stood, oh so slowly. His ratty, sharp face was blank. He moved to pick up the cloak he'd laid on the bench beside him. The way he gently felt for it told me there was probably a weapon under its folds.

"And you can leave that. Hardcastle here will bring it for you."

Lovell laughed. "Everything had better be there when I get it back," he said.

"We shall give you a receipt," I said.

Hal pulled the table out gently and waved him through; we watched as the man adjusted his belt, straightened his tunic, smoothed down his hair.

"And you can also give Hardcastle the knife you have just taken from your waist, Lovell. You won't be needing it in the gaol."

Lovell tutted, looked up to the rafters and handed over the small knife.

Then he slid gently from behind the table.

As he did so his booted foot caught the leg and it stuttered across the wooden floor with a screech. Lovell bent and quick as a ferret with prey, he'd retrieved a knife from his boot top.

He straightened up, to find my knife pointing at his eye.

"You can still tell me what I need to know, Lovell, with one eye."

"Aw, My Lord Belvoir, you don't think...you can't think that I would...."

"No," said Hal, "but I can! Now git movin." He took the knife from him.

Hardcastle grabbed the small man's left arm and Hal his right.

"Yard please, Hal."

"Right you are, sir."

Master Green nodded to me. "Much obliged, m'lord. If you should ever find yourself in need of a pint..."

"I'll bear it in mind," I said, shuddering at the thought.

I poked my head out of the front door.

"Sir Andrew...backyard. We have him."

Andrew was leaning on the wall of the alehouse. Two others stood to attention close by.

"You heard the Constable...backyard," he said and they jog trotted past the few houses which lined the road here and disappeared down Angel Lane.

I went back through the alehouse, nodding to Master Green.

Castleman, Harry and Hal, plus Pearson who had been at the back door, had Lovell up against the outhouse wall.

"Right, shall we start again?" I stood in front of him. "Ed, can you search him for more weapons please?"

"Ere, you watch where you're putting your hands, you filthy..." moaned Lovell as Castleman searched his body for more weapons. No more knives but one lethal looking razor-sharp flat metal strip and tucked into a small sheath at the back of his hip there was a long nail which had been sharpened to a murderous point.

Hal took charge of the weapons.

"So, you were here in town the day of the riot on Southfields?"

"Who says I was? He's a lyin' toad who says I was."

"You deny it?"

Lovell squinted up at me. "My, my, was there a riot? I can't tell you anything because I don't know when the riot…."

"You know, because you were there, Lovell," said Hal, "with a damn great bit o' wood."

"As I was askin'...." said Lovell in a very friendly way, "when was this riot? If you'll let me know I will think back and tell you where I was on that day. Hmm?"

"Well, to help you remember," I turned my back, "we'll just tickle you a little in the midriff."

I heard the air expelled but had no idea who delivered the blow.

Andrew and the others came in the back gate and sauntered over. I lifted a hand in acknowledgement.

"Well, hello again, Lovell. Oh dear. Have you hurt yourself?" he asked, grinning from ear to ear.

"Well I ain't punched meself now 'ave I?" said Lovell. "These bullies...." but he lost his breath before he could finish.

"Bullies? Dear sweet Pearson? No, surely not. He's kind to dogs and grandmas, aren't you Pearson?"

"I am indeed," said Pearson, showing his teeth and the gap where the two front ones were missing.

"And I know that Castleman wouldn't hurt a fly. He doesn't even know how to fight...do you Ed?"

"No sir", said Ed, chuckling. "I'm far too busy doing my embroidery, to practise, sir."

Glanville Lovell glowered at us under his disordered fringe.

"I told you, I weren't there."

I took Andrew by the shoulder and turned him round so that neither of us could see who hit Lovell again.

"By the way Andrew, did you ever get that new sword you..."

"Ooomph," said Lovell and this time he landed on the floor on his knees.

I turned back. "Oh, how careless you are, Glanville. Falling over like that. Here let me help you up."

I offered him my hand. He stayed down.

"As you please. So where were you that day of the riot then?"

"In - Oare - I expect."

Hal shook his head. " Trouble with you is..."

"Oh yeah...?"

"You have no manners. It's 'in Oare I expect.' MY LORD!" yelled Hal into his ear.

Glanville Lovell jumped up grimacing. "You might think yer poncy Constable Belvoir is a Lord but I..."

This time I saw Hal hit him.

"Oh deary me Lovell," I said, smiling sweetly. "If you will keep falling over then we shall have to take you up to the castle for the good of your health. Obviously, the ale in this establishment doesn't agree with you."

"You can't take me in if I i'n't done nothin' and that's a fact. You i'n't got any proof." I was surprised the man could still speak but he was a tough creature with muscles like house beams.

"Well, I think that can be arranged can't it, Andrew?"

"Oh yes," said my friend, joining in the game wholeheartedly. "Evidence can be planted. It would be no bother, no bother at all. In fact I'd quite enjoy it."

Lovell grinned nastily. "It i'n't what it seems, no, not at all..."

"What isn't?"

"Me at the riot."

"Oh so you *were* there?"

"I mighta bin."

I folded my arms. "Come on then...what's the story?"

Lovell shook himself and pulled the hair from his eyes.

"Like I say, it weren't how it looked."

"Oh and how did it look?"

"Me with, what did you say..a damn great bit o' wood."

"So what were you doing with it then?" asked Hal.

"I was tryin'a stop the young lads and apprentices from getting hurt and hurting their elders and betters."

"Were you now?"

"I heard as you came in all fire and flame and laid about you with the flat of yer sword. Well, I was doin' the same earlier. Only with a bit o' wood."

"Aw c'mon, Lovell," said Andrew laughingly, "You seriously expect us to believe that?"

"And it just so happens that you accidentally hit the senior, nay the King's gardener over the head Lovel, with your bit o' wood."

"Did I? Aw…well, if I did I am very, very sorry. It was an unavoidable accident."

I shook my head. "And then a little while later you went up to his house..."

"Ah, where's that then?"

"And you stuck a knife into the poor man because you knew he could identify you."

Lovell stood stock still.

"No, sir. I never did. By Holy Mother Mary's milk, sir. No. It wasn't me." His face had a white and frightened look at last.

I glared at him.

"I like the idea, Glanville. I like it a lot. So much so, I am going to arrest you for the murder of Master Olivier Green and take you up to the castle."

"Aw no, sir. Don't do that. You'll be making a huge mistake, sir."

I nodded to Castleman and Pearson and they both took Lovell by the arms and marched him out of the gate.

We made for the High Street and turned left to go up to the castle.

It was hard going, for there were children running about and matrons with their shopping; carts veering to the roadside to avoid oxen pulling lengths of timber, barrels and bales of thatching straw.

A running man bumped into Lovell and momentarily distracted, Hardcastle and Pearson slackened their grip.

Lovell headbutted and then elbowed the one in the guts and kicked the other in the cods and was off down the High Street in a flash of sky blue.

I heard his laughter as he veered off and barged his way through a shop selling cloth. As he went through, he pulled everything from its place. Shelving and tables went flying. Bolts of cloth unrolled along the floor tripping and tangling feet.

Women screamed as he pushed his way through them. Mistress Fleschier who was in the shop was spun around and ended up on the floor in a snarl of skirts and fabric.

We followed.

We heard a crashing and breaking sound as no doubt, the private quarters of the mercer, whose shop and dwelling it was, was invaded, Lovell wreaking havoc as he fled.

Finally we gained the back of the shop, thundered through the garden and made for the river. Lovell was ahead of us running and leaping over obstacles like a startled deer.

We pounded on.

A townsman approached as I shouted "Ware! Harrow harrow..felon, stop him." The poor man was punched in the teeth for his pains and went down on the grass moaning.

Lovell made for the small path at the banks of the river which led around the back of the Priory of St Margaret of Antioch.

We followed though I yelled at the two men behind to go back and run along the High Street to come out at Southfield.

Lovell ran on, picking his way carefully but swiftly, between the plants of the bank side.

He reached the priory wall and risked a look back. We were still following and I saw him mouth an obscenity.

On he ran along the wall. I wondered if he would double back at Figgins Lane but no, he ran on, slipping and sliding and eventually made Southfield where the gardeners were working once more. Single file owing to the narrowness of the river path, we ran after him and we saw Glanville Lovell stagger onto the field.

I shouted again, “Harrow harrow, felon escaped.”

A couple of brawny men hefted their spades and ran at Lovell but he dodged them and was away before they could catch him.

He ran on up the slight slope and risked another look behind him.

I heard his laugh as he dodged yet another man. I saw Farmer and Petersen, my two guards who'd run up the High Street, come out from the cover of the houses. They ran onto Southfield and attempted to head Lovell off. The gardeners seemed to get in the way, shifting first this way then that. At last, the obstacles cleared, they herded Lovell towards the main part of the site which was beginning to look quite like a garden. The beds were dug, the lawns shaped and to one side the foundations to the dovecote lay open to the elements.

On ran Lovell. One more look back and then... he disappeared.

Lungs bursting, Hal and I reached the place where he'd vanished. We looked down. There in about two feet of water, floundering and breathing hard was Glanville Lovell.

“Ergh!” he said as he sank deeper into the mud at the bottom of the pit. “Erghgurgle.”

I laughed with what breath I had left.

“First a grave and then a pit for a dovecote, Hal!”

“Aye sir,” said Hal, his hands on his knees, taking huge gulps of air. “But 'a course...it i'n't how it looks is it sir? Oh no.”

“Oh for goodness sake Lovell, keep still and we'll pull you out!” I said. “The more you struggle the more you'll sink.”

Lovell was now throwing obscenities at me, by the dozen.

Andrew ran up puffing.

He put his hands on his hips and laughed out loud. "Well, Lovell. What are you doing in there? Taking a bath?"

"Oh yes..very funny!" spluttered the felon. "I didn't mean to fall in here did I. "As if I'd do this to meself, heh?"

Suddenly the world around me lurched away and silence descended. My brain buzzed. My belly felt as if I'd been punched.

I saw Hal mouthing words at me but could not hear what he said.

He had said "You all right,lad?" apparently, but I didn't register it.

No, I was not alright.

I had just worked out who had killed Garner, Master Green and poor Edouard Picot. And I thought I knew how.

I shook my head.

Hal said once again "Aumary, you hearin' me?"

"Yes, yes, Hal." I stretched up to my full six feet in height. "I can hear you."

I sighed.

"Get him out and take him to the castle gaol. Clean him up and dry him off. Charge him with the harming of Master Olivier Green with a stave of wood. However, we cannot lay the death of the master gardener at his door."

"No? Aw that's a shame."

"No, Hal. I have just worked it out. I know who killed him. I know who killed Garner, stabbed Edouard, struck Percy and wounded Congyre" And I turned away to walk to my office at the castle and once there, I locked the door.

Chapter Thirteen

I took a piece of parchment and scribbled for all I was worth for about the time it takes to sing vespers. My writing grew spidery and illegible. No matter. When I was satisfied, I took a pumice and scrubbed and scrubbed till everything was erased. Then, I sat back and stared at the wall.

I heard Hal scratching at the door and rose to open it.

He stood in the doorway stroking his long forked grey beard.

Yes, he always did this when he was worried, Paul.

"You all right, lad?" he asked. "Not like you to go off just like that, like a maid with the mopes."

"No, Hal. I'm so sorry. Sit and I'll tell you what I think I've discovered."

So for some time, until Father Columba rang the bell of the castle chapel for vespers, I told Hal what I thought.

His jaw dropped.

"No lad... it can't be."

"I do think it is."

"How're we goin'a prove it?"

"I'm not sure, old friend, but prove it we shall."

"Well I 'ave to say, if it is as you say and..." he snorted almost in disbelief, "then I wouldn't be as calm as you are. I'd be angry as a wasp in a wimple so I would."

"I am, Hal. It's just ....I don't know. I don't know what to think."

Hal looked past me at the bare piece of parchment. "You bin writing it all down?"

"As I usually do but I can't bear to look at it, so..."

"What're you goin'a do then?"

"I don't know yet, Hal, but I'm sure of one thing..."

"Hmmm?"

"I am not going to let any of it pass unpunished."

*****

We trudged up the keep steps and Peterkin Gayle, the gaol master, opened the door for us.

Glanville Lovell sat on the stone plinth which ran around the wall of the pit dug into the base of the keep.

I leaned against the flint and chalk wall and folded my arms.

Lovell didn't rise but shook his gyves and called out, "I won't be goin' to vespers in these now, will I?"

"You? Goin' ta church? Don't make me laugh, Lovell!" said Hal.

I smiled at the banter. "No Hal, he won't be going to church. It would take Father Columba far too long to shrive him. He'd miss all the services from vespers to sext."

"If you're gonna hang me then I gotta be shriven," said Lovell cheekily.

"No Lovell, I shan't hang you - today."

"Ah, well then."

"I shall order some other punishment for you."

"Like what? And anyway I gotta be tried first."

"I'm the law here if the Lord de Neville is absent. I say what happens."

"Ah but you're a lenient man sir, so you are."

"So what do we think, Hal? Shall we rid him of his nose? His ears maybe. His hand?"

"His cods, sir... that'd be better."

"Now steady on..." said Lovell, paling.

I sat down on the stone plinth beside the felon.

"Lovell. This is the second time I've had you in here. I promised last time to hang you if I needed to see you again in my gaol."

"But you said..."

"You struck a man down. Assaulted him with a stave. That act must be punished."

"Ah, but he didn't die, sir. And it were an accident as I live and breathe."

"No, you didn't kill him. Someone else did that."

"Ah, so I see you have come to your senses at last, sir," said Lovell grinning. "I didn't kill him. No."

"One little thing might save your miserable cods. Or your ugly little nose."

"Or your sticky out ears," added Hal.

Lovell glared at us "What's that then?"

"Tell us exactly what happened the day of the riot. Who was where. Everyone you recognised. Describe those you didn't know...."

"I might not have a great recollection of it all, sir, as I was laying about me.... erm trying to prevent too much damage to folks and not takin' much notice."

"Drunk you mean," said Hal, chuckling.

"Ah well, I might've had a wee drink in the Green Man but that doesn't mean that..."

"I shall send my scribe to you. Harald will write down everything you say. It had better be the truth. I have other witnesses with whom to confer."

"Like the bastard what told on me, eh?"

I shrugged. "I am particularly looking for those who incited the uprising. Name them. Describe them and I'll be lenient."

I got up to walk away and turned in the doorway to look back at him.

"Men from your neck of the woods, Lovell, perhaps."

The felon cricked his head to one side. "Oare, sir?"

"Places close about."

I had my foot on the bottom step of the stairs when Lovell shouted after me. "And I can go free without any punishment?"

I stood and looked up at the sky just visible as an oblong of blue.

"Oh no, I didn't say that, Lovell."

"Then I i'n't sayin' nothing."

"All right. You can stay here till you rot." I reached the door and banged it shut. Gayle locked it.

"Good bye, Lovell. It was nice knowing you."

*****

Harald came to me a while later.

"Sir, I have the confession and the list that the man in the gaol dictated to me."

"Well done, lad."

I scanned the young man's perfect Latin, his steady penmanship.

One name jumped out at me.

"You got what you wanted, m'lord?" asked Hal.

I sighed. "Yes, I have it, Hal."

"What do we do with Lovell, sir?"

"Lash him, Hal. Ask Andrew to organise it. Tomorrow and then send him on his way. But make sure a perfect record is kept. I want no accusations later."

"Right you are, sir."

He screwed up his face "And you, sir?"

"I shall be at Johannes' tonight. Look for me there with Bayard tomorrow morning."

It was growing dark as I trudged up the High Street towards the house behind the High Cross.

I went into Church Lane through the short alleyway and hesitated as I turned into Johannes' yard. I'd thought to go into the church and pray. Pray for guidance; for inspiration, for God to steer me towards the truth. However, dismissing the thought, I veered off into Johannes' yard, scratched on the kitchen door and entered.

Little Agnes was there preparing supper.

She smiled and then cocked her head on one side. I knew this meant, "What's the matter?"

"Oh don't worry about me, Agnes," I smiled. "Is Johannes at home?"

She shook her head and pointed to the yard. Johannes was out.

"Is the Lord Pewsey and his wife still here?"

Yes was the answer and she pointed to a tray where she was laying out bowls of food and drink.

I nodded. "Might there be one more for supper?"

Agnes grinned and took down another bowl from the shelf.

I sat by the fire, a mug of ale in my hands and thought.

In a few heartbeats Johannes entered. He took off his blue cloak and folded it neatly onto a stool.

I looked up. Johannes' face was grey, drooping and tired.

"Bad day?"

Almost ignoring me he turned to his maidservant and said, "She didn't make it, Agnes. I'm so sorry."

Agnes' shoulders drooped and she bit her lip. I jumped up and, offering her my stool, guided her to the seat.

"A friend, Agnes?"

She nodded.

"I'm so sorry."

"One of the maidservants at the Snap household," said Johannes.

"Ah."

"A failing of the lungs."

"I suppose there's nothing you can do when..."

"No, nothing. She was so young." We sat in silence for a while.

Then Agnes jumped up and began to ladle out the stew.

When she had loaded her tray with food and drink, she dried her eyes on a corner of her apron, smiled at us and was gone through the door into the front room to take food to Percy and Frida.

"How's Percy's wound?"

"Healing well. I don't think it was as serious a knife wound as that which Congyre sustained."

"No, I think you're right. How is your other patient?"

"Doing well, despite my dire predictions. I've consulted my books and I went up to the Jews on Silver Street and looked at a few of theirs. You know that Ezra has a few good books on anatomy up there?"

"Yes. I do know that." This was something I'd discovered two years ago when I'd had cause to go and help the Jews against a party of town and castle folk intent on pillage and arson.

"Congyre was certainly sheltered by the hand of God when he was struck, Aumary. I didn't expect him to survive. It's almost as if Foreman, if Foreman it was, knew that to strike him there would not be fatal."

"Perhaps Foreman didn't manage to penetrate the man's body as fully as he might have done if he were at his full strength," I said.

"No, that was certainly true of Sir Percy."

"Another wound that didn't kill."

Johannes eased off his boots.

"So what's the news?"

Agnes came back in with her tray and started to cut up bread and bustle about the kitchen.

I told Johannes about our apprehension of Glanville Lovell.

"That man is a menace."

The doctor poured himself some wine and one for me too.

"I have ordered him flogged," I said.

"Not hanged?"

"I have commuted the sentence of hanging or mutilation to flogging because of information the man has been able to give me about the riot on Southfield. But truly, as you know, it's not my place to hand out punishments."

"Oh?"

"He was witness to something important." And I began to tell him the rest of the story as I saw it.

Johannes put down his cup slowly.

"Oh Jesu. And all the time..."

"Yes."

"Why?"

"That is what I shall attempt to find out next. So no word about anything for a while."

Agnes was standing with her mouth open and the ladle dripping gravy onto the flagstone floor.

"Agnes...that's our supper!" chuckled Johannes and jumped up to mop the floor.

*****

I slept in the workroom that night, if sleep was the word for it. I tossed and turned on the pallet and heard every creak and groan of the old house. Sherwyn was a silent sleeper on his little pallet in the corner. Frida slept upstairs and Percy was in the other room downstairs.

In the darkest time of the night, I heard the door of the front room open. Silent steps came towards the workroom; the door was being tried. I had locked it behind me and if it were Johannes looking in on his patient, he would have opened it with the key but no key clicked in the lock. I held my breath. Quiet feet padded away and the world was left in darkness with Sherwyn Congyre's even breathing punctuating the silence.

The next morning I broke my fast on ale and manchet bread fetched fresh from the baker. These were small white loaves which were seldom made and only the wealthy could afford them. It spoke of the prosperity of our little town that there was a market for such foods here.

Using my duplicate key, I quietly re-entered the workroom where lay Sherwyn Congyre. He opened his eyes when he heard the door open and smiled. "My Lord Belvoir. Are you here again?"

"I haven't been home, Sherwyn."

He nodded. "Such are the responsibilities of your office, sir."

I chuckled. "John gets his pennies worth from his officers, it's true. Or would, if he paid them."

Sherwyn smiled.

I sat down by the bed and stared down at my father-in-law's brother.

"I think I now know what happened to you, on the rooftop."

"Ah yes, sir. I thought maybe you'd work it out eventually. It was all very hazy to me before. Now I remember more clearly."

"Good, then tell me as much as you can remember."

Sherwyn shifted. "The doctor told me that the Lord of Pewsey…is alright…."

"Yes. He is a friend of mine. He should go home today, whilst you will stay a little longer here under the care of Dr. Johannes."

"This matters not to you, sir? What I have to say?"

"It matters greatly but I will have the truth, Congyre."

And so he told me.

*****

Percy was waved off to Crofton, the nearer of his two manors, a short while later.

One of his servants had come to guide them home and Johannes was satisfied that his patient was well enough to travel.

We parted with a promise from him, of a visit very soon.

Hal came up from the castle with our two horses accompanied by Jem.

In a short while we too would be on the road.

Meanwhile I had Sherwyn dictate to Harald, a castle scribe, all that he recalled about the scene on the rooftop. I sealed the parchment as he lay back, wearily.

"Sir, did I hear right that someone tried the door last night?"

"Yes, Sherwyn, they did."

"My life is still in danger, isn't it, m'lord?"

"After today you will no longer need to be guarded. I promise this."

He nodded. "Thank you, sir. I have not deserved your care."

I smiled. "Now all we need is for you to get better." And I patted the bedclothes as I left the room and locked it again.

Jem was positioned once more outside the door with instructions to be careful and Hal and I mounted and turned our horses' heads to the forest.

We reached the turning to Durley within a short time but carried on riding past the lane.

We passed through the village of Burbage which also lay in the forest and turned off on the road which eventually led to Bedwyn.

The manor of Crofton was a small one, not the main residence of the Lord of Pewsey but one which he and his wife favoured.

We left our horses in a stand of trees at the back of the house and made our way on foot to the walled garden, where weeks before we had enjoyed the hospitality of its lord. The door was open. There was no one in sight but I thought I knew where Percy would be.

His garden was his overwhelming passion and I felt it would be the first place he visited once he returned to his manor.

We crept quietly towards the small door in the wall which upon our previous visit had been locked.

Gently we turned the handle.

Percy was standing, leaning on a stick, his feet wide planted, looking up at a plant which had been trained up a wooden archway. Naturally it was a rose and unlike its fellows this one was still in bloom.

The many petalled, striped and blotched pink flowers cascaded over the arch like a coloured waterfall. Blooms in abundance grew from one stem and the weight of them dragged the heads down.

We saw Percy lovingly caress the lowest bunch and bring them to his nose.

Around him was the same paraphernalia as we had seen in the secret garden of the Lord Garner. Pots, cuttings, piles of rose heads and seeds.

Oh so quietly we entered and shut the little door with a click.

Percy turned.

"I have almost been expecting you, you know," said my friend.

"You 'ave?" said Hal, looking at me with a perplexed expression.

Percy sniffed. "There was never much you could keep from Aumary, Hal, even when he was a boy. Now he's a man, he's twice as nosy."

Hal tried not to smile and fingered his twin moustaches instead.

"Is this the same rose as is in the copse at Whitehill, Percy?"

"Not quite. It's taken me over three years to get it like this. Of course it's now better than the wild one. You must admit, she is a beauty."

"I have seen nothing to rival it, Percy," I said honestly.

"Come let's go up to the hall and we shall..."

"No. We stay here," I said forcefully. "And you tell me all about that silly piece of acting on the church tower."

"Tower?"

"Aye. The killing of Foreman, the wounding of Congyre."

"I am sure I don't know what you mean." He laid the stick on the bench.

"Congyre was meant to die wasn't he?"

"Die? Foreman was the one who...."

"No!" I shouted and my voice raised a few birds from the tall trees behind the wall.

"Oh, he was a murdering man, of that we're sure. But he did not strike Congyre and he didn't strike you."

"I can assure you..."

"No Percy, you cannot."

"What has that Congyre man been saying? Has he poured poison in your ears...?"

I shook my head. "No, Percy. I know the truth of it now."

"Congyre was defending me when he threw that piece of metal..."

"No!" I shouted again, "He wasn't. He was defending Foreman."

*****

Percy smiled and scuffed up the earth with the toe of his boot, his hand on his hip.

"Honestly Aumary. I don't understand you. How long have we known each other?"

"Almost thirty years Percy, but you are not the boy I knew at five, six, not even at eleven. That boy would never have grown to be the man who killed for his obsession."

Percy opened his arms. "Whom have I killed, Aumary?"

"Firstly, the Lord Garner."

"Pah!" Percy looked away. "Why? Why would I stoop to kill such a piece of offal? He was beneath notice."

"Perhaps he was until you found out that he too had a garden and that he had discovered a rose in the forest, a rose beyond compare. One he was nurturing and planned to grow in his own garden. One such as you have now here in your secret space. One you denied knowing about. You must have argued with him, fought over it I suppose."

Percy glowered. "I might also grow such a rose. Indeed, I have." He pointed to the rose growing up the wooden arch. "I am sure I have made a much better job than any he could have made."

"You killed him because he somehow found that you had caused some basket weave arches to be made and he coveted them, moreover asked for them to be copied."

"I found him wandering around in here one day. Stupid Frida had allowed him access, thinking to show off a little, I think. Pah. I sent him packing."

"And not long after you sent him packing completely. Didn't you?"

Percy sighed.

"A knife in the ribs. In town. A man in a blue cloak. I saw you not long after that in town, in your blue cloak. You pretended not to know Garner but you knew him, oh yes, you did. You knew him and hated him. He had what you wanted."

"And what was that?"

"The secret of how to cross the rose in the forest with another to make one like you have here. One which will, if I can quote my friend Master Jardine, not revert. For that was always the problem, wasn't it? Any rose you bred would, after a while, revert to its original parent. That is why you have so many of them on the arches outside. All failures. But this one....this one was your crowning glory and had to be kept a secret."

Percy laughed out loud. "Oh Aumary, don't be so serious."

"Perhaps Garner wrote down an account of his work. How to form this rose. Did you pay Foreman to get it for you? Was he a traitor to his lord for thirty pieces of silver?"

Percy shook his head. "Oh my you do let your imagination overrun you, don't you?"

"Foreman did not abduct Sherwyn Congyre. Congyre saw you dragging Foreman along and singing as if you were drunk. The fingermarks on his arms are bruises you gave him when he was dragged along. Other bruises which he suffered as he was forcibly hauled up the tower steps were masked by his fall. He could never have walked up those steps unaided."

You entered Johannes' house. Foolish Edouard Picot opened the door to you. And why not? You were no threat. You knifed him by the kitchen door, got the key and took Foreman and dragged him - there was no way on earth that the man could get himself even the short distance to the church - to his death on the tower top. He couldn't be allowed to live, could he?"

"Rubbish!"

"Congyre followed you there, wondering what on earth you were doing with the man. He had no cause to love Foreman but he knew that he was injured and was not capable of looking after himself. When you realised you had been seen, you stabbed Congyre and then when you knew you had been heard shouting at both Foreman and Congyre and that someone was following you ...Hal and I... and these words can barely pass my lips, Percy, for the deception is...evil; so evil, you took a knife, your own knife, and measured carefully, three fingers' breadth from the breastbone and knifed yourself. Then you attacked Foreman once more making it seem to us that you grappled with him, when truly the man was powerless in your grasp, and toppled him over the parapet to his death. One knife, Percy. There was only ever one knife."

"Stab myself... whyever should I do that?"

"It's a good trick if you can pull it off, Percy. And you had been studying the books. Johannes tells me that you went up to see Ezra the Jew not too long ago."

"To obtain some monies, that's all."

"No, to look at his anatomy books. Where might I stab myself and frame another for my attempted murder, should I need to do so? The books told you how and where. I shall ask Ezra. He will tell me."

Percy's face darkened. "Oh Aumary, don't be so foolish."

"You don't think it foolish to be so governed by your passion for something that it drives you to kill over and over?"

"Foreman was a louse!"

"And Congyre?"

"A meddler! Now come, Aumary, let's go up to the house and I will show you..."

"No, Percy, I'll have the truth from you." I put my hand on the pommel of my sword. Percy wore no sword today.

"Master Green. You did incite the apprentices to strike him. Why? What was he to you? The man was no threat but I think you heard us talking about consulting him, taking him to the garden owned by Garner and you couldn't have that, could you? The knowledge that Master Green might work out what you had been doing was hard to ignore. So he had to die."

"Oh Aumary, you still don't understand, do you? The King wants a garden here in Wiltshire. I can't have that. THIS is the only garden in this area, in Wiltshire. It will be the only real garden in the county. Mine! Mine! I couldn't have Master Green ruining my plan. Nor that man Garner! "

"Sir Percy. That's mad," said Hal suddenly, "Plain mad."

"Aye Hal. I think he is mad."

"Mad you say? Mad?" He licked his lips and came a step closer.

"Is it mad to want to be the only one and the best at something? Is it mad to strive to create perfection as God has done? And succeed. Think of it. Succeed as God has done."

Hal crossed himself. "Aye it's mad, sir. Some might think that God will strike you down for such blasphemy, I'm sure."

"It's mad to kill five times to obtain this satisfaction, Percy," I said quietly.

"Five times?" said a voice.

I turned; Joscelin was standing in the doorway.

"Father?"

"Go back to the house Jos, this doesn't concern you," said Percy.

"Father, I heard the Constable..."

I looked carefully at Joscelin of Pewsey. "Do as your father asks Jos, go back to your mother."

Joscelin looked at me with wide, pale eyes.

"I am sorry, sir, to disobey you." He came through the doorway, "but I want to know what is happening."

"Jos. You do not need..." began his father.

"Oh but I do, sir," said the young man. "I heard you, M'lord Belvoir, say that my father had killed five times. If it is untrue, I want to hear that it is from his own lips and I want to know why you think he has murdered, sir." He gave a small nod of a bow.

Hal stepped forward "Now come along, master..."

"No, no, Hal, let him stay."

Hal shrugged. "Right you are, sir."

"Your father is accused by me of murder, Jos. I wish that, God I wish, that it was not my job to unmask him but unmask him I have and now it cannot be undone."

The lad's face grew grim.

"Is this true, father?"

"Of course it isn't true, Jos. The Constable is sadly making some big mistakes and has no evidence," said Percy with some levity in his voice.

Jos turned to me again. "What is your evidence, Sir Aumary?"

"I have the testimony of two people who say that they saw him at the riots about the King's garden in Marlborough, stirring up the apprentices to violence. Later the master gardener was knifed in his own home by a man in blue. Your father was wearing blue that day.

"He often does. It's his favourite colour. But there are many men who wear blue, sir."

"Yes. That is true. He all but admitted before you arrived, Jos, that he hated the gardener and that he wished to be the only one in the area who owned a garden such as this one. He did not wish the garden on Southfield to be built and so disposed of its creator."

Jos' face screwed up at that, as he took in the words.

"He also knifed a man called Garner in Marlborough High Street, for the man had stolen one of his horticultural ideas and he wanted revenge. At the same time he wanted to acquire the knowledge this man had. The knowledge about this rose here; how to grow it successfully. He wanted to remove all competition."

"He is passionate about his roses, sir, but I cannot see him killing to protect them."

"You cannot? Master Congyre accuses him of trying to kill him on that church tower and last night I witnessed him trying to finish what he started there in the town. He left his bed with the intention of coming into the workroom of Dr. Johannes and murdering Master Sherwyn Congyre as he slept. He didn't know that I was also in the room and had locked the door. I think this is the second time he's tried it for on the first night, he feigned a sleepwalking incident and came into the room where the injured Master Congyre lay. Hal here intercepted him."

"Aye, I did, lad," affirmed Hal.

Percy sighed. "I left my bed with the intention of going to the privy, Jos," he said in exasperated tones. "And I have no recollection of walking into that room on a previous night."

"No Percy, you tried the door of the workroom and then passed back to your own bed, thwarted in your intent. You didn't go out through the kitchen door to the privy."

Percy shook his head, laughing.

"With my own eyes, Jos, I saw your father struggling with the man on the top of the church tower where he, according to the man Congyre, had dragged Foreman. I watched as he threw him over the edge. So did Hal here."

"No, Jos. Don't listen. This man Congyre lies for some reason and the man Foreman was trying to push me over the edge of the tower. It was unfortunate he went over instead. It was an accident."

"He killed one of my castle guards in the corridor of Johannes' house, knifed him in much the same way as he did the Lord Garner...."

"The Lord Garner has been here, father, has he not? I remember you walking around with him and...."

"No lad, you're mistaken. Your mother let him in when I had expressly forbidden it. He was trying to steal my ideas."

Joscelin looked confused. "No sir... I remember it well, you were laughing and joking and..."

"Joscelin, in order to throw us off the scent, your father wounded himself. Oh, it wasn't a mortal wound but it was intended to make us think that Foreman was the murderer. Congyre wasn't meant to survive but by the grace of God and the ministrations of Doctor Johannes, he did, to give up to me his version of the story."

"Is this a lie too, father?"

"Of course it is, Jos." said Percy.

Joscelin looked very uncertain.

"Your father had been up to the Jews on Silver Street to look at medical books they have there, Jos. Why would he do this? His interest is in gardening, not anatomy."

Joscelin started to shake his head.

"And he has lied to me several times. Me, his friend of over twenty years. He lied about not knowing about the riots, he lied about not knowing Garner and he lied about this little garden and the knowledge of the rose in the forest."

"I did not," said Percy in a sulky tone.

"A place where you 'ave a midden and keep poisons you said, m'lord," said

Hal.

"Your tests and searches, your trials, your infant plants, father. This is what this garden is for. Why would you lie to Sir Aumary?"

"I didn't, lad. I just didn't want anyone to know what I was really doing here. You know how important my work is to me."

"Important enough to kill, father?" said Jos in a quavering tone.

"Joscelin, you must believe me."

"Why would the Constable lie, father? He is your friend, as he has said. He has no reason to be unkind to you in such a way."

"Ah, but that's where you're wrong, my lad," said Percy, stepping forward with a sneer. "You know what? He wants to build a garden. A garden at Durley...."

"As you encouraged him to, sir? I heard you."

"Aye well. I was a fool, I'll admit it. He wants to outdo us, Jos. He wants this garden to fail, he wants to destroy it so that his may thrive...."

"Why cannot they all thrive, father, all gardens?" asked Jos, turning his head inquisitively.

"Your father had already destroyed the garden where Sir Jacques Garner carried out his trials on roses, Jos. Hal here and I were in this garden when your father came after us, no doubt wondering what we had found out. He locked us in after hearing us say we were to consult Master Green, the King's gardener. Then he returned shortly after and took an axe to the plants and benches, destroyed the roses and arches. Destroyed everything the Lord Garner had there."

Percy's eyes flashed "I could not let it survive, could I? Mine was to be the only garden...Why should I let someone else...?" He stopped and his eyes flew to his son.

Joscelin opened his mouth to speak and then with a look of horror on his face he stepped forward and swallowed.

"It's true isn't it? Every word?"

"You must understand, my son..."

"No sir. I cannot understand. This love of roses above all other flowers has turned your brain. You have lost your mind over it, father."

"You cannot comprehend, Jos, what it's like to give your life to something and then have some clodheaded idiot steal your ideas...those you have laboured over..."

"You are right, father I cannot understand. Why couldn't you share your knowledge?"

Percival shook his head. "Share it? Noooo. I have to be the best. My garden has to be the only one. The best. It was MY rose I tell you, MINE!"

"You killed to protect our garden? This?" said Jos throwing his hand up. "Father, it's only a garden...a thing of nature."

"No! No! You have to understand, I have tamed and bent nature to my will!"

Percy looked at his hands.

"I have rivalled God with these hands." He stretched them further out in front of him. "I have played God."

"No father. You have been tempted by the devil!"

Percy stepped forward and before I knew what was happening, he struck Joscelin hard across the head with his fist.

The boy flew sideways and hit his head on the wooden staging close by him. He crumpled in a heap.

I took out my sword and brought it up to Percy's throat as he attempted to get to Jos, horror on his face at last at what he'd done.

"Back away, Percy," I said.

I gestured that Hal should see to Jos.

Percy stepped back a pace. His body drooped. His eyes lost their flaring anger.

Hal stepped up quickly to Jos and leaned over him.

Percy moaned, his hands dangling by his sides.

"Have I killed him, too?" he whispered.

"No sir," said Hal, kneeling by the broken body of Joscelin of Pewsey, "I don't think so. He's not dead yet. But we need to get 'im to some 'elp and that 'elp needs to be quick "

Percy gave an enormous groan which rang up into the trees surrounding the walls.

"I've killed him! I have killed my own son!" he wailed, falling to his knees.

He covered his face with his hands.

Hal was busy lifting Jos from the ground, trying to protect the boy's damaged head.

Jos moaned quietly and opened his eyes....

"Wha..."

"Jos...Jos!" cried Percy and, regardless of my sword pointing at him, he leapt up, barged into me and pushed past.

Joscelin saw him coming and tried to scream but it came out as a whimper. He writhed in Hal's arms.

I grabbed Percy's shoulder and tried to draw him back so that he wouldn't hamper Hal.

"We'll get him into the house. Quickly," I said.

Percy was not to be thwarted however and lashed out at me. I felt something sharp gouge my cheek. I tasted blood on my lips.

Suddenly Percy turned and the anger and spite was back in his eyes.

"Come on then, Belvoir."

He crouched and waved a wicked looking grafting knife in front of me. (I had learned from Master Jardine this was the curved knife favoured by those who prepared their own plants for bonding, one to another). Somehow he had managed to pilfer it from the wooden bench at his side.

"Come on then. We haven't fought for nigh on fifteen years."

"And I am not going to fight you now, Percy," I said.

He gave me a grin which was intended to irk me, I'm sure, but I drew back, dropping my sword point and simply looked him in the eye.

"Afraid are we?"

"Not in the least, but I will not fight you, Percy."

"Father..." moaned Jos.

Percy made a pass at me with the knife. I jumped back. Unbeknown to me, there was a wooden crate behind me and I caught my heel and went over, my sword spinning away. Percy came on and lunged at me.

I caught his hand as he lowered himself onto me and brought my knee up to his damaged midriff catching him a blow which momentarily stopped him.

Even so, the knife came closer to my windpipe.

From the corner of my eye, I saw Hal set down a wavering Jos and take out his knife.

I did not want Percy harmed but I had no breath with which to yell.

Closer and closer to my windpipe came the grafting knife.

"Father...father, Sir Aumary is your friend," screamed Jos. "You cannot kill him. No!" and he broke away from Hal's grasp and threw himself shakily onto his father's back.

They rolled onto the gravel of the path.

Hal stepped on Percival's wrist and the knife went skittering away.

Jos lay on his back, his chest heaving, tears streaming down his cheeks; his eyes with that look which denotes shock, pain and dizziness. I noticed the gash on his head just above his left eyebrow trickling blood into the gravel. Then he passed out.

I jumped up and went to him. Percy lay on his back a few feet away from his son, his knees raised. Hal had recovered my sword and it was now pointing at his chest.

"I'm very sorry, my lord," said Hal "But I am going to 'ave to ask you to stand up and do as I say."

Percy said nothing at first but then burst into wailing cries.

Tears sprang from his eyes. His face crumpled. "Oh God!" he said "I have just tried to kill my son and my best friend. Oh God!"

*****

I am coming to the end of my tale Paul, my scribe. The tale of how my childhood friend, his mind turned by jealousy and pride, covetousness and selfishness, killed five people to protect nothing more than a rose. A flower. Both Jacques Garner and

Percy became completely deranged over a sweet smelling and beautiful flower and it was their undoing.

Yes, it is rather like two men fighting over the love of a fair maiden Paul - it's true.

Jos was delivered to his mother and before we left had regained consciousness again. We didn't allow Percy in the house but took him up on his horse and rode him back to the castle in Marlborough. He was completely limp and biddable and confessed to everything. He wept bitterly over his striking of his son and showed true contrition for this act of anger. We put him in the keep in one of the better rooms, as befitted his status in life. He was tried by the justices four months later, found guilty and sent to Winchester to be tried by a greater court there.

No, Paul he didn't hang.

The King intervened and stripped him of everything he owned, for John was a king who needed money more than he needed to make an example of a murderer of the knightly class. Percival was sent packing abroad with nothing more than the clothes in which he stood. I heard later from one of my Irish cousins that he fetched up in Ireland and later died in some Irish bog.

His wife, mourning him greatly, was not allowed to accompany him. The manor of Crofton was given back into my keeping. I allowed the steward to govern it for me and I permitted the Lady Frida to continue living there with her son Alfred and of course, Jos.

Jos recovered from the large gash on his head and still bears the scar. He will not talk about that time, as if it had been wiped from his memory, but I know he carries the hurt deep inside even unto this day.

He is master of Pewsey now with a fine wife and two lovely daughters. I managed to prevail upon John to allow the manor to be taken by him when he came of age. There was no justice in denying him his birthright and John was well pleased with how he managed his assets. He does seisin to me for Crofton, much as his father did. However the garden is now gone back to wilderness.

I still have the scar on my cheek given to me by Percy with that grafting knife. It's only small but when I have clipped my beard, you can see it.

The garden at Southfield was built and yes, the Queen did come and stay, several times. The fair which Marlborough had been granted in 1204 carried on but was moved to the Green on the hill. This wasn't ideal but it too prevailed and the town has not lost by the removing of the field. In fact, when the Queen was not in residence, the King allowed the good people of Marlborough access to the garden on certain days. This practice continues to this day, though for how much longer I don't know. The twice yearly day of the archery contest and other martial competitions was moved to the Common and no one has complained about it as far as I know.

I say we are almost at the end of our tale. *Ah yes....you remind me, Paul.* We have one more little snippet to add, so let us carry on writing.

Chapter Fourteen

Leaving Sir Percival in the care of my friends Andrew Merriman and Peterkin Gayle and with my paltry hurts salved by the castle doctor, the next day I saddled up Bayard and with Hal clopping along on his large grey Grafton, we made for home. As was my habit, I sat in my study that afternoon and wrote everything down, as I had experienced it.

The swifts were screeching over the courtyard looking for the evening flying insects when I at last finished and sanded my account.

Now I would go in to supper and explain to Lydia and to Hawise that my good friend Percy, Lord of Pewsey and Crofton, was a murderer five times over.

Johannes had ridden into the village and he now sat with Lydia at the top table. I knew Hal, had said not a word about what had happened and he lounged with Hubert the farrier and Alfred Woodsmith on a lower table, laughing in hushed tones at the antics of Hubert's little white dog Aura. Even so, some facts were known for there was a quietude to the hall not normally present at supper.

My own dog, a white gazehound called Holdfast, trotted up to me and I patted her silky head as we walked up to the table.

Lydia stood, came down from the dais and took my arm.

"Oh Aumary, we are so sorry. No one would have thought..."

"No."

I looked up at my daughter who had been crying.

"What will happen to Jos, father?" she said, her large green eyes full of tears.

"Nothing, my angel. He will continue to live at Crofton, if I can convince the King to let them stay there."

"If not?" asked Lydia.

"I have a mind to move them all to Bedwyn."

I looked round the gathering. My thoughts flew to the little village of Bedwyn.

"Where is Evisa? Has she returned home?"

"No, my love, she is in the church."

"She spends a lot of time in the church now, dada," said Hawise. "Moaning and crying. She is very unhappy without grandfather Toruld. I have tried to make her happy...but..."

I nodded. "I understand, Hawise."

I jumped up onto the dais and pecked her on the cheek. "I shall go and see if I can make her happy then."

I pinched her cheek gently.

"Wait for us. I'll bring her back in to supper."

"She isn't eating, Aumary," said Lydia. "She says she cannot face food."

"No, she told me that she doesn't eat much anyway," said Hawise, "She said old ladies don't eat like they used to when they were younger but she doesn't even eat as much as Holdfast does."

My little white gazehound was noted for being a very fussy eater, picking at her food and then leaving a good proportion. Hubert's dog Aura usually feasted on her leavings.

"Well, let me see if I can tempt her to eat with us."

I strode down the hall and met our priest Crispin in the doorway. He looked distracted and worried.

"Ho there, Crispin. You look like you've just had a summons from the bishop!"

"Aw no, nothing like that," he said. "I'm just...a little...."

"Hungry!" shouted Hawise laughingly. It was a known fact our priest enjoyed his food, though he never put on any flesh. I knew that he denied himself his full portion and kept some back for the poor and needy of the forest.

He laughed. "No not today, Lady Hawise. I'm just a little - preoccupied - that's all."

"I'm off to the church to see if I can tempt Evisa into the hall for supper with us."

Crispin looked up at me and smiled but made none of his usual witty rejoinders.

*****

The sun was dipping over the trees on the road to the west as I jogged up to our little church and opened the door.

Evisa was on her knees, mumbling in front of the altar.

"Mother-in-law," I said quietly. "How long have you been here? The sun is setting. Come; it's supper time."

She finished her prayer and tried to rise. I gave her my arm and grimacing, she struggled upright.

"Oh Aumary. Are you back now?" The hand on my arm was cold.

"Yes, yes I am and I won't be going back to town for a while if I can help it," I smiled.

"Have you managed to conclude your business there?"

"Yes, I have, though perhaps not in the way I would have liked."

"Oh dear."

"You remember I told you about the man Garner being killed in Marlborough High Street?"

"Did you, dear?" she asked.

"The man who was supposed to inherit Whitehill Copse and surrounding land."

"Ah yes, I remember now."

"I have arrested his murderer."

"Have you dear? Oh."

"Evisa, are you all right?"

"Yes Aumary, I'm just a little tired. Old ladies you know, don't sleep like they used to. I wake in the night and I come in here to pray."

"Wyot Gatekeeper lets you out of the wicket, I suppose."

"Yes, he does. He is such an accommodating man."

"Well! You will be tired if you do not eat and even though the day is warm, you are cold. Come, let's go back to the hall."

"Oh I'm not hungry, Aumary."

"Well, then come and see Hawise, she wants to talk to you."

I covered her thin arm in its sleeve of pink with my hand and tucked it through my elbow.

"But Aumary, I have come in here to pray and I haven't had the chance to do so yet."

"Evisa, they tell me you have been here quite a while."

"Oh no. I've only just come in. You go ahead my dear and I'll stay and..."

"No, Evisa. Come." I started to walk her down the nave. "We miss you too much. You can come back a little later." Though I knew that this was untrue for I would ask Annie, her maid, to take her to her bed after supper.

We walked a short way, slowly to the church door.

"Where is Father Godfrey, Aumary? He should be here at this hour lighting the lamp and the candles."

"You are at Durley, Evisa. Father Crispin will light ours after supper, when he comes to compline."

"Oh yes."

She tottered along beside me. I opened the church door.

"I had better go and find Toruld. He would hate to miss his..." She stopped. "Oh...Toruld is dead, isn't he?"

"Yes, mother-in-law and you are at Durley. There is nothing to worry you here. Come, let's go and find Lydia and Hawise."

We began to walk slowly back to the manor. I noticed how frail my mother-in-law had become in a very short time. The downhill walk, though only a gradual gradient, was difficult for her.

"You told me that you found out who killed the Lord Garner, didn't you, Aumary? Who was it?"

"Oh no one you know, Evisa." Though of course she did know Percival of Pewsey for they were quite close neighbours to Bedwyn.

"And the will, did we find the will?"

"Yes, we did, Evisa."

"Oh good. Does this mean we can bury Toruld now and perhaps I'd better go home?"

"Oh no, do stay a little longer, Evisa. Hawise and Lydia love having you here."

"Oh well, if you insist."

I opened the wicket gate for her, for Wyot had closed the main gate. She shakily ducked through.

"I do like your priest, Aumary. He is such a sweet man. I made my confession to him. He is such a good listener."

"Crispin? Yes. He's a good soul. He used to be the Bishop of Salisbury's secretary you know."

I knew that she did know this but was looking for something to say to keep her mind on setting her feet one in front of the other.

"And he came back to Durley to be our priest even though he has such an important job there."

"He told me he'd had enough of it."

I chuckled "Yes, the politics of the church."

We crossed the yard slowly. The swifts were now roosting up on the wall walk and in the various barns on my property. The bats had taken over the hunt for insects.

We looked up and watched them for a while.

"Oh, we are going the wrong way, Aumary. I should be going to the church, to pray for Toruld," said my mother-in-law suddenly.

"Supper time, Evisa," I smiled.

"I'm not hungry - really."

"Never mind. Hawise wants to see you."

"She is so much like Toruld you know."

"And yet she favours you and her mother in colouring."

"Is Cecily at home? And Geoffrey?"

"Oh God," I thought, "please don't let this be happening to her."

"Cecily and Geoffrey have been dead a long time, Evisa. You remember?"

Evisa swallowed. "Ah yes."

Her veil fluttered in the evening breeze. "She suffered so in the end didn't she?" she said suddenly brought back to the present.

"Aye, she did, but now she's at peace."

"Toruld suffered too."

"Yes, I know he did."

We started up the steps to the hall. In order to rise safely, my mother-in-law grabbed a handful of her dress, leaning heavily on my arm and her other hand grasped the rail tightly.

"You know he begged me at the end to help him."

"I know that Dr. Johannes was giving him some medicine which helped with the pain."

"But it didn't really help."

"No, sadly."

"Not at the very end."

"No."

"He begged me and begged me to help him."

"Help him do what, Evisa?"

"Help him die."

We were passing the door of my study. I took out my key and opened it.

"Come in here for a moment, Evisa. I just need to get something."

She followed me willingly like a faithful dog.

"Toruld had a room much like this one," she smiled.

"All us men have a place where we go for business, Evisa. It's where we work."

"Toruld couldn't work in that last year of his life."

"No, I know. Do sit down for a moment." I lit a candle. "But Matthew is very good at running the manor of Bedwyn, isn't he? There was no real need for Toruld to work. Matthew Steward managed perfectly."

"Yes, yes he did, though Toruld fretted so."

"I'm sure he did. He held Bedwyn for nigh on forty years. Of course he worried about how it was being run."

I sat down and eased my mother-in-law next to me on a padded bench.

"Tell me about Toruld's last day, Evisa. We haven't really had the time to speak about it. His brother came to see him. Sherwyn."

"Yes, and they forgave each other."

"I know. Sherwyn told me. He also told me that he did not kill his brother."

"No, he's right, he didn't."

"Do you have any idea who did kill Toruld, Evisa?"

She turned her lined and pale face up to me in its white wimple. Her eyes were guileless.

"Yes, Aumary. I know who killed him."

I took a deep and shaky breath. "And so do I, mother-in-law." I said, patting her age spotted hand. "So do I."

GLOSSARY

Barber surgeons - Doctors who were little more than hairdressers and bloodletters.

Baxter - A female baker.

Bothy - A small round wattle and daub building with a beaten earth floor.

Burntwine - Brandy.

Bride Piece - Sometimes called bride wealth, also known as bride token. Money, property, or other form of wealth paid by a groom or his family to the parents of the woman he has just married or is just about to marry. Often kept for if and when the woman becomes a widow.

Cods - Genitals

Coroner - (Sometimes called crowner). The man appointed by the Crown to deal with unexpected deaths. The coroner was the man who drew up the jury of twelve men to decide the cause of death and if need be, impose fines.

Cott - Cottage

Cotte - A long sleeved shift or tunic. A coat.

Faddle - Mess about.

First finder - The person who first discovers a crime.

Free woman - Peasants were tied to the land and lord and had to work on that land in return for the opportunity to grow food and have lodging. If a female peasant married a free man, she automatically became free. Permission had to be sought from the lord.

Gimpy - Unsafe, broken, lame.

Gurning -Grinning without smiling, pulling a grotesque face.

Jakes - Primitive toilet.

Kirtle - Dress.

Lincoln Green - A mixture of the dyes, woad and weld, peculiar to the town of Lincoln.

Manchet loaf - A small loaf of good quality white flour which might be held in the hand rather like a roll.

Morpheus - God of dreams and sleep

Pallet - A mattress sometimes laid on a crude bed frame.

Pax - Peace

Reeve - An official elected annually by the serfs to supervise lands for a lord.

Rouncey - A smaller horse used as a workhorse often ridden by servants. Rounceys were not fast but they were possessed of great stamina.

Seisin - possession of lands.

Sext - Sixth hour of the day before or about noon.

Screens passage - The corridor between the hall and buttery and pantry in a manor house

Scrip - Pouch worn at the waist or sometimes a larger bag.

Shriven - Forgiven of one's sins having made confession to a priest.

Solar - A private room reserved for the lord and his family, often positioned to catch the sun for much of the day.

Stampcrab - Heavy footed, clumsy person

Undercroft - The space like a cellar under a manor. Usually used as a storehouse.

Vert and Verdure - Greenery of the woods.

Villein -Peasant, serf, churl.

Warren - A manmade place where rabbits live and breed.

Withys - Strips of willow with which baskets are woven.

AUTHOR'S NOTE

This tale is one of greed and obsession and is based on the Tulipmania of the 17th century, when people were killing each other for possession of the bulbs of the tulip; that new fangled plant which came from Turkey and the Near East. This obsession nearly bankrupted governments and ruined many people.

Roses of a very basic nature were known in Britain very early on but the Crusaders brought more highly perfumed plants with larger blooms to the country from the Middle East. I like to think that there might have been the same rivalry and obsession about roses in the 12th and 13th centuries, as there was about tulips in the 17th.

The rose I mention is, in fact, my favourite rose - Variegata di Bologna. This is a modern rose by rose standards, dating from the early 19th century. However the Rosa Mundi and other striped roses were around earlier. We see them depicted in manuscripts. I hope purists will allow me to invent a mediaeval rose like this very special one.

Rose breeding was known about though obviously nothing was known about DNA or genes in general. People just accepted that things happened. It was an act of God. Hal of Potterne says that some thought that one shouldn't meddle with nature and this is quite true. It might have been considered unnatural and the result of devilry. Magic.

A garden was built in Marlborough and was loosely attached to the castle but I am unsure of the exact date. It seems to have been situated on Southfield. Now a housing estate, this part of town runs down to the river on its southernmost side and is bounded by the Pewsey Road on its western edge. The High Street meets its northern edge at the mini roundabout. Figgins Lane runs along its eastern boundary even today. Marlborough College is now on the site of the castle and all that can be seen of the keep is a tree topped mound within the college grounds. Now cordoned off with a barrier, when I was a girl one could go into the car park and stare at it.

Not all murderers were hanged, especially if they were noble. Kings were much more interested, at this stage in history, in acquiring coin. It was quite common for a man to be banished and beggared. Many of them fled abroad and were allowed back after a while. Some died there.

Medicine was in its infancy. Some books did exist, many of them coming from the more advanced Middle Eastern nations. Anatomising cadavers was expressly forbidden by the church. Knowledge of the human body was poor but there were some whose training allowed them to understand it a little better than their compatriots. Johannes, having trained at the very advanced school in Salerno in Sicily, would have access to books and to knowledge far greater than the barber surgeons of the day, most of whom couldn't even read.

Now to Aumary. He is a minor lord, not terribly wealthy and more a businessman than pure aristocracy. As warden of the forest he has quite a practical job and needs to know about the forest and its trades. He is a knight - yes, but first and foremost, a forester. I have made him a sympathetic character as so many folk of his class are portrayed in novels as proud, haughty and nasty. I fail to see how many of them could be so. They were dependent upon their peasants for their livelihood. If the peasant didn't prosper, neither did they, at this level of society. Grander folk perhaps could be less amenable. Aumary takes every man as he finds him and isn't averse to rolling up his sleeves and getting on with it.

ABOUT THE AUTHOR

Susanna, like Aumary Belvoir has known the Forest of Savernake all her life. After a period at the University of Wales studying Speech Therapy, she returned to Wiltshire and then moved to Hampshire to work, not so very far from her forest. Susanna developed an interest in English history, particularly that of the 12th and 13th centuries, early in life and began to write about it in her twenties. She now lives in Northamptonshire with her husband and two small wire haired fox terriers called Delphi and Tabor.

TITLES IN THIS SERIES

Belvoir's Promise

She Moved Through the Fair

Down by the Salley Gardens

I Will Give my Love an Apple

Black is the Colour of my True Love's Hair

Long Lankyn

One Misty Moisty Morning

The Unquiet Grave

The Lark in the Morning

A Parcel of Rogues

Bushes & Briars

Please visit the website for further information

https://susannamnewstead.co.uk/

0143

01329 552440

Printed in Great Britain
by Amazon

61218219R00169